MW01236257

# Cowboy Lover

# Cowboy Lover

## EROTIC STORIES OF
## THE WILD WEST

⎯⎯∞⎯⎯

### EDITED BY
### CECILIA TAN AND LORI PERKINS

THUNDER'S MOUTH PRESS
NEW YORK

COWBOY LOVER:
*Erotic Stories of the Wild West*

Published by
Thunder's Mouth Press
An imprint of Avalon Publishing Group, Inc.
245 West 17th Street, 11th Floor
New York, NY 10011

AVALON

Compilation copyright © 2007 Cecilia Tan and Lori Perkins. Introduction copyright © Cecilia Tan and Lori Perkins 2007. "The View From Where I'm Standing" copyright © August MacGregor 2007. "The Maginficent Threesome" copyright © Elspeth Potter 2007. "The Unattainable" copyright © Livia Llewellyn 2007. "Gentling" copyright © Shanna Germain 2007. "Hard Lessons" copyright © Teresa Noelle Roberts 2007. "When the Rancher Needs a Loan" copyright © Andrea Dale 2007. "Pistol Packin' Mamas" copyright © David Shaw 2007. "Angel to a Cowboy" copyright © Laney Cairo 2007. "Ace in the Hole" copyright © M. Christian 2007. "A Dying Breed" copyright © Rakelle Valencia 2007. "Two Visions" © copyright Connie Wilkins 2007. "The Branding of Miss Charlotte Babington" copyright © Anna Black 2007. "Celestial" copyright © Stephen Dedman 2007. "Cowboy Cocksucker" copyright © Clayton Holiday 2007. "Reverse Cowgirl" copyright © Rachel Kramer Bussel 2007. "The Stake" copyright © Lee Crittenden 2007. "The Barning" copyright © LUCypher 2007.

First printing June 2007

All rights reserved. No part of this publication may be reproduced or transmitted in any form or by any means, electronic or mechanical, including photocopy, recording, or any information storage and retrieval system now known or to be invented, without permission in writing from the publisher, except by a reviewer who wishes to quote brief passages in connection with a review written for inclusion in a magazine, newspaper, or broadcast.

Library of Congress Cataloging-in-Publication Data

Cowboy lover : erotic stories of the Wild West / edited by Cecilia Tan and Lori Perkins. --1st Thunder's Mouth Press ed.
    p.cm.
  ISBN-13: 978-1-56858-330-3 (pbk.)
  ISBN-10: 1-56858-330-3 (pbk.)
  1. Erotic stories, American. 2. Short stories, American. 3. Western stories. I. Tan, Cecilia, 1967– ii. Perkins, Lori.
PS648.E769 2007
803'.01083538—dc22

                                2007013248

        9 8 7 6 5 4 3 2 1

Book design by Pauline Neuwirth, Neuwirth & Associates, Inc.

Printed in the United States of America
Distributed by Publishers Group West

# Contents

# Introduction

IF YOU HAVE picked up this book, you are holding in your hands a radical concept in erotica. We bet you noticed that there wasn't a seminaked woman splayed alluringly across the cover. In fact, you picked this up in spite of the fact that the object of desire was a man.

Cowboys have always been sexy—the outlaw loner in tight jeans with a gun and a lasso is a true American icon of masculinity. *Brokeback Mountain* brought his smoldering sexuality smack dab into middle America and for this generation of western readers it's all about what lies under those chaps.

This new generation of cowboy lovers is surprisingly diverse—more than half of these stories are written by women and a few play fast and free with gender. They are a far cry from the westerns of Louie L'Amour and Larry McMurty, and they uncover the sublimated sexuality of classic Hollywood westerns, examining a rife milieu for sex and desire.

We were worried that the stories we received might be too clichéd or too similar to one another, but we were quite pleased with the range we had to choose from. Although there are by necessity some familiar figures, you'll find, for example, that the tongue-tied cowboy and schoolmarm in "Hard Lessons" are quite different from what you might expect. You'll find the requisite saloons and gunfights, Indians and ranchers, but we assure you they will all be in very different circumstances than the last time you encountered them. You'll even find an appearance by our old friend the Marlboro Man. We made him brush his teeth first.

*Cecilia Tan and Lori Perkins*
EDITORS

# Cowboy Lover

# The View from Where I'm Standing

AUGUST MACGREGOR

MICHELLE HAD SEEN similar views in magazines and western movies—spaghetti and otherwise—but nothing could match the real thing. Some movies got close to showing the grandeur, with a huge screen to respect the mountains and a musical score to lift you up.

The valley unfolded in a bright green swath until hills rose and kept rising up to mountains. This was the real deal. Not Italy for a cheap budget, but Wyoming to show the rugged American spirit.

The morning air smelled crisp, and the coffee tasted damn good. No Starbucks here (she didn't think to bring any), but that fancy stuff would've been out of place with the scenery.

Standing on the porch, Michelle envisioned a cowboy riding out of the prairie dust, his figure barely seen in the distance, then becoming larger and clearer as he and his horse gradually got closer. Of course music played in the background, the music that seemed to be the same in every western. With her luck, he wouldn't turn out to be a young Clint Eastwood with a bellyful of pasta and squinting in the sunlight, but a weary, old prospector with a month-long beard. He would glance to both sides, then lean in close to her and utter a crazed whisper between parched lips: "There's gold in them thar hills."

"Mornin' ma'am."

The male voice startled her out of her daydream.

The speaker, wearing full cowboy attire, stood on the ground in front of the porch. She had seen him around the ranch and took him to be one of the authentic cowboys that worked on the place. He had boyish good looks that had yet to be weathered by sun, wind, drink, women, and worry. More cowboy than cowman.

"Didn't mean to scare you," he said. "Just saw you on the porch and wanted to say hi."

"Oh, no," Michelle said. "No, it's okay. I guess I was lost in the view. We don't have anything like this in Chicago. It's gorgeous."

"Yes, ma'am. But not as good as the view from where I'm standing."

She thought, *Are you for real? Isn't it too early in the morning for flirting?* "Um, you don't call me ma'am. Makes me think you're talking to my mom."

"Well, I'm sure she's a real nice lady." His grin grew from one corner of his lips. "My name's Mark." His forefinger and thumb tipped his hat in that classic cowboy way straight out of the movies.

"Good to meet you. I'm Michelle."

"Are you with the cigarette people?"

"Not really. None of us are actually cigarette people." She liked his phrase and imagined crowds of cigarettes walking the streets. "We're an advertising agency. The tobacco company's a client. So we work for them, but we're not really the cigarette people."

"And all those pictures you're takin' are gonna be on billboards?" Mark asked.

"Uh-huh. And in magazines. We're even shooting a TV commercial for foreign markets."

"Not for here?" he asked.

"You'd never see them in America. But they're okay in other countries. There's nothing quite like seeing a dubbed commercial of cowboys. They're riding horses, throwing lassos, but you hear Japanese. And you still hear Japanese after their mouths stop moving."

"Ah," he said with that lopsided grin. "Like the Godzilla movies."

"That's right." She liked his grin and was glad she inspired it.

Mark pondered that for a couple of seconds. "Now what do you do for this advertising agency?"

"I do makeup for the models. The guys modeling as cowboys."

His eyebrows floated. "Really? Men wearing makeup. Huh."

So this man in training had already mastered the art of distilling minutes of conversation that might actually help his listeners understand his meaning to the lone syllable of "huh."

"Yeah," she said. "It brings out their features. Covers up any blemishes. And I do their hair, too."

"Never had a woman cut my hair."

"You should try it sometime. Might get a better haircut."

"How 'bout you, ma'am?" Mark asked, and his devil-may-care smile appeared when Michelle frowned. "Oops, 'scuse me. That one slipped through. Are you free after your work? We could get a bite to eat."

*You won't fluster me again, pardner.* "Have to say no on that one. Thanks for the invite, though."

Her rejection didn't seem to hurt him at all. He just took it in stride. "Well," he said, drawing the word out longer than it needed to be, "I better be going. It was real nice talking with you."

"You, too."

Mark tipped his hat again. "Have a great day now."

"You, too."

Michelle watched him walk away and marveled how good a man's butt could look in jeans. Nothing held the male posterior quite like denim. This butt, like the other authentic cowboys around there, was probably uncomfortable sitting on anything other than a horse, pickup truck, or bar stool. She wondered how his butt felt. Wondered how a firm grip of each cheek felt as she kissed his lips.

*Enough of that,* she thought. Back to the male models with butts used to finer materials and richer modes of transportation. They were more like filtered cigarettes compared to the unfiltered ones of the cowboys.

—∞∞∞—

DURING THE DAY, Michelle couldn't get Mark out of her mind. She tried to focus on her work and the scenery, but her thoughts kept floating away from the fake cowboys with makeup and going to the real one with plain good looks and a killer butt. Images kept popping into her head: Mark tipping his hat, his one-sided grin, his Levi-covered ass walking away.

Maybe it was the distasteful thought of another night alone in her room decorated in a country-kitsch style. From the outside, the bed and breakfast was a beautiful, rustic house. Inside was another matter. Apparently, someone thought baskets made for quaint decorations. A lot of baskets. The canopy bed and the wall border of lassos added to the ambience.

Maybe a change of pace would be refreshing. In her recent dates, she was too concerned if the men sitting on the other side of the table were marriage material. There were some hot ones, true, but they all turned out to be bloated with boastful talk and empty promises. No backbone of responsibility.

Mark would give her an honest-to-goodness one night stand. It was straightforward. It was simple. And it just might be a helluva lot of fun.

*What was in it for this cowboy? Besides the obvious. Did he already conquer all the young things in town and need fresh meat? Not much to do in this town but drink with your buddies, so maybe he's looking for a different adventure. See what a city girl feels like.*

*And I get to see what a cowboy feels like.*

The more she thought about it, the better of an idea it became.

—∞∞∞—

WITHOUT HIS HAT on, Mark kept running his hand through his brown tousled hair, which didn't need cutting and looked sexy in its disheveled state. The kind of effect city boys spent hours and globs of hair products to achieve, but was natural on Mark.

Michelle was pleasantly surprised at their good conversation over decent beers, mediocre salad, and fantastic steaks at the nicest restaurant in town. *What did I expect? Monosyllabic dialogue?*

He smiled that one-corner smile during dinner and—probably picking up on her surprise—said, "Cowboys have opinions about everything. We have plenty of time to think."

She did have to push herself to be patient and not try to finish all of his sentences. Mark took his time saying his piece. He spoke much slower than the rapid-fire conversation she was used to. When she pulled the reins on her inner rush, she was much more at ease. Like taking a leisurely walk rather than hurrying to jump in a taxi and zip to the next appointment.

More than his speed of speech put her at ease. It was his whole manner, a slow and easy way about him. He was comfortable in his own skin. And he seemed to have the attitude that you could take him or leave him. City mice were always looking to impress everyone: check out my car, the title on my business card, the address of my apartment. Not this one. If you didn't agree with him, well, that was just fine.

*Should've been chasing country mice all along.* For the first time, the general idea of a one-night stand with Mark transformed into a specific, colorful vision: his grinning face above her, his hard warmth inside her, his soft butt cheeks in her hands. Tingles danced up her body.

Mark drove them back to the bed and breakfast in his pickup truck. In the tighter quarters, she enjoyed the view of his blue jeans and black shirt. The aroma of his spicy cologne mixed with remnants of cigarette smoke. *I hope that's from his friends.*

As he parked, she said, "Come up to my room."

If he was surprised at her bluntness, he didn't show it. He was one smooth cowboy all right.

Once they got to her room and the door closed behind them, he bent his head down to kiss her. But Michelle backed up, showed him the palm of her right hand in the universal stop sign, and said, "Hold on."

"Huh?" Cowboy startled. Finally.

"You smoke." The scent on his breath and clothes was much stronger with him so close.

"Well, yeah, of course. Don't you?" Cowboy incredulous.

"Nope."

"But you're doing all this work with the cigarette people."

"Yeah, but that doesn't mean I smoke. They do. I don't."

"Oh. Sorry 'bout that."

"Brush your teeth." Her head lifted in the direction of the bathroom.

Mark frowned. This wasn't how he had planned. Surely, the women around here weren't pushovers. He said, "Um, well, I didn't exactly bring my toothbrush."

"So use mine. And use mouthwash."

As he brushed, she sat on the bed and removed her brown boots. Her heart galloped with anticipation. A silly urge caused her to imagine him swaggering across the room and saying in a John Wayne drawl, "Hey there, little lady. My little pilgrim wants to get in your pants." But he didn't. He also didn't gargle, just swished the mouthwash. She thought only a belch and a fart could've topped gargling in the unromantic department.

Still, his dental hygiene was an improvement. Kissing him was not only tolerable, it was downright fun. The gargle and tobacco breath slipped away into memory. Now, if something could be done about the tobacco stink on his clothes.

He made the first move by releasing the top button of her blouse, then it was open season on buttons. Their hands impatiently rushed from one button to the next, causing their arms to bump against each other and their lips to kiss faster. He went straight for a bra strap rather than the hook. Used to male clumsiness, she reached behind her and undid the thing so the bra fell free.

"Well, now," Mark said with twinkling eyes staring at her chest. "Would you look at these beauties."

*Who says shit like that?* But goddamn, did it sound good. Especially with his drawl. More Brad Pitt than John Wayne.

Then his hands and lips were upon her breasts, squeezing and sucking. It was quicker than she normally liked, but she enjoyed his eagerness and still glowed from the compliment about her beauties. Foreplay was an art form few men appreciated anyway. Besides, his fingers weren't the only impatient ones; hers worked at his big silver belt buckle. They paused for a moment to slide along the ridges of the buckle's design.

*Hmm, what's on here?* Michelle realized she hadn't looked closely at the buckle, and she wondered what was on it—lasso or horse or mean-looking bull. *Ah, plenty of time for that later.*

The buckle unhinged smoothly. His zipper went down easy. She reached into the opening and touched skin and a thrill raced up her spine, that same thrill every time she met a new cock. She helped the poor guy out of the tight confines of the jeans. Mark inhaled sharply when her fingers clasped his erection. The feeling of hard warmth never ceased to amaze her.

She was amazed, too, over his ravaging of her breasts. As if he hadn't felt enough tits to shift into a calmer gear and give them a polite reception. But she wasn't complaining. She enjoyed his energetic adoration while softly stroking his dick.

Finally, he came up for air. Maybe he was struck by the realization that there was more to her than nipples and globes of spongy flesh. His face held a naked, let's-get-it-on quality.

"Jesus," she said. "You like boobs, huh?"

Mark's cheeks turned dark pink. Very cute. "Um, uh, yeah."

*Doesn't like being called on it.* "Hey, don't worry. It's flattering."

He looked relieved. "I told ya they're beauties."

Her turn to blush. She blurted out "Yeah" in a spontaneous half-chuckle. Then she backed up a step, lest he set about ravaging them again, and swallowed to regain control of her voice. "Thanks." She nodded at his erection poking out of his pants. It looked wildly pale next to the black jeans. The rest of his skin looked sunbeaten, but his dick stayed safe behind a layer of protective denim. "Not too bad yourself, partner."

His face brightened, and he doubled over with laughter.

*Gotcha. Might as well throw you a bone.* She giggled and began stripping off her jeans. *'Cause you're gonna throw me that bone.*

"You're a lively one," Mark said through a wide smile, then followed her lead. While Michelle slid out her pants, Mark shoved his down.

In no time, they were on the bed with his warm naked body pressed on top of her. In no time, he slid inside her. His hips roared to life, moving with all the grace of a bull unleashed from rodeo gates to buck madly in the open field. His breaths shot short bursts of air on her neck.

"Whoa, whoa," she said. "Hold on. What's your rush? Slow down, stay awhile."

His face turned crimson. "Um, uh, sorry 'bout that." The mumbled words were far from his usual confident banter.

At least he listened. His hips eased to a slower pace. He took longer, more patient breaths.

"There you go," she said. "Much better."

*Used to wham-bam-thank-you-ma'am? Not here, pal. Not this city mouse.*

She loved his muscular arms, chest, and abs as they rubbed against her body with his thrusts. Plenty of her dates back home boasted about belonging to gyms, but their naked bodies proved it either was a lie or they just never went. Just as she was beginning to settle in and enjoy his cock, he came. She tried to mask her disappointment and chalked it up to overexcitement.

*Maybe he's never had a city mouse before.*

At least he was polite enough to wash his cock. Maybe he cleaned it in the hopes for a blowjob, but Michelle mentally told him, *Never on the first date. Not this girl.* She took the chance to investigate his belt buckle. It was a running horse flanked by feathers, all framed in an oval of twisted pewter to look like rope. Following the intricate design with her fingertips felt surprisingly intimate. As did feeling the design of wheat stalks flowing over his wide, reddish brown belt.

"Like my belt?" Mark asked as he saddled up next to her.

"Yeah. Better than what the models are wearing."

"Well, that's good. Guess I can't smoke?"

"Not if you don't want to be kicked out of bed—and the room."

"Ah, well. Guess I'll have to find somethin' else to do." He leaned over and kissed her.

She dropped the belt to the floor, and he climbed aboard her, not missing a beat with his lips. He was a good kisser. This intermission before the next performance struck her as very familiar, as if they had been lovers for months rather than three minutes. Smelling his cologne mingled with sweat and musky sex fueled her anticipation for another round. *Just make it longer!*

"How old are you, anyway?" she asked after their lips broke for a rest.

His patented mischievous grin mere inches away. "Guess."

"Oh, I don't know, twenty?"

"Close enough."

"Come on. Really. How old?"

Other men might wear a smirk, but Mark was having honest fun. "Old enough to know better, but young enough not to care."

"You're not going to tell me, are you?"

"Not unless you tell me how old *you* are."

She frowned and said, "Yeah, right. That'll never happen."

"Didn't think so. I figure we're old enough to do what we just did. And if I have my way, we're going to do it some more."

She liked his brashness. "Really? Confident about that, are you?"

His smile finally grew on both sides until it practically stretched from ear to ear. "Sure am. You haven't kicked me out yet. I figure you want me to stay for a bit. Don't worry. I've got plenty of strength for this race."

"Just don't run so fast, okay?"

He winked.

*You kidding me? When's the last time a man winked at me in bed? Or anywhere?*

He was a good listener—and a quick learner. Strong, slim body above her, he started thrusting slowly, then increased to a steady and wonderful pace. As his cock pushed forward, she lifted her hips to meet him. Thankfully, his endurance lasted much longer this second time. And a third.

⚬⚬⚬

DRY LIPS KISSED her cheek, then her forehead, then her lips.

"Huh? What?" Michelle groggily mumbled. "What's going on?"

"Mornin'," Mark whispered.

"What time is it?"

"Never mind. C'mon. Get dressed. I want to show you something."

Whatever time it was, darkness greeted them outside. In the chill of the crisp morning air, her drowsiness subsided and her senses awakened a little. Seeing the frosty clouds from the nostrils of the horses made her glad she was wearing a thick sweater.

He tossed a saddle on a horse and said, "Now these aren't the trail hags they let you ride the other day. These're young and strong. You're gonna get a little wind in your hair. So be careful. Hold on real tight."

Mark was right. Eagerly pacing, this horse was a world apart from those that the ranch owner let them ride during a break in the modeling shoot a couple days ago.

She patted the sleek hair of its neck, said, "Giddyup," and felt silly for it.

Then they were off, rushing forward in the morning chill. The animal's effortless grace amazed her. Beneath her, its strong muscles beat a rhythm that she found sensual and exhilarating. Her hungry lungs drew in the crisp air. Moisture flecked on her cheeks. Whether from early mist in the air or drops of dew kicked up from Mark's horse in front of her, she didn't know.

Soon she was lost in the horse's motion, the wind whisking by, and the clomp of hooves. Whisked away were her worries over this one-night stand and lingering worries in the background about the modeling job. The horse's muscular rhythm mixed with a childish joy as if she were in a storybook fantasy and a carousel horse had come to life and carried her away, over the rolling hills with her prince.

As the clouds brightened, his purpose dawned on her. Pinks and purples painted the bellies of the clouds high over the mountains. The immense beauty awed her. If this was a dream, she didn't want to wake up.

———— ∞ ————

THE HOURS TRUDGED by in Michelle's weariness. Like the day before, focus on her work kept slipping from her hands. Today was even harder, as the sensations of Mark on and in her were fresh in the memory of her muscles and skin. But she was a pro and had been doing makeup and hair for so long, that she could let her fingers go on autopilot.

After she was done, she sat and watched the models play as cowboys. *I'll show you wusses a real cowboy.* Occasionally, a photographer called out for her to touch up a model, but mostly she could relax and remember the morning and last night. She was impressed by Mark's sweetness on taking her to the sunrise. He didn't have to do that. He could've simply woken up, had a cup of coffee, cut another notch in his saddle, and never talked to her again. But he didn't. Instead, he took her on a gorgeous journey. When they had returned to the stables, they made plans to get together tonight. The heat of anticipation built inside her throughout the day. She barely knew Mark, but this was a man who put her at ease and rapture. This was a man who could do *things*. And she wanted to do things to him.

*I'll make this a night you won't forget. Show you a gorgeous journey.*

The photographers, models, and art director wondered what Michelle was smiling so much about.

⸺∞⸺

DINNER WAS TAKEOUT taken back to her room. Sitting at a restaurant seemed pointless at this point. In the eagerness of the moment, the boxes of food were stacked on the TV and forgotten. Hungry hands tore at the buttons on each other's clothes. Unfortunately, Mark repeated his speedy performance of last night. His hips drove a nice, steady gait, but his dick bucked and spent much too soon.

"Sorry," he whispered. "Too excited, I guess." His blush wasn't as red as before.

"It's okay. As long as you make up for it." She was glad for the chance to give him an impish grin. "Let's eat. Get your strength back."

The hamburgers and fries were lukewarm, but Mark and Michelle wolfed them down. She had never had such good hamburgers as she had in Wyoming. Not the fast-food nonsense, but the real stuff from restaurants that didn't cheap out on any ingredients. Her bed made for a fun spot to eat. Mark loaded a french fry with a glob of ketchup at the end and swabbed her nipples with it. She was so surprised, she couldn't decide if she should be disgusted or turned on. The weirdness of it faded as his tongue licked off the red goo, and her pride tingled with her nipples over his slurping. This man *loved* her boobs. She enjoyed his mouth and hands for a while, then it was time to move on.

"Let's take a shower," she suggested softly.

He looked up with a nipple sunk inside his puckered lips. He winked. Tingles showered down her belly and legs. He released her and said, "Next to godliness."

The shower was all kisses and hands caressing soap suds on various body parts. Michelle's hands kept returning to massage his balls and cock, just as his hands paid loving attention to her breasts. The hot water invigorated her. As did the protein from the hamburgers. She was more than ready for more action. Mark clearly shared her readiness, as evidenced by a cock so good and hard that she had to be careful of its pokes.

*Is that a cowpoke?*

Dripping from the shower, they vigorously rubbed themselves dry with towels. Michelle dropped hers in front of Mark. He looked down at the fluffy pile at his feet with a questioning gaze. Her answer came when she lowered to rest her knees on the towel and kissed the head of his cock. He gasped. She took more of him in, tasting his cleanly scrubbed skin. His dick wasn't as juicy as the hamburger, but his rigid meat inside her mouth gave her a wicked thrill. She bobbed on him. His moans hastened in urgency. She scolded herself for not going slower.

*You're as bad as he is.*

Her mouth let him go. Her hand took over. She slid to the side. On her palm, she felt the thick pulse on his cock's underside. Naughty delight tickled her as he ejaculated onto the ivory tiles of the bathroom floor.

His face was priceless. Awash in wide-eyed pleasure. But there was something more, like the situation was perplexing to him. Sure, *she let me bang her and all that, but a hummer? I'll have to wait months of dating for* that. *Now this.* The cookie jar was empty. The crumbs were all over the floor.

She stood and kicked the towel on top of the white blobs.

He said, "I . . . uh . . . geez . . . wow."

*Nice compliment. He can't even speak!*

"What's that?" she asked and touched a fingertip on his lips. "Thanks for sucking my dick? That was the best blowjob I ever had?"

He burst into laughter. "Sweetheart, you're one of a kind." He leaned down and picked her up, surprising a gasp out of her, then carried her to the bed. Gently, he set her down. Gently, he parted her thighs. Gently, he kissed her pussy.

Her turn to moan. She took it all in: his forehead and tousled hair between her legs, one callused hand resting on her thigh, his tongue licking up and down on her skin that was wet from the shower and lust. Closing her eyes, she focused on his tongue and the pleasure waves it caused. On the shore of her forehead, the waves washed a vision of the early morning ride and the strong horse moving underneath her. Phantom wind coursed over her face and through her hair. Mountains rose to mountains of clouds flush with every shade of pink and purple. Like his cock in her hand as it had spurted. Like her pussy.

Mark was *damn* good. Either he had a huge stroke of beginner's luck or someone had schooled him well. And he took his time. An unselfish giver! She wished she could say the same. Apparently, he had forgiven her for the rapid blowjob. His tongue leisurely slid across her folds in different angles. It flicked across her clitoris, thudding with a strong rhythm. Her horse brought its hooves thudding on the hard morning ground.

Michelle reached down and held his hair as she had done with the horse's mane. His head nodded, silently saying "Yes" as if to mimic her real cries. An orgasm rivaling the sunrise burst through her. Mark stayed right there with his wonderful warm mouth until her cries dissipated into moans and her moans faded to a glow. She opened her eyes to see him standing and stroking himself.

*Getting ready. I owe you.*

"Give me your cock," she whispered hoarsely. "My mouth. I'll go. Slower. This time."

*Monosyllabic. Didn't I think that about him? Way back?*

She scooted to the edge of the bed. Still on her side. He moved over, brought his dick to her face. It was quivering and rising. She held his balls while watching. She didn't want to miss this gorgeous journey to hardness. The view was better than front row; the tip nearly touched her cheek. She imagined the blood in his cock bellowing, "C'mon, boys! Yee-ha!" and a stampede rushing up his shaft. Finally, she wrapped her lips around his mushroom cap. Soft and plush. She just held him there, resting on her tongue, as her fingers fondled his balls.

He seemed not to mind her lack of oral action. Other men might've tried to fuck her mouth. Instead, he leaned over, cupped her pussy, and rubbed it tenderly.

*Oh God. Back for more.*

She released him. She kissed his shaft with little kisses. Mixed in slow, short licks. Careful to not toss him over the brink.

He had other plans for her. His fingers had a love affair with her clit. His mouth had given so much to her tits and pussy, and now it was his fingers' turn. Soon, another orgasm engulfed her. She rested her head on the bed while her hand, on autopilot, rolled his balls. Her first orgasm had zapped her strength, but this one invigorated her as the hamburger and shower had done.

She looked up at him, past his patient erection, to make eye contact. "Lay down," she commanded. No whisper this time.

He didn't hesitate to climb aboard and headed for her.

"Uh-uh," she said. "On your back."

That pleased him. "Yes, ma'am. You got it." After he flipped over, his grin was wide enough to fly.

Her eyes narrowed. "Bastard." Now she wanted to fuck that grin off.

Still, she took a brief moment to admire his lean muscles. Scrumptious. Best of all was the cowpoke standing tall. She gripped it, held it steady, and lowered herself with a relieved sigh. *This* was what she was aching for all day. Filled. Filled up with good, thick cock. Straddling him, she looked down at Mark with great satisfaction.

*I'm in control now, stud boy.*

She simply rocked to and fro, wanting to draw out this delicious moment. Mark had no complaints. The guy was a pig wallowing in heaven.

*Why not? His dick got sucked. He's getting fucked. Doesn't have to lift a finger. Just his dick's got to stand up. And it's standing up just fine. Just fine, thank you, ma'am.*

The memory of the morning's ride appeared again in her imagination. Again she tasted the air, wind, horse, dew, and clouds. With the imagined senses swirling, her hips tried to mirror the gait of the horse in her memory—an effortless rising and falling like the smooth cycles of carousel animals.

Her eyes flitted open. The baskets on the shelf near the ceiling greeted her. Much better was Mark's face, the picture of relaxed pleasure. She leaned in and presented her breasts to him.

"You like my tits?" she wondered.

"Yup. Love 'em. Love those beauties."

*I'll never get tired of that.*

His big hands filled themselves with her breasts as his lips found a nipple. A simple invitation was all it took for him to show him how much he loved her beauties.

She pushed harder on him, grinding circles on his cock. The reins of control began to slip from her tight grip. Everything felt too glorious to command a certain speed. Different parts of her body leapt to mutiny and followed their own desires. Hips raised and lowered. Pussy nodded appreciation with the cock now in motion. Tits thrust closer to Mark's eager mouth. Hands clenched the headboard. Groans escaped her throat.

"Don't," she panted, "ever fucking call me ma'am."

He sucked harder on a nipple. His hips, no longer satisfied on remaining still, pushed up. Once, twice, his hips joined the gait of fucking. Skin slapped skin. His hands grabbed her ass. But his lips didn't let go of her nipple. A herd of slaps pounded the prairies of their loins. Like last night, the third time was a charm for his stamina. He saved the best for last. His cock had turned into an unstoppable steel rod as it rammed throbs through her, all the way up to her swaying hair. Her thighs pistoned, slamming her hot cunt down on him. Aerobics classes at her upscale gym never gave this good of a workout.

Michelle grunted through gritted teeth and could only manage "Oh God" over and over again.

Then he came. Her muscles hugging his dick felt the jerks before warmth flooded and spurred a mixture of disappointment and delight in her. She was glad for his orgasm, but it was difficult to slow down after the wild bucking. From the depths of savagery, becoming tame was hardly fun. She sat up straight, sliding her breast from his mouth, and returned to an easy-does-it rocking motion. Sweat dripped everywhere. Hair plastered on her forehead. Her chest heaved.

His grin was gone. He looked as wiped out as she felt. "Darlin'. . . darlin', that was . . . *wow*."

Not a shout the way an excited guy would yelp, but a soft voice that spoke volumes of genuine wonder. It was the biggest compliment she had received in a great while.

She collapsed on him and kissed him with the energy she had left, like embers still glowing in a fire that had once raged for the cowboys and cowgirls sitting around it. Even though darkness and sleep grew, they looked forward to the crisp, hopeful air of dawn.

With her head on Mark's shoulder, Michelle whispered, "Wake me up tomorrow. Take me riding again."

His grin looked hazy through her tired eyes. "You got it, pretty lady."

# The Magnificent Threesome

ELSPETH POTTER

The One-Eyed Man saloon was not providing the entertainment DeVille was waiting for. His companion, Harcourt, hunched over a small bound notebook, turning his stub of pencil over and over between his big, blunt fingers. DeVille doubted the numbers would change tonight. The next town along was hosting a fandango after a performance of the traveling Grand Ethiopian Minstrel Choir, and the streets had emptied by noon. Not a soul had entered who was interested in playing cards or hiring guns; the patrons, all two of them, came in, drank, gave him and Harcourt a suspicious glance, and left. He'd seen pitched battles that were friendlier.

He fluttered his deck of cards between his hands in a never ending stream while he pondered how best to irritate Harcourt, and thus distract him from his obsessive accounting. It wasn't getting them to San Francisco any sooner.

"It's closing time," the saloon's owner Miss Kitty said, leaning over their table. A tuft of dark hair poked out of the lowcut bosom of her red dress, and she needed a shave. DeVille had been surprised, when they'd first arrived two days ago how few of the customers seemed to mind Miss Kitty's eccentricities. Then again, it was the only saloon in town.

"I know you must get your beauty sleep every night," DeVille commented. He gathered the cards into one hand and smiled up at her.

Miss Kitty laughed like mountains crumbling and tapped the back of his head. He grabbed for his hat. She said, "You are a caution, Mr. DeVille. Are you sure you don't want to spend the night?"

"I am so sorry, ma'am, but me and the captain here have other plans," DeVille said. "Right, Harcourt?"

Harcourt put away his notebook. He looked up long enough to say, "Yes." He pushed his chair back and stood.

DeVille knew what the locals thought: Harcourt looked dangerous. A colored man with deep-set eyes and lean cheeks, he wore black from hat down to scarred cavalry boots. The grips of his two low-slung Colt revolvers gleamed with use, and he didn't hide the Bowie knife sheathed at his back. His voice was as deep and rough as his appearance.

DeVille, a round-faced white man with a tidy moustache, knew he looked as if he'd come from another country entirely, though both men hailed from Holmestown, New Jersey. He made an effort to look less dangerous and more prosperous than Harcourt. Today he wore snug fawn pantaloons and a brocade frock coat the color of good red wine. His embroidered gold waistcoat glowed over a minutely pleated cream linen shirt with a string tie. He reached into his breast pocket, but Miss Kitty laid a giant hand on his arm.

"I'll run you a tab," she purred.

"Why, thank you, Miss Kitty," DeVille said. "And I've been thinking—why don't you call me Virgil? It doesn't seem fair, me using your Christian name and you not knowing mine."

Miss Kitty giggled. This sound was more like rocks tumbling down a mine shaft. "Oh, you sweet thing," she said. "Don't you forget to have a drink with me next time."

"I most surely would never forget!" DeVille said. He bowed and kissed the back of her hand. Harcourt rolled his eyes. As they exited, a slender young cowboy entered, battered hat in hand, his longish blond hair tied back into a stubby queue. He wore a long sourdough coat, stained dark with waterproofing. DeVille gave him a second glance, and then a longer, more appreciative one as he hurried into the saloon, graceful in his high-heeled boots. Harcourt elbowed him. He sighed and let himself be drawn out the swinging doors.

They'd gone barely ten steps when Miss Kitty bellowed after them. "Virgil! Captain Harcourt!"

DeVille looked at Harcourt, who lifted his eyebrows. They retraced their steps. The cowboy sat at their vacated table. Seeing his face clearly for the first time, DeVille was startled by the softness of his features, though he was clearly no longer a young boy. Without beard or moustache, his lips had a plush curve, just waiting for someone to press with their thumb.

Miss Kitty poured the cowboy a glass of whiskey and placed it in front of him, but he didn't drink it. Miss Kitty said, her expression fierce, "Some rowdies attacked the Widow Larimer's spread, just outside of town. Austin here's her wrangler, and he thinks they'll be back."

The Widow Larimer was a colored lady and DeVille imagined she hadn't been interested in the so-called "Ethiopian" minstrels. Before Harcourt could say they'd risk their lives for free, he named their rates.

Austin looked up at that. He was beardless, but no fool, that was clear. "She told me to hire Captain Harcourt."

"Where he goes, I follow," DeVille said. "Ever since we were boys. But I'm only half his price, since he's the better shot."

After a little haggling, DeVille stowed away their advance money. Austin would ride ahead; they had to retrieve their horses from the livery. As they headed for the Widow Larimer's ranch, Harcourt said, "You only follow me because it suits you. You've been getting me into trouble ever since we were boys."

"He paid up, didn't he?"

A few moments later, Harcourt said, "You keep your hands off the widow."

"What if she's pretty?"

"She's respectable, Virgil. God knows, you could inveigle a snake into bed with you, much less a defenseless colored woman. I don't trust you farther than I could throw you."

"What if I inveigled for the both of us?"

"Virgil."

"Is it because she's colored? Are you afraid I'll—"

"We were hired to protect her, not seduce her."

"That tart back in Boise stick your saber up your ass?"

"Virgil."

"Jesus. You didn't do her at all, did you? You wasted my money and didn't do a damned thing."

"She appreciated your *money*, not me," Harcourt said, wryly.

"I paid her triple," DeVille said. "She claimed she would make you so happy you'd be singing for a week. She had this thing she did with her—"

"I didn't ask you for your help in getting a woman."

DeVille muttered, "If you're not careful, your cock's going to dry up and fall off."

Harcourt remarked, "Yours will wear out first. And remember, hands off the widow."

The Widow Larimer did not look as if she needed protection. It was clear she would repel seduction attempts with the shotgun she cradled competently and lovingly against her incredible bosom. A second shotgun leaned against the porch railing beside her. She was a veritable goddess. DeVille moaned softly.

She called out, "I don't need that fool gambler. I don't care how cheap he is."

"Boudicca!" DeVille rhapsodized. "Penthesilea! Mrs. Bridger the Sunday School teacher back home!"

"Quiet," Harcourt growled out the corner of his mouth. To the widow, he said, "An extra gun can never hurt, ma'am."

Austin stepped into view, cradling a rifle. "With all respect, ma'am, you sent me for some extra hands, what with everybody gone over to Destiny for the dancing."

The widow snorted, audibly. "You keep them out of trouble, boy. And they're sleeping in the barn."

DeVille murmured to Harcourt, "*He's* got a pretty face. Can't be more than twenty-five. Wonder if he needs someone to teach him the wonderful ways of the world?"

Harcourt eyed him sourly. "Hands off the wrangler, too."

—⁂—

AUSTIN DIDN'T HEAR their exchange, too busy wondering if the two men were going to be more trouble than they were worth. At least they had guns. And the colored man was right, more guns were better, though he looked like, alone, he could whip his weight in wild cats. Austin would have bet a month's pay he'd been in the War. What Harcourt was doing with a dandy like DeVille, Austin couldn't fathom. Perhaps he was DeVille's bodyguard. If DeVille was anything like Austin's daddy had been, he would have a lot of reasons to need one, but it wouldn't help him in the end.

Austin watched the visitors quickly care for their horses. The horses liked them, and they didn't stint on the work. Knowing that some men cared more for their horses than for other people, Austin relaxed a little.

DeVille glanced over as he gave his gelding's nose a final stroke. "How'd you come to work for Miz Larimer?"

He probably had his eye on the widow, or at least on her ranch. Since a gambler didn't seem likely to have money, maybe he was hoping his nice teeth would recommend him. Austin said, "How'd you come to be a dandified flatterer?"

DeVille said, without seeming to notice the insult, "Some are born to glory. I, however, am the son of the worst ruffian in Holmestown, New Jersey, saved from disgrace only by the good offices of Captain Harcourt." He plopped down on a hay bale.

"The archangel Michael couldn't save *you* from disgrace," Harcourt said.

His tone was familiar and absentminded, as if this sort of remark was common to him. They were friends, then, and not employer and employee? A strange pair. Austin said, "Don't let Miz Larimer hear you blaspheming. If she's your goal, that is."

Harcourt said, shortly, "I have no interest in the lady."

"She's rich," Austin said, testing.

"Is she?" DeVille asked. "Rich *and* a warrior queen. I think my heart just might leap out of my chest."

Harcourt thumped him on the back of the arm. "Later," he said.

A pistol slid into each of DeVille's hands. "Yessir," he drawled. "I'll take the cookhouse, sir, and cover the back. Austin, you coming with me?" He smiled and winked. Austin startled; the smile charmed, and the wink had looked almost seductive. Some men would go after anything that moved, true, but surely not if it moved in pantaloons.

"I'll take the well," Harcourt said.

Outside, Austin settled with one hip braced against a water barrel while DeVille paced endlessly up and down the side yard between house and cookhouse, talking endlessly as well, his voice clearly audible across the yard.

"Speak up, I don't think they can hear you in town yet," Austin said.

Cheerfully, DeVille replied, "The widow seems to have an itchy trigger finger. I can't enjoy my money if she accidentally blows my head off."

"And Harcourt?" Austin asked. The other man was only just visible as a dark bump on the well house, if one knew where to look. It was too bad he wasn't over here, chatting. Austin had never seen anyone like him before. "Why's he hiding, then?"

"He's in reserve in case things get difficult," DeVille said. "So, Austin, you like poetry?"

"No!"

"Well, how about this one? You might like this one, it's better than you think." And without letting Austin interrupt, DeVille charged into a recitation, and then another, and another.

Just after midnight, the attackers ran into the yard, whooping and firing pistols. Austin had never heard more than a single gun firing at once. The noise was bone shaking.

DeVille appeared unaffected, apart from dropping Alexander Pope in the middle of a rhyme and plastering himself against a corner of the house. "How kind," he said. "They brought friends. At least they're not on horseback."

"Miz Larimer," Austin said, from behind the water barrel.

"Hush," DeVille said. "Stay hidden."

"I thought hired guns were supposed to be brave."

"Only an idiot nominates himself to get shot."

The widow's voice rang out. "Get off my property or I'll pump you full of buckshot."

A foul reply from the yard was followed by her shotgun blast. Shouts and pistol cracks, and more shotgun blasts, covered any more dialogue. Austin followed DeVille's slow creep around the corner and was nearly knocked down by a reeling, brawny figure wielding a flaming branch in one hand and a pistol in the other. The intruder swung the pistol at the side window; Austin leapt at him, wrestling for the torch before he could shove it through the hole in the glass and set the house afire. The torch went flying into the yard, but the big man still had his pistol. He shoved Austin backward and aimed.

"Down!" DeVille yelled, and leapt. Both landed on the ground. Austin struggled free and sat up. The attacker fled, along with two others Austin hadn't seen, in a confusing melee overflowing with drunken curses.

"Cowards!" the widow yelled.

Harcourt stepped into view, rifle to shoulder. A hat flew into the air as if jerked on a string; its owner kept running.

"Great shot!" Austin said, feeling strangely euphoric.

"I was *aiming* for his—Virgil, you all right?"

In the sudden silence, DeVille's voice trembled. He still lay on the ground. "I can't believe, after all I've been through, some brain-less lickfinger son of a bitch—"

Harcourt shoved Austin to the side and yanked open DeVille's coat. "No blood," he said.

"Jesus Christ, something sure hurts. Right here."

The Widow Larimer loomed over the men with a lantern. "Do not take the Lord's name in vain, for if you died right now, you would surely go to the fiery pits of hell."

DeVille squinted up at her. "I don't think I like you any more."

Events came together in Austin's mind. "Miz Larimer, I think he saved my life."

Harcourt produced a dented silver case from DeVille's coat. "And this saved his. Virgil, you don't smoke!"

Austin took the case and examined the bullet mashed into its tooled surface. The case would barely pry open. It held not rolling papers at all, but pornographic playing cards. He said, "Captain Harcourt, do you think they'll be back?"

The widow said, "If they do, I've got a whole case of shells right next to my coffee and my thunder mug. You men can leave my property to me, now. Go on, get."

There was no arguing with her. Austin carried Harcourt's rifle and the silver case, then lit and hung a lantern while Harcourt assisted DeVille back into the barn.

Once inside, DeVille snapped, "Get your damned hands off me!" and shoved Harcourt away. He spun his hat onto the pile of saddlebags, followed it with his gloves, ripped his necktie loose, then sat down, hard, on the same bale as before, wrapping his arms around his chest. He'd seemed perfectly collected while bullets whizzed by, but after his outburst, Austin could see him shaking.

Austin said, "I think we could all do with a drink."

"In my saddlebag," Harcourt said.

Austin had not imagined spending the night sitting around the barn on hay bales, passing a flask from hand to hand with two men who had been, at suppertime, complete strangers. DeVille didn't speak for a long time, only took two gulps of the smooth whiskey for Harcourt's every one. The two men sat shoulder to shoulder and wore still, tight expressions that made them seem oddly alike. Austin took the flask from Harcourt's hand and sipped, just enough for flavor and a touch of heat, and to try and ease an unexpected trembling.

At last, DeVille said, "That damned harpy is paying me double. You can tell her."

Sympathy evaporating in a flash of steam, Austin snapped, "Don't talk about her like that!"

DeVille snatched the flask, gulped, then upended it, looking disgusted when nothing dripped out. "She was awfully mean to me. You only like her because you think females have to stick together."

Austin's breathing stuttered. "What?"

"I've landed on more than a few women in my time," DeVille said, still vainly shaking the flask. "Also, you smell better than a cowboy. Doesn't the widow know?"

Austin glanced at Harcourt. He looked mildly curious. Austin took a deep breath and said, "The widow don't hold with women wearing men's clothes."

DeVille shrugged. "Lot of people don't hold with me being friends with Harcourt."

"The reverse is also true," Harcourt drawled. "What point are you making, Virgil?"

DeVille smiled, though Austin noted the smile wasn't as brilliant as before the fight. He said, "If nobody knows about Miss Austin, here, I thought it might be a relief to her to let her hair down for an evening. So to speak."

Before Austin could reply, Harcourt had thumped DeVille on the arm. "I told you, hands off the wrangler!"

"She's not paying us," DeVille pointed out. "What d'you think, Miss Austin? Care to be entertained by two fine and discriminating gentlemen?"

DeVille appeared to be completely serious. Harcourt said, "Now wait just a minute, I never said—"

DeVille held up a hand to stop his words, in a graceful gesture like an actor on stage. "We can't leave you out—"

"This woman is not a—"

"Don't say it. You have some cussed strange ideas about women—"

"I respect women!"

"So do I!"

"You respect them right into bed with you!"

"Jealous? That's not my fault. I sure as hell invited you along enough times!"

The two men glared straight into each others' eyes as they argued. DeVille wore a strange half smile, which appeared to enrage Harcourt more every second. They were sitting so close they could, Austin thought dizzily, lean forward and kiss each other with no effort at all. Such a thing had never occurred to her before. She hadn't even known she wanted to see it, until now.

She sprang to her feet. "It'll be both, or none!"

DeVille snorted and shoved at Harcourt's shoulder, then grinned. "I was right. They always like you best."

Harcourt glared at him, then stood and took off his hat. "Miss Austin, don't let that silver-tongued rascal talk you into something you might regret. Please understand, we'll keep your secret, there's no need to worry about that."

Rough as it was, he did have a lovely deep voice. She could've listened to him all night. Now she'd have the chance. "That's mighty kind of you," she said, looking him up and down. His shoulders were broad and strong; his torso narrowed down to a waist more slender than hers. His thighs looked hard beneath his worn black pants, and when she looked at the bulge his cock made beneath the fabric, her mouth watered. "But it's you who don't understand. I was married once. Earning my living the way I do, though, I haven't been able to think about the pleasures of the flesh in a long time, because for sure, somebody would talk; and nobody's going to put a woman, a fallen woman, in charge of their remuda. You two don't have anything to do with that, do you? And I might as well make up for lost time." She looked at DeVille and smiled.

He said to Harcourt, "You can't complain about this one's intentions, can you?"

Austin took a step closer to the men and tipped her hat back on her head. "You ain't scared, Captain Harcourt?"

He glanced at DeVille, then back at her. His fingers tightened on his hat brim. "You two might want to speak in private. Perhaps I should take my leave."

"Don't," Austin said. "Please?"

DeVille reached out and slapped Harcourt's leg. "Come on, Harcourt. For the lady."

Austin stepped forward quickly, tugged Harcourt's hat from his hand, and pressed her lips to his, interrupting whatever he had been about to say in protest. Her hat fell off. His lips were far softer than she'd expected, and he tasted like whiskey with all the burn gone.

She dropped his hat in the straw and ran her gloved hand up his chest. That was nice and firm. She scrubbed her palm across a nipple, but she could barely feel it beneath his clothing. His fingers closed over her wrist and lifted it. "Are you sure about this?" he said. Flickers of lantern light reflected in his eyes and glistened off the new dampness on his lips.

"As sure as shooting," Austin said. "Get over here, DeVille."

"That'd be Virgil to you."

"Then I'm Sarah. Sarah Jane Austin." Her free hand, ignoring the pleasantries, shaped Harcourt's narrow waist and rubbed next to the knife sheath at the small of his back.

Harcourt's eyes closed for a moment, then he grinned down at her, a quick flash. "Virgil, this lady is compromising me."

"I'll protect you," he said, solemnly.

Preparations took little time. Harcourt opened out the men's bedrolls atop their canvas tarps, with enough straw beneath for cushioning, while DeVille skimmed off Austin's coat, knelt, and unbuckled her chaps. His fingers danced along her hipbones, then slid down the outsides of her thighs and cupped her knees above her boots. He tipped his head back to look up at her and said, "It's a nice change from petticoats and corsetry. Downright inspirational, in fact."

Austin swallowed and said, "You've got considerable clothes yourself. Harcourt, you going to help me with this?"

"Give me his coat, and I'll hang it up."

That wasn't what she'd meant. She stripped off her gloves and, before laying her hands on DeVille's coat, cupped his face instead. Stubble rasped her palms; he turned his head to press a damp, whiskery kiss into her palm before she reached his mouth. He was more skilled and intent than she'd been prepared for, and when she finally tugged away from him and shoved his coat off, her vest was off and her shirt had been unbuttoned to the waist, and pulled mostly out of her pants. She didn't linger over DeVille's waistcoat buttons as she'd intended, fearing she'd find herself ravished and sated before she'd even extracted his watch from its pocket. That would hardly be fair to Captain Harcourt.

DeVille helped her with the shoulder holsters he wore, laying his guns carefully away on a big silk handkerchief. Austin then glanced at Harcourt, whose hands went to the buckle of his gun belt, letting it slither down his hips until she caught the worn leather and laid the weapons aside.

She said to Harcourt, "You take his shirt off."

A pause. DeVille said, "Lady's choice, Aaron." Their gaze met and held in silent conversation. Austin tried imagining using Harcourt's Christian name herself, and couldn't quite conceive of it.

Harcourt took a moment, visibly collecting himself, then went to work in businesslike fashion on DeVille's cuffs and collar. He hesitated again. "You sure about this?"

DeVille shrugged. "I don't think our Sarah's that delicate, are you, honey?" He licked his lips, though, and looked away while Harcourt's hands, suddenly gentle, worked the linen over DeVille's shoulders and down his arms, and pulled off even his undershirt.

Austin understood, then. The bruise from earlier wasn't showing except as a red mark, but DeVille was scarred all over his ribs and belly, as if he'd been peppered with a giant shotgun. She forced herself to look away from the damage and saw he had a good pair of shoulders on him. He said, "It's from canister shot, down in Virginia. You got anything to say?"

"You look fine to me," she said. She elbowed Harcourt aside and set to DeVille's pants buttons. He didn't seem to mind her fumbling there, so she fondled his cock and balls through the fall of his pants before dipping her hands inside and drawing him out. His rosy cock had a pretty arch to it, and she imagined with suddenly dry mouth how it might feel inside her cunny.

Harcourt moved behind her and unknotted the thong binding her hair, spreading it over her shoulders. He burrowed his callused fingers down to her scalp and massaged, a pleasure that brought tears to her eyes. By the time she had DeVille fully naked, her own shirt had disappeared and Harcourt had his arms around her waist from behind, nuzzling her ear while neatly flicking open the buttons on her pants.

Harcourt lifted his head long enough to say to DeVille, "You first," and returned to her ear, her cheek, her throat, her shoulder, each kiss or nip making her tremble. She shuddered when she felt him hardening against the small of her back, and squirmed against him. He breathed raggedly into her neck and squeezed her to him more tightly. She wondered why he hadn't wanted to go first himself. So long as she had him eventually, she supposed it didn't matter.

Austin tugged DeVille forward by the arm. "Kiss me," she said, just before his mouth closed over hers. His clever fingers delved beneath the bandages she used to bind her bosom, and a moment later she felt another set of hands join in. Cotton fluttered down her sides and to the floor, and for the first time in six years, hands other than her own touched bare skin. She whimpered and sagged back against Harcourt, who cupped and held her breasts for DeVille's hot, delicate mouth.

She twisted in their grip for an eternity, until DeVille muttered something and Harcourt lifted her off her feet, with no more effort than she would have used in picking up a kitten. DeVille, she realized, was yanking off her boots, then her pants. She had just enough presence of mind to grab, but she wasn't quick enough to prevent him from seeing the rolled bandage that provided the other element of her male disguise. He grinned up at her and kissed her right on the quim. "Maybe it's time for those bedrolls," he said. "Harcourt, do take off that blamed knife. And the rest of it, while you're at it."

Austin lost some details after that. Both men seemed intent on making her lose her mind. She had never felt anything so good in her life as strong male bodies pressed both to her front and her back, their hands seeking out every sensitive spot she had. For a long time she did nothing but hold on and respond to whomever happened to be kissing her at the time. She could tell them apart even with her eyes closed: DeVille's artistry and the scrape of his moustache, Harcourt's smoother skin and more aggressive tongue and teeth. Harcourt's hands were more direct, too, which she appreciated as she began to feel more and more wild for release.

His blunt, callused finger delicately traced down the line between her buttocks, then stroked the folds of her quim. She cried out. The finger pressed upward, opening her with impossible gentleness. The tip of the finger curled inside, and she cried out again. Harcourt said, sounding out of breath, "I think she might be ready for you, Virgil."

"Goddamn—hold her for me—"

She didn't want to wait for anything. Austin grabbed DeVille's cock. "Hurry up you son of a—" She lost her breath as he nudged himself inside, stretching her deliciously; then Harcourt's hands shifted her hips in some small way, and DeVille slid in even more deeply, until there was no more space between them at all. He rolled his hips, rubbing deeply into the center of her pleasure, and she gasped, "Again!"

"Anything for a lady," he said, and after a little more of this she crested with a sharp cry, clinging to him until the waves of pleasure ebbed. She felt wonderful, but still wanted more. She squirmed between them both, sliding her hands from DeVille's shoulders to his hips and back again. She could still feel him inside her, harder than before, and Harcourt's cock like a iron bar digging into her waist.

DeVille said, tightly, "I need her on her back right now."

Harcourt took her head in his lap. She hadn't had a good look at his cock before now. She rubbed her cheek against it and kissed his velvety skin; after a muttered curse from him and a strained chuckle from DeVille, Harcourt took her shoulders firmly in his big hands and shifted her down, so she could no longer reach. She braced her feet on the blanket for what she expected would be a wild ride. Tense as he'd sounded, though, DeVille took his time, each stroke long and slow and sweet, punctuated now and then by his mouth on her breasts. Austin eased into a trance of pleasure, spiraling around DeVille's cock and Harcourt's gentle fingers playing in her hair and stroking her forehead and lips.

She didn't think she could come this time, but she reveled in DeVille's gasping breaths as his thrusts gradually turned short and ragged. She squeezed her passage tightly on him, on his next push; it felt even better, and DeVille's back arched, his fingers tightening on her hips. She did it again from then on, keeping up the torture until, with a soundless exhalation, he spilled his pleasure inside her. At the end, as he began to soften, he wedged two fingers into her and stroked up and forward, just enough hardness and pressure to wring another crest from her, this one deeper, seeming to flood her from the inside out.

After that, she drifted, barely aware of Harcourt shifting her more fully into DeVille's embrace, then sliding down behind her and throwing his arm over them both. His cock was soft; she hadn't seen him come, but perhaps he had, while she was occupied by her own pleasure. That was good, it meant there was no rush to satisfy him. She dozed a little then, and she thought DeVille did, too, for when she opened her eyes Harcourt had propped himself on his elbow and was stroking his friend's brown curls. As if he'd felt her eyes, his hand abruptly stilled.

"I was just remembering something," he said, withdrawing his hand and pretending interest in the door of the barn. He shook DeVille's shoulder. "Wake up, lazybones!"

"But she tuckered me out!"

Austin grinned. "I want to tucker *him*, too." She eased her backside against Harcourt and found him ready for her. He growled and

grasped her hip, holding her there for a stroke or two. She said tentatively, not sure if he would allow it, "I'd like a taste of you."

Harcourt's breath whooshed out against her neck.

"Lady's choice!" DeVille said, gleefully. "You can't say it's wicked
if she offers." Austin was relieved he didn't seem to mind he had-
n't received the same; she hadn't even thought of asking until that
moment. Maybe after this round, they could. DeVille leaned down
and kissed her, smiling against her mouth. "You are one fine
woman," he said. He drew his finger down the length of her nose.
She couldn't help but smile at him.

Austin turned in Harcourt's arms and said, "Just a little taste?"

His lips parted, but he didn't speak, only nodded. He laid his
hand on the back of her head as she crouched and licked the length
of his erection. His legs trembled, and his hand fisted in her hair.
It was something amazing, to have power over a man like that.
Holding his cock steady with one hand, she lapped his balls, then
dragged her tongue up his length again and pushed back his foreskin. She traced his rim before pressing tiny kisses onto the head.
The slit leaked clear fluid, and she drew it between her lips. He
tasted salty. She pressed her lips around the head and sucked. A noise
like a howl burst from him, and she jerked back, startled.

"Enough," he gasped. "Virgil, quit laughing!" Harcourt yanked
her toward him and kissed her feverishly.

He seemed to want her on top of him. Austin was happy to
oblige, stretching out on his muscled length, pressing her bosom
to his strong chest and matching up her quim against his rigid cock.
She rubbed against him and moaned into his mouth, hungry as if
she hadn't already come twice that night. Harcourt kneaded her
backside and DeVille stroked the rest of her, from one end to the
other. Harcourt's cock was insistent, though, and she began to feel
hollow, so she sat astride him, lifted up enough to get a grip on his
cock, and slid down. Harcourt reached up and played with her nipples, panting but not thrusting into her. "Lady's choice," he said.
DeVille settled on his heels next to them, apparently content to
watch for now.

Austin laid one hand on Harcourt's belly, letting her fingers stray down into his curls, and then touching where they were joined. "I want a good, hard ride."

He grinned, a flash of teeth she would've missed if she'd blinked. "That'd be a mercy just now, ma'am, but you please yourself."

Austin found herself smiling. "I'm not aiming to have any mercy," she said, and squeezed her passage on him. She could have sworn she felt the pulse of blood moving in his cock and throbbing against her inner walls. She bit her lip and rocked against him while he steadied her hips with his hands.

DeVille reached between them and laid his warm hand over her mound. His thumb nudged between her folds. "You want a little extra?" he asked.

"Yeah," she said. "And—" Harcourt's hands went to her breasts before she could ask.

Her ride lasted longer than she'd hoped. They were all weary, and even with DeVille's skilled touch, her pleasure this time took longer to build, but it was worth it. Her crisis wracked her with spasms from feet to scalp. She cried out, and soon after, Harcourt followed, holding her tightly in his arms. When it was over, he pressed his mouth to her temple and held it there for a long moment. His fingers feathered down her back, and she blinked back tears, though she surely had nothing to cry about. She kissed his mouth softly and rested her forehead against his.

All three of them lay spent for some time, until DeVille said, "That was some pumpkins."

Austin laughed. She didn't want the night to end. She hesitated, then decided to ask for what she wanted. When else would she have the chance? "I want you two to kiss. Because I ain't seen it before, and I want to see it now."

Harcourt opened his mouth, then closed it again. He didn't look so dangerous with his eyes so wide and shocked.

DeVille grinned. "Come on, Harcourt. Where's your grit?"

Austin touched his face. "You don't mind so much, do you? I've just got a powerful curiosity."

"I noticed," he said, dryly. "All right." He gave DeVille a quick, sliding glance.

DeVille said, "I never thought I'd see the day. They must be sledding in hell right now."

"Maybe I should change my mind," Harcourt growled.

"Don't," DeVille said. He slid a little closer on the blanket, eyes downcast. "Listen to me."

Harcourt's brow wrinkled. "What's all this solemnity?"

"I don't want to joke about this." He looked up, and Austin's breath caught at his steady gaze, though he wasn't looking at her. "You know if you asked me, I'd do just about anything for you, don't you?"

"You don't have to do *anything* for me. If you think *that*—"

Austin put her hand on his arm. "Let him talk."

DeVille went on as if she hadn't interrupted. "I didn't say anything about *having to*. I only—will you let me do this my way?"

"You're serious about this. You really want—why?"

"There's a difference between us, Aaron. Not color, or money, or bravery. You had a family, at least you did once. All I ever had was you. I've always wanted you to know that." DeVille caught Harcourt's face between his hands, dragged him close, and kissed him, openmouthed.

Even weary as she was, it was downright exciting, seeing others engaged in intimacy at such close range, and so emphatically. DeVille's hand snarled in Harcourt's hair almost immediately, as if afraid he would escape; but after Harcourt's first instinctive flinch, she could see his shoulders relax as he let DeVille taste him. Then Harcourt's hand lifted, and she'd never seen anything so tender in her life as when his big square hand fitted itself to DeVille's cheek, his thumb stroking. A moment later, he leaned forward, moving into the kiss, and DeVille made a tiny sound in his throat.

Austin slid her hand down between her legs. Harcourt reached back, blindly, and grabbed her arm, pulling her toward them. He dragged his mouth away from DeVille's, looking dazed, and kissed her hungrily. Then he turned back and kissed DeVille, who made a sound like a whimper, then Harcourt was tugging them both down to the blankets.

The night wasn't quite over yet.

When morning came, Austin found herself rolling her few extra clothes into a saddlebag, not quite sure how DeVille had talked her into going with them to make their fortunes in San Francisco.

# The Unattainable

LIVIA LLEWELLYN

. . . ONE THOUSAND ONE . . .

THERE'S A DREAM I once had long ago, a girlish fantasy I'd almost forgotten—and now I'm remembering it again, today of all the lonely days I've lived. I stand alone on the flat dirt of an arena. The flame-eyed stallion stares me down, foam-flecked lips curled back. He rears, slams his weight into the earth. I don't move. I know that by seeming not to see or care, I make myself the unattainable, the thing he longs for most in all the world.

And after time passes, the wild thing approaches, fear subsumed by curiosity. We dance in the empty center, limbs weaving rhythms hesitant, intricate, until I've mounted him. Now I'm astride his wide torso, hot muscles shuddering between my legs. He bucks beneath me, fights my weight against his heart. Yet I hold on; I will his fear to pass.

And it does, because he wants to be under my command, he wants to be broken. But it's only when I've ridden him pain-wracked to the ground, and still he pleads for my touch, do I know I've won. In the calm center of submission, when all that binds him to me are the reins of trust and love, I press against his steaming neck, and whisper in his ear:

"Now you're mine."

Of course, there are no feral things in this world. There are no flame-eyed stallions, no dragons to bestride. Nothing wild exists, and I'm old. Twenty years of bad jobs and nothing to show for it, except to turn tail and run across America, back to my old hometown. I'll fall into the void of my twilight years, and no one will remember me. At least, that's what I'm thinking as I drive the long curve of 97 into I-90. The hills part, and Ellensburg appears in the valley, backlit by the gold of the setting sun.

Twenty years haven't made a difference. College buildings still rise like neo-Gothic queens from the flat expanse, challenged only by the subtle mound of Craig's Hill and the white alien spine of the stadium. Cars stream ahead of me, ruby lights flowing into the town's throat. I roll down the window; hot air rushes over my face in dusty sheets. It's a wide and clean smell, like the scent of my first lover's skin, the night I lost my virginity on a sagging dorm room bed. He was a corn-fed stud, thick limbed and heavy cocked. I forgot how much I loved that smell, the taste of it in my mouth and lungs. I've forgotten so much, I realize.

Bright hoops of lights shine at the town's darkening edge, candy-colored tops gyrating above houses and trees. They disappear as I drop farther into the valley, but now that I've seen them, I know what to listen for. Calliope music, high above the hum of traffic and wind, laced with the roar of a grandstand crowd. The sounds and lights mean the fair is in town, and with the fair comes the rodeo: horses and horn-crowned bulls, and all their men.

Tomorrow I'll cross the Cascades, drive to the house I was born in, slink inside. I'll sit by the window, remember all the things I lost in life because I was always dreaming of something else. This little town below me is the last bead on a necklace that's been falling apart for years—soon it'll slip off with the rest. All I'll have left is the wire that binds me to nothing, except useless childhood dreams.

That's when the old fantasy floods my mind, pushing reality aside. I shift in my seat, trying to shake off the weight of the late-August heat. Sweat trickles under my clothes, pools between my legs. I need a shower. Something wild, that's what I need. A pleasurable ache blossoms inside as I think of cool water, the rough hands of a stone-faced stranger running soapy hands over my breasts, while I lift one leg, guide the red tip of his flesh into—

A burst of horn snaps me out of the daydream. Wincing, I fall back, letting the car I almost back-ended disappear in the traffic ahead. I rub my hands on my dress, clench the wheel, and concentrate. And yet, my mind drifts. One thing I never did in Ellensburg, all those years ago. One last bead, one last sparking jewel. One last chance to catch it before it falls.

Hotel names float through my mind, but they'll probably all be full. It doesn't matter. I already know, wherever I end up, I'm going to stay the night.

. . . ONE THOUSAND TWO . . .

Parking on the north campus lot takes half an hour, and the ride to the fairgrounds just as long. By the time I stumble down the shuttle steps, it's that odd hour before twilight, when a thin veneer of silver coats the shadows, sharpening the edges of everything. I pay the price and walk through the gate, stopping to look at the brick-red back of the grandstand. Crowds surge and disappear inside. The bulls will be in the arena tonight, the rankest beasts in the nation. Only eight seconds for each rider to hold on in order to place—but I know too well how eight short seconds can turn into a lifetime.

To my left, Memorial Park has been transformed into the midway, with Tilt-a-Whirls whipping screaming kids through the air. The stately O of the Ferris wheel hovers like a portal to another world. Odors of popcorn and sawdust, barbeque and leather saturate the air. It's like a big family picnic. I feel out of my element, clumsy—a middle-aged woman in a limp cotton dress, trying to get out of everyone's way. Wandering through the stalls, my eyes fix on men young and old. Men with children, men with wives and girl-friends, men with their buddies and friends. Stetsons and Levi's, clean-shaven faces, and light-colored button-down shirts. All of them with someone. A couple walks past, high school kids. The boy's hand is hooked into the girl's jeans, revealing smooth, tanned skin. Her hand rests on the back of his neck, playing with strands of hair. They're in love.

In a panic, I slip to the side of a cotton candy stand, away from everyone. What was I thinking? I don't belong here. This little fair isn't the Puyallup, where the midway blots out half the sky, where crowds of ten thousand clog the grounds. I could get lost there, unseen in the crush. But here, I stand out for what I am. A big-boned woman on the make. Floozy. Whore. Inside my dress pocket, the grandstand ticket crumples into a tight ball. Somehow it slips to the ground as I walk away.

A volunteer tells me where the exhibits are. She also points me to the beer garden—the look in her eyes tells me this is a woman who knows about the booze, because she'll be hitting it after the midway shuts down. I thank her and move on, determined to reach the stock barns before they close. Maybe I'll find someone there, some dirty stable hand who won't mind five minutes of humping in a cobwebbed corner with a desperate woman on the run from herself. It's a depressing thought, but it keeps me going.

I pause at the racetrack surrounding the stands. Behind the high chain-link fence, a horse approaches at bridle pace, the rider steering her down the dirt. A rush of noise from the grandstands drowns out the announcer's metallic voice. Did someone get thrown, or did they win? I turn away, just as the cowboy catches my eye. Not that I wasn't looking. But it's the horse that makes me pause—a roan, glossy and tall, perfect form. She's a wonder, and when the boy hears my gasp of pleasure, he smiles.

Yeah, a boy. Barely out of his teens, so bright and flush with youth that it hurts to stare at his face. Yet when he winks, I blush and grin like a little girl. He's not my type, he's far too pretty and young, but I'll take what I can get, nowadays.

"She's beautiful," I say. The horse tosses her head, dark eyes looking me over from under a fringe of hair. *I don't submit*, her mouth implies, firm against the bit.

"Don't let her know that," the boy replies, as he steers her over to the fence. "She thinks too much of herself."

"May I?"

"Sure. She's gentle." The boy watches as I stroke the long muzzle, his eyes never leaving me.

"You do know you're headed in the wrong direction," he finally says. "Rodeo entrance is that way."

I point in the opposite direction. "Yes, well, the beer garden's that way." The boy laughs, and touches his hat.

"Well, ma'am, maybe I'll see you there later."

"I highly doubt it. You don't look old enough to drive."

"I'm driving her, aren't I?"

Now I laugh. "Oh, I think you have it backward."

The boy winks. "Believe me, I'm old enough to do a number of things. I just might prove that to you later on." He guides the roan away, leaving me rolling my eyes even as I revel in the flattery. Turning away, flustered and unseeing by my small victory, I run smack into—

The words freeze on my tongue. The man standing before me stares me down with a face so sharp and cold, it's like being punched with black ice. By the time I've caught my breath, he's slipped into the crowd. People push past as I stand transfixed, shivering in the heat. All I remember of the face under the dark Stetson reminds me of Mt. Everest, in the black slits of his eyes, the weathered angles and peaks of his profile—a face I could kill myself on. And why I should care to remember what he looks like, I don't want to think about. Yet, I can't stop.

At some point I'm moving again, although I don't know what my destination is, or what will happen when I arrive.


. . . ONE THOUSAND THREE . . .

I can't see the land around us, when his truck finally stops. But I know I'm near Kittitas, the small town just east of Ellensburg. I found him in the barn with the Black Angus bulls, and it took longer than eight seconds to get his attention. Yet somehow I convinced him, made him take pity on a woman with no home, no place to stay the night. So when the floodlights dimmed and the gate closed, he let me follow him out of Ellensburg and down quiet roads to his home—a small white bungalow surrounded by large trees and endless clear sky.

I cut the engine. As it ticks the heat away, silence blankets me, the kind found only between mountains, in the sleeping valleys and plains. It's like someone just took the pillow off my face, and let me breathe again.

He's already out of the truck, a large sheepdog groveling at his feet. A peaceful pleasure radiates from his face, erasing the sharpness of years. I watch him caress the dog's soft ears. Goose bumps and prickling nerves, like my skin is on fire, like my first date in high school—I never thought I'd feel that way again. I grab my bag and get out of the car. I'll make him forget about that dog, if only for this night.

Following him across the dirt drive, I walk up several steps to a sleeping porch. Face hard again, he opens the door, motions me inside. I slip past, feeling a bit like I'm trespassing. Honestly, I didn't think I'd get this far. He drove to his house so fast, I was chasing him most of the way.

"Have a seat." As I perch on a worn brown couch, he hangs his hat up, runs his hands through his hair. Without the wide felt curve framing his eyes, he loses a bit of the severity. He wipes his palms on his jeans, stares at the floor. One boot rubs at something invisible. Is he nervous?

"Beer?"

I nod, and he disappears into the kitchen. I sit for a minute, all polite and mannered, then decide he's giving me a chance to snoop. So I circle the room, gleaning for clues. What kind of man is he? Well, he's not stupid. The bookcase next to the TV set is full. I run my fingers along the spines: Pynchon and Kerouac sit next to

McCarthy. Below them sits a shelf of thick technical manuals on agriculture. Several posters hang on faded cream walls—country landscapes, an Ansel Adams photo of the Rockies. No photos of him, though—nothing personal at all. I still know nothing about him, other than that he wants me here. I think, that is. If he wants to fuck, he hasn't shown much interest.

"You a reader?"

He stands in the doorway, beers in hand. There's a look on his face—amusement? Well, I can't pretend I wasn't snooping.

"Not much anymore. I got rid of most of my stuff when I had to move. The books were the first things to go."

He doesn't reply. Anxious to keep the conversation going, I slide one of the manuals out from the shelf.

"*Guidelines for World Crop and Livestock Production*. Light reading?"

"I'm not a light reader." He sets a beer onto the coffee table with a thump. The conversation on books is over, it seems. Frustrated, I sit back down on the couch. He returns to the edge of the door and takes a long pull from the bottle, his eyes never leaving me. I drink my beer, feeling self-conscious. It's like he's sizing me up, the way he'd size up a horse before deciding if it was worth the ride. It's a territorial stare.

Gathering up my courage, I stare back. His hair is longer than I thought, but there's also more gray in it than I noticed before. Dark brown eyes, and fine lines running from nose to mouth. My age, maybe older. Not beautiful, but compelling. His mouth *is* beautiful, I decide. Not the plump wet lips of a boy, but hard and dry, experienced—the mouth of a man. A sudden urge to feel that mouth moving over my breasts, between my legs, sends a violent shudder through me.

"Cold?"

"No," I mumble, playing with the label on the bottle as a blush warms up my cheeks. He saw me stare, knows why I shivered. Time to act coy. "I'll need sheets for the couch, though."

He shoots me The Look. I know that look. It's a sardonic half-smile, accompanied by raised eyebrows and the slightest of eye rolls. It's the look my mother used to give me when I lied about not touching myself. I knew he wasn't going to make up the couch, that I wouldn't be spending the night there. We both knew it. And so he gives me The Look. It's like waving a red cape before a bull. I sit up, back stiff, face tense.

"What." It's not a question. It's a challenge.

He says nothing. Now it's a contest. But my impatience makes me crack. I keep my voice light, but I can't disguise the anger.

"What? What did I say that's so amusing?"

He shakes his head. "Please. You didn't follow me all the way out here just for my couch."

"Well, I didn't follow you out here because I'm a slut, if that's what you mean." I spit the words out like bullets. My mistake. His whole body shifts, like a snake's casual recoil before striking.

"Don't pull that shit on me." His low voice oozes polite menace. I ignore it.

"What shit is that? Enlighten me, please."

"Acting like you don't know why you came here. You're far too old to pretend you don't know what's going on." A slight twang has entered his tone, a bit of the country. I'd laugh if I wasn't so unnerved by him—yet I can't stop goading him. Fucking up my life overcomes my fear, every single time.

"Well. If I'm too old to understand you, then I guess I'm too old to fuck. Problem solved." I sit back and pound the rest of the beer.

"Put that down, bitch, and get over here. I don't have all night." He eyes his watch. "Some of us actually work, you know."

That's it.

"Fuck you!" I slam the bottle down and grab my bag. It's only five steps to the door, but I don't make it. All of a sudden he's just *there*, arms around me, same way he's probably done it a thousand times with animals wilder and stronger than me. As he spins me around, covers my face in hard kisses, I'm surprised by how good it feels to be grabbed, to be handled. There's no poetry in it, it's all need. I still want to hit him, but I was oh so right about those lips of his, and my whole body rocks with the desire to fuck him. He slams me against the door—I match the grind of his hips, panting as I spread my legs, rub my crotch against the hard bulge in his jeans. But when I reach for his zipper, he breaks away and drags me across the room, hand clamped firm on my arm. I stumble behind, lips and cheeks burning from his rough stubble, as if a ghost of him remains locked against my face.

The bedroom is dark, and he keeps it that way. The moon is bright, though, and I see everything: hard muscles, beads of sweat, the flame-red spark of his eyes. . . .


. . . ONE THOUSAND FOUR . . .

There's no foreplay. He takes off his clothes with absolute economy of movement, while I let my dress fall to the floor, pushing it aside in a flowered crumple. I fall back on the bed, but I'm barely off my feet before he's crouched over me. Two thumbs hook into my panties, and they're ripped apart, gone. He's not looking at me, not touching me, not caressing me. I'm not here.

In the dim light, I see the ragged line of a scar across his lean stomach, glowing white against tan. It reminds me of that last sliver of light above the mountains, before the sun disappears. He spreads my legs wide, then places a hand against my shoulder, as if he thinks I'll bolt. He's not wrong. This isn't what I wanted, though—he's in complete control, there's no taming of anything happening here. Straining my neck, I catch a quick glimpse of his cock, long and hard as he strokes it, before he lowers and blocks my view. I close my eyes, grimace as he enters me. One expert stab, and I'm pinned to the sheets like a butterfly on wood. A gasp of pain escapes my mouth, but the hint doesn't take. He's fucking the hell out of me, and he won't slow down. But he doesn't make a sound—no grunts or groans, nothing to indicate pleasure.

The spackled ceiling overhead catches moonlight from the open window. I watch shadows dance in tiny patterns but they can't distract from the pain. I raise my arms, thinking if I put my hands against his chest, he'll slow. The movement triggers a violent reaction: he grabs my wrists and holds them against the mattress. I kick out, but he ignores me, probably doesn't even feel the blows. His cock pumps in and out, methodical and sure. Instinctive, against my will, my hips arc up in slight thrusts. My traitorous cunt contracts, grows slick. The pain doesn't lessen, but it doesn't grow worse. I'm not thinking of the ceiling anymore.

He presses down harder, crushing my breasts. Sweat trickles from his hot skin to mine, and I smell him, sharp and musky. A foreign scent, not unpleasant. He buries his head into my neck and hair. Hot breath floods over my skin as his mouth moves against me, murmuring some strange language I can't hear. Fear and anger dissipate, replaced with slow wonder. He's gone, somewhere so far away that I can't follow. Does he see me there? Am I in that dreamscape of his? He chose me. Even with that face, those dagger eyes, he could have had anyone. He wanted me. But, he's not with me.

"Stop," I say. He doesn't, and I try again. "Just stop for a second. Where are you?"

His sudden grab at my face is the last thing I expected. Two large hands hold my head tight. His lips brush mine as he speaks.

"What are you talking about?"

"Wherever you are, I'm not there. I'm right here."

He doesn't answer, only sighs before thrusting in again, like an engine that can't stop. I struggle against him, trying to keep him still, but he's too strong. He pushes down, pinning my arms between the both of us.

"You're hurting me," I say.

"Then make me stop. What are you afraid of? I can take it." The intensity of his words, the clotted growl of need and desire confuses me. Now I'm the one with no answer. Does he want me to punch his face, twist his balls until he does what I say? That's not my fantasy.

"Please, just slow down a little."

"Make me."

"What?"

"*Make me.*" Pleading.

This is unsettling. "I can't *make* you. You're twice as strong as me."

"Goddamn, you're stubborn." Is he laughing at me now, or is it from despair?

"Fuck you. I'm not livestock. You can't break me."

"I've broken everything." Desolation and sorrow in his voice, so deep I don't think he even knows they're there.

"You can't break me," I repeat, voice cracking. Tears well in my eyes, but I refuse to cry. "You won't win."

A moment of silence. Then, out of the dark: "I always win."

His mouth covers mine, tongue sliding inside. Protestation forms in my throat, but it dissolves. His cock demands my full attention, hammering away as if it had never been interrupted. God, it's so painful, and it feels so good. I can't help it—it's the way he moves his hips, the way the base of his cock and coarse hair rubs up against my clit, the slick pole of flesh filling me up. A perfect fit, like he was born for me. My nails dig into his back, barely able to keep a grip, mouth biting his shoulder as I come, thunderstruck into stiff spasms. A few more thrusts, and he stops—abrupt and matter-of-fact, like he lost interest. He rests on me, our hearts pounding in time together, with my muscles wrapped so tight around his cock, he couldn't leave me if he tried. All that, and he never uttered a single moan. He never came.

His head lies against my shoulder, breath light and untroubled. Do I dare? With the lightest touch, I caress his damp hair—a cautious attempt to show warmth. But the moment he feels it, he lifts up and pulls out of me, then rolls over, curling against the side of my body like a child.

He's asleep.

. . . ONE THOUSAND FIVE . . .

I stare at the ceiling. Beyond the roof of the house, stars run across the cloudless valley sky in silent flight. Everything sleeps below, dreamless and deep—horses and horn-crowned bulls, and all their men. Everyone safe at home, except for me. My hand creeps down to the matted hair, the throbbing folds of flesh. No one's ever fucked me as hard as he did, but I've never come like that before. I think of waking him, hoping he'll slide his arms around me, hold me tight—but the thought of his impersonal brutality keeps me still. And why didn't he come? Why did he fuck me with such violence, and for no apparent pleasure of his own, save that he could?

Well, that must have been the point: the bastard could. Leave it alone, I think. Let him sleep, before he wakes up and beats me to a pulp. I was lucky he didn't—I haven't been so lucky in the past. Rolling away from him, I slide the edges of the sheet over my worn flesh. I shut my eyes, concentrate on the wind in the trees, the passing of the stars.

But the hours drag, marked by electronic ticks of a digital clock on the bedstand beside me. I can't sleep, and now I have to pee. He hasn't moved, except to slip one foot over mine as he sinks further into dreams. If I get up, I'll wake him. But I really have to go, so I move, trying not to rock the bed as I pull my hair from under his head. He shifts, says nothing. I don't look back to see if he's awake, as I creep into the pitch-black bathroom. Only when the door's shut do I fumble for the light switch, and let out a sigh of relief.

The bathroom is sparsely decorated, much like the rest of the house. Under the glare of the light, I sit on the toilet and stare at the plain shower curtain, the half-curled tube of toothpaste on the counter, a chipped glass holding a single splayed-bristle toothbrush. Nothing on the walls except a mirror over the sink, and a small wreath of dried roses and crumbling greens. Not something a man like him would have bought in a million years. There was a woman here, once.

Flushing, I hobble to the sink and run the water till it's lukewarm. Wetting the corner of a bath towel, I pass it between my legs, ignoring the pain. It'll pass. In less than a day, I'll be home, and this will all be a distant memory, just another foolish, fucked-up dream—

I pull the towel away. The dull ache pulses like a second heartbeat. It's blood, rushing through all the secret places he once was. It's all I have of him, the pain of where he filled me up, where he left me. Do I want to erase it so quickly?

I empty the chipped glass and fill it with water. As I drink, my reflection catches my eye. The woman staring back is a strange but familiar one—the young girl of my past. A quicksilver ghost, fine-lined around the eyes and mouth, but all the more beautiful for aging. A pale face, surrounded by messy brown hair, red-tinged cheeks where his stubble burned the skin off, and a bright sheen drifting across dilated pupils. A drop of water hangs from my swollen lower lip. Is this what he sees? I imagine him standing behind me, hands cupping my breasts, mouth pressed against one shoulder in soft worship—an image so strong, I glance to my side to see if he's really there. I look back at the mirror.

*What I could be, with him. If I want it to be.*

"Stop it, Katherine," I whisper. "It's just another dream."

But the image, the feeling, remains.


. . . ONE THOUSAND SIX . . .

A knock at the door—the image dissolves. "I'll be just a minute," I start to say, but he's already opening the door.

"You all right?" He looks up and down my body, his face neutral.

"I'm fine. I was thirsty."

"Took long enough." He gestures, indicating that he wants in. I let him take the glass as I sidle past him, careful not to indicate my impulse to run.

"Don't fall asleep," he says before closing the door. I notice he keeps it open a crack. The thin line of light guides me across the mattress to the headboard, where I curl up and listen to the sounds of running water. Night pours in through the window like a river, in the rustling of leaves, the distant howl of a dog. The light flicks out, and I sigh. I don't want this again, all this rough handling, the impersonal stabbing of flesh. My heart pounds, unmoored and drifting—I curl up tighter, afraid it'll break through my ribs and float away.

He moves across the room, graceful and invisible. My body senses him standing over me, staring. I'm clutching myself like a child hiding in the closet from the monster outside. I want to shout *no*, my muscles ache, I'm battered and bruised. I want to cry, having him kiss the tears away. But he won't. He lowers.

The second time is like nothing I expected.

My hair slides back from my face—he's caressing it in careful strokes as he tucks it behind my ears. My eyes have adjusted, and I see all the sharp angles of his face softening. One finger traces my jaw line, moves up to my lips. His other hand rises—I brace myself, but don't turn away. His fingers suss out a length of hair, separating and smoothing it into three pieces. Something catches in my throat as I recognize what he's doing. He's braiding my hair, gently working the pieces into a single plait. His touch is comforting—inch by inch my legs unclasp, fall against his. Together we sit, heads bowed. Static crackles, and he licks his fingers before slicking the unruly strands down. My mother used to do that.

When he gets to the end, he ties it off—a hard and neat knot my fingers wonder at, while he turns my head and starts another braid. I shift closer, draping one leg over his. His knee rests against my cunt, soothing to the sore flesh. My left hand lowers onto his thigh, casual. He doesn't push me away. Inch by inch he works the plait, and I glide my palm up to the dark center, where he's all silky curves and tight curls. My fingertips find a home in the tangle of hair right at the base of his cock.

He ties the knot, then runs his hands over my face. Heat flares inside my cunt. His knee shifts, and I press against it, leaving his skin wet. He thrusts his hands into my hair, grabbing the braids, drawing me in. I don't have to see to know where his lips are—I draw his hot breath in on a sigh, let seep back from my mouth to his.

"Don't go," he whispers. "Don't go." Each word is a kiss, a sigh, a plea.

"I'm not going anywhere." Inside, my heart sinks. Is he going to start this all up again? But his response surprises me.

"Don't go home." More kisses, and his hands drop to my waist, running over the wide curves. "Stay here."

"I can't stay, I have to get home—" The sentence trails off, disappearing in the other conversation between our lips.

"Your home's not there." His words are cruel, but true. Firm palms slide up to my breasts, where his fingers and thumbs begin rolling my nipples into stiff points. "You're running to nothing."

I have no answer, for him or myself. Just let him have his say. It's worth it. My hand travels up his hardening cock, to the plump tip. I rub at the small hole, working silky liquid out over the soft skin. He gasps, but shifts away, his cock sliding out of reach. Lips move to my nipples, then lower. As I fall back onto the pillows, his wet mouth courting my cunt into delicious submission, it finally sinks in: this is a competition. An event. He's going to make me come like the animal I am, then walk away before I can give him one second of pleasure because he's the one in control. And I'll be left naked in the dust, pleasure and pain ringing my bones like bells.

*I've broken everything. I always win.* Isn't that what he said?

He wraps himself around me, sinks into me, and once again I drown. He doesn't come, and he won't tell me why. Hot tears and pain follow the orgasm, but this time he holds me, rocking me like a child as the night bleeds into pink dawn. Exhausted, liquid-limbed, I sink into delicious half-sleep, floating through fragments of dreams. The land lies all around me: I am the Cascades, ice-capped peaks covered by his star-shot skies. And somewhere in between, three words thread their way through us, a radio whisper of the heart drifting from one slumbering body to the other. *Let me submit.* I reach the black lands of sleep, a frisson of fear pushing its

way in with me, as I realize I don't know where the words came
from—from me or him, from the mountains or the sky.

### . . . ONE THOUSAND SEVEN . . .

Sunlight and bird song. Before I stretch out, open my eyes, I can
tell he's already gone. The wake of his leaving fills the whole house
with bittersweet calm.

A thin plaid robe lays on the edge of the bed. It wasn't there last
night. Folds pressed into the fabric tell me it hasn't been worn in
years. I slip it on, and raise a sleeve to my nose. His faint scent clings
to the fabric. I smell him on my skin as well, and in my hair. My
tongue glides over my lips. He's there, too.

I pad through the living room, reverent this time, as if I'm in
church. The windows are shut, and dust motes hang in the air like
dead stars. From the kitchen, a clock ticks out the seconds. I follow
the sound. Midday sun drenches the room, bleaching the curtains
white. I smell coffee and the sulphur whiff of eggs. A mug sits next
to the pot—I pour a cup and lower myself into a chair, still a bit stiff
from last night. I don't feel bad, though. I haven't felt this calm, this
balanced, in years.

He left a note and a map on the table, under a candy-red apple.
I slide the note toward me, and read. Neat cursive letters in blue pen
rest on the lines:

Working the fair today. There's a plate for you in the oven.
Take what you need from the fridge.

I'll be home around eight.

A plate in the oven—I swing around, catch the handle, and open
the oven door. Warm air hits my face. A plate covered in alu-
minum foil sits on the rack. I grab a dish towel and pull it out, peel
the foil away. Bacon, eggs, and toast. He made me breakfast.

I pour another cup of coffee, and start to eat, staring at the note all the while. No "thanks for everything," no "it was great." Well, it's not his way. I unfold the map. He's drawn a dotted red line from the middle of nowhere, through Kittitas up to I-90. A note, an apple, and the way out. After all his protestations, he wants me gone. He wants me—

"Home," I say to the ticking clock. But the word doesn't sound right anymore. Maybe because, when I think of home, I don't know what it is I'm supposed to see.

My dad once told me that no man could live in an oasis. He could stop and drink, rest a bit, but then he had to move on, find his way home. This is only an oasis, I say as I wash the dishes and place them in the plastic rack. It was a place to lay in the shade, away from the burning sun. I stand in the shower, curtain open, staring at the wreath on the wall. It was only a place to get a little rest, before pushing on. The braids grow fat with water, and I don't undo them. My eyes blur—from the soap. I smooth down the sheets and plump the pillows, pressing each soft feather mound to my face before laying it on the bed. He'll sleep on them tonight.

I have to go.

I could have snooped through all his things, but I don't. He deserves better from me. But on the way out, I peek into the second bedroom, unable to resist. A flick of the light switch reveals boxes and cartons, an old steamer trunk, musty sheets covering tables and chairs. I lift a sheet, revealing a short bookcase. Trophies, plaques and ribbons, all proclaiming the same thing for the same event. *first place. first place. first place.* The dates—he won some of these in Ellensburg, the same years I lived here. We fought and bled and slept in the same little town, under the same starry skies. I let the sheet drop.

An open box sits high in a pile—I pull it down, and flip through a series of photos in cheap frames. A young man, jet-black hair framing a stern and determined face, riding bull after massive bull. Behind him sits a sea of faces: judges and grandstand crowds, with floodlights shining down on man and beast. Odd to see so much power and rage, muted behind framed glass. In one photo, the bull's kicked back so high, his hind legs are higher than the rider's head. But none of the photos show the rider falling. He's marking out his eight seconds, every goddamn time. The rage in the photos is the rider's, not the bull's. This is a man who always wins, who never lets go of the reins.

And yet he let go of me.

I pack the photos into the box, and balance it back on the pile. I'm careful to close the door behind me, just like it was before. My watch says two o'clock. I have to be on the road. A good six hours of driving is ahead of me, and I want to cross the pass before dark. The lights are off, the windows shut, and everything's tidy in the kitchen. I take the note and the map, leave the apple behind. I struggle to lock the front door, then realize it doesn't, and probably never did. There's no need for it out here. Amazing.

Throw the bag on the seat, rev the engine, and don't look back. It feels good to be on the road again, to be free. So it didn't turn out quite like I planned—when did anything? Buildings whoosh past in a blur as I speed through Kittitas, up to I-90. It was an adventure, something I'll remember when I'm old, when there's nothing else left to remember. One last bead from the string, flame-bright like the eyes of some rough stranger, caught in the palm of my . . .

. . . I stand by my car. It's parked on the lookout, a half-oval of dirt next to the highway, high above the valley. From here I see Ellensburg, see the glimmer of the Ferris wheel, the sparkle of windows and headlights caught in late afternoon sun. Kittitas lays to the east, a green jewel in a strand of ancient land left scrubbed by the Cordilleran floods. To the left sits Cle Elum, another small treedappled town. And in between, rivers of roads, a patchwork of farms and ranches. The land teems with life from the horizon's edge up to the snowy Cascades. This is no oasis. It's an empire.

*I'll be home around eight*, the note in my hand says. I've been staring at it for three hours now, almost four. My skin burns from the sun. *I'll be home.* He's a careful man, economical with words. That much I know to be true. Three things he wrote that I needed to know, and left the map for leaving. What purpose, then, in telling me when he'll be home? Why should I care if he's home around eight? That's when I'm supposed to be back— I won't make it now. He's won again. Has he ever lost?

Night's closing in. The sun's still high, but the light's changed. I look beyond the mountains and see nothing, feel nothing. The only thing I feel is in my hands—on a slip of paper, in a single cryptic sentence. Turning around, I reach through the open window and pick up the map. A dotted red line with two round ends. The circles look like the eyes of a bull, burning through paper streets. An animal who's always won, who's never been allowed to surrender. What would his fantasy of love be, then? What would be the unattainable for him?

*Let me submit.*

Traffic's a bitch. The fair's closing, and horse trailers and RVs clog the streets. I inch my way through Ellensburg to Kittitas Highway, then gun the motor till I'm back at the house, tires spraying gravel across the scraggly lawn. The windows glow pumpkin orange from the setting sun. Early evening winds whip the braids across my face as I unlock the trunk, root through boxes. At the bottom: thin leather straps and bronze workings, attached to six erect inches of polished wood. I could be wrong. What if he hits me—or worse? The note is damp with sweat. I clutch it, praying I'm right as I stumble up the steps into the house.

Everything's as I left it. I open the windows, turn on a light. He'll see my car, I can't hide. I don't want to. Let him know the rider is ready, the event's already begun. I leave the bedroom dark. By the light of the setting sun, I slip off my clothes, strap the harness around my hips, and climb onto the middle of the bed.

The clock ticks, the wind sighs. Shadows stretch across the room. I wait, patient—the apple at my feet. The clock hands near eight. An engine, faint in the distance, growing nearer, until it throbs through the open window, then cuts. I don't breathe.

Footfalls against the earth, running. The slam of the door, the pound of boots against wood. He's rushing down the hallway, down the chute—

. . . ONE THOUSAND EIGHT . . .

There's a dream I had long ago, a girlish fantasy I'd almost forgotten—and now I'm remembering it again, tonight of all the lonely nights I've lived. I wait alone on the flat white plain of the arena. My flame-eyed stallion stares me down, lips curled back in rage or shock. I am unmoved. Arms outstretched, erect, I look away. I know that by seeming not to see or care, I make myself the unattainable, the thing he longs for most in all the world.

And after time passes, the wild thing approaches, shy fear subsumed by curiosity, kissing my hands, my feet. I wipe the sweat from his skin, run my fingers over his body, passion flowing where once only loneliness lived. We dance in the empty center, bodies weaving rhythms hesitant, intricate—until, slowly, gently, I've mounted him. Now I'm astride the lean torso, hot muscles shuddering under my legs. He bucks beneath me, fights the pain, fights my weight against his heart. Yet I hold on, I will his fear to pass.

And pass it does, in the shower of pearl-studded pain, because he wants to be under my command, he wants to be broken. But it's only when I've ridden him pain-wracked to the ground, and still he pleads for the pleasure of my touch, do I know I've won. In the calm center of submission, when all that binds him to me are the reins of trust and love, I press against his tear-streaked neck, and whisper in his ear:

"Now you're mine."

# Gentling

SHANNA GERMAIN

I HATE HORSES. Goddamn big hooves, sharp as pickaxes and power enough to crack your nose with a kick or break all your five toes with one of their accidental/on-purpose step-downs. Tail full of wires slapping your face. And them teeth—'bout as long as saw blades but hidden behind a soft little nose, so you don't find out they're there until they've already opened up and split your skin.

This horse in the stall in front of me I especially hate. Darnassius Starblaze Sugarback, it says on the big gold plaque above his stall. Sugarback, my ass. I don't know who the hell named him, but I hope nobody ever asks that guy to name their kids. Devilstallion. That's what I'd like to name him. Painintheassius Devilstallion. You can write that on his official papers.

Damn horse got it out for me, though I've been nothing but nice. Nice and full of carrots and oats. He don't care. I hold that carrot out flat in my hand, same as all the other hired help. He nuzzles it off them just fine, but goddamn if he don't open right up and try to eat my fingers like they're the fucking carrot. Like he don't know the goddamn difference. Which he does. Asshole of a horse, but not stupid. I know that much.

See, right now even, Devil horse banging those slamslam hooves against the wood, just cause he can. Just cause he knows I'm out here with nothing but a limp old carrot to protect me.

I want to like him. All the other horses, I do. Before this, I did a stint down at Homestead dairy. I liked them Jersey cows easy enough. They got big soft brown eyes and no teeth on the top, which makes them look like little old ladies. Sure, they got sharp hooves, too, but you know how to get down next to them on your stool and pull on them teats just soft and talk to them like you might be their calf, and they're more than willing to leave them hooves in the straw where they belong. But then the dairy farm went mechanical—milk machines and automatic feed—and there wasn't any more to do over there. Now I'm on to these horses. I'm grateful for the job, but horses. Jesus.

Bruce—he's the main man round here, the main reason I'm still here—that's the first thing he wanted to know when I got here, if I was afraid. Henry, my boss at Homestead had told to go look for Bruce here if I wanted a job, but nobody told me what to look for: tall, thin, balsa-wood looking man, like if you stepped on him, he'd crack right in half. Big brown eyes doping on you through square wire glasses. Took me forever to find him that day, had to ask around until I seen him standing in a stall under the curved neck of a big black stallion.

I didn't want to interrupt—figured he was focusing all his attention on being that close to a horse so big—so I stood. Tried not to shuff my feet back and forth, the way I do when I'm nervous. The sound of my work boots back and forth on floor, it's comforting somehow, though I'm the only one that thinks so.

Bruce noticed me right off though. Maybe it was the leather bag over my shoulder, or the haying gloves I was holding, but he figured I was there for a job without even asking.

"Are you afraid of horses?" he asked. Kept his eyes on me while he talked, like he didn't even notice the way that horse kept throwing his head around, kept picking those hooves out of the straw. Reminded me of those guys who put their heads in the lion's mouth, looking at the crowd the whole time.

I knew I wouldn't get the job if I said yes, but I said it anyway.

I'm lots of things, probably not half of them good, but I've never been a liar. I looked at him standing skinny under the wide neck muscles of that big, black horse. "I might be," I said.

"Good," he said. "You should be." Bruce reached up to stroke the horse's black neck, and I saw the muscles in his arms, too, in his forearms, the way you could tell he used them all the time. And I saw why Henry sent me to talk to him: he turned to men the way I would turn to men if I wasn't so damn afraid.

And then I was a little afraid of him, too. Not in the same way as the horses, but in the way that I knew he could crush me, with his hands and his teeth and his hips, could push me up against the wood until I couldn't breathe, wouldn't want to breathe. I shivered a little, just down in my belly where I thought it didn't show.

"Animals can smell your fear," he said right then and I thought maybe he could smell my fear, too. Or maybe he was just talking about the horses. "So you just need to show them that you are not afraid."

And then he told me to come back tomorrow morning, ready to start. When I left, he was still under that big neck, showing that black horse how not afraid he was.

Next day, Bruce started me on the mares—big and fat and slow with babies. Then running around with the foals, currying out their winter coats and lunging them in bigger and bigger circles. All the time, me learning from the way Bruce bends his body to those horses, enough to say, "I'm not a threat," not so much to say, "I'm afraid of you." Learning from the way he tangles his fingers into the wire mane of some unruly colt. And from the way he waits for the skittish ones, sitting stock-still to make him a no-threat, until they come to him. He moves these boys and horses around and around him, their center. No matter he's littler. And smarter. He's got them all eating out of his bucket, his cupped hands. And, me, I'm ducking my head blind right down there with the rest, even though I can feel that big cougar sneaking up on me, waiting to pounce.

Couple of months like that and then, yesterday, Bruce puts his hand right on my shoulder and says, "It's time." Those eyes doping at me through the lenses like I should know what he's saying. "I'd like you to start working with Sugarbuck." Takes me a second to realize he means that Devil horse. But I can't say no to Bruce, not the way he asks me things, not those big brown Jersey eyes. Not with me wanting to impress him so he'll put his hand on my hair like he does some of the boys, the ones who've been here the longest.

So here I am, standing in front of this stall, stalling. From inside, Devil stallion takes another whack at the wood. Beneath the sound of those slamslam hooves, I whisper, "I ain't afraid. You hear that, you devil dog? I ain't afraid of you."

I suck in deep, smell the horse shit and wet straw and wood breaking down from where that Devil's smashing up the inside of his stall. And then I put my hand on the metal latch, slide it up until the door can swing open and I can step inside. Devil's got twenty hands, which basically means he's one tall fucker. Skinny Arabian head, all curved muzzle and banana ears. White blaze that skinnies up his nose with a baby star on top. You see this horse from far away—out to pasture running with his neck all arched—and man, he's glory. You see him up close like this, and I'm telling you, he's one big mountain of sharp teeth and pointed hooves.

The door shuts behind me and it's just me and him and my carrot between us. "Hey, Dev," I say in my lowlow voice. "We're gonna be friends, ain't we?"

He shows me the whites under his eyeballs and snuffs at me, nostrils all open. His ass is tucked back in the corner of the stall, nothing to aim at but wood, and still he's got one foot cocked up out of the straw.

I put the cold carrot on my hand, my fingers as flat as they'll go, bent backward if I could. "Look, brought you something." I gotta keep talking, keeps that shivering inside me almost laid still.

But he don't want it. First he wants to bite off all my fingers like they're golden carrots, and now he don't want the damn thing. Just stands there dropping his head the way they do, pawing the straw up with his front hoof.

"C'mon, c'mon, you big fucker." I don't really mean what I'm saying, I show him I don't really mean them bad things—please you big goddamn horse don't kick my fool head off—by keeping on my sweet, soft, lowlow voice.

Devil horse steps toward me, lowers his head so it's right at my face, my little teeth to his big ones. My foot goes up, like to take a step back, and my hand is already sneaking behind me, aiming for the latch.

And then I think about Bruce. How you can't show them you're afraid. I think about his Jersey eyes behind his glasses, the way his hair is the same color as them cows, tawny like.

But all those thoughts don't matter none. They don't stop what happens. Devil stallion gives his head a shake, opens his mouth. My hand moves back, lifts the latch, opens the stall door. I throw the carrot down on the straw. My work boots shuffling, not comforting now, not this way, backward, away from the hooves, the teeth.

My back hits up against something halfway out the door, and goddamn if I don't let out some kind of shriek. The noise is high and loud and it's coming out of my lungs and lips. And even as I let out that sound, I smell somebody like warm hay and hand-rolled tobacco. It's Bruce against me, bending, not bending. His chest to my back, pec muscles pressed to my shoulder blades, his waist against my ass. My body rising, so fucking fast, how do you stop something like that, the way the blood fills everything?

"Fuck," I say. I try to pull away to spin around and face him, but Bruce has got those skinny, strong arms around me and I know how those damn colts feel when he puts his fingers in their manes, holds them there, inside all that anger and fear. Afraid of what's in front of them, afraid of what's behind.

"What happened?" Bruce asks, and his voice is right by my ear. He turns me so I can see Devil, backed into the corner of his stall after my yell. The carrot's still in the straw where I threw it, and

Devil's eyes go back and forth—me, carrot, me, carrot. I realize he's
as afraid of me as I am of him. Maybe more. Warm shame spreads
up my chest, all the way up to my forehead.

"I got scared," I say.

The muscle in Bruce's chest jumps against my back, tic tic.
"No," he says. "You've always been scared. Try again."

I don't know where the anger comes from, that fast, like it's been
sitting in my blood, waiting. But it's enough that I can break free of
Bruce's grasp. My arms are shaking, and I cross them over my chest.

"You fucking left me," I say. "What good is it, you being there
through the mares, through the babies, and then the big shit comes
down and you send me in on my own?" I can't catch my breath after,
as though I haven't talked this much in my whole life. I'm already
thinking how you don't talk like that to the guy who pays you. I'm
already thinking how I'll pack my things, maybe try to find a job
down in the next town over. There's a feed store there. No horses,
just back-breaking bags of oats.

Bruce steps toward me, and I step back. The lines between his
eyes make vees.

"Do you really think I'm not here?" he asks. He opens his arms
up, and somehow it makes him twice as big. Then his voice goes
soft. "What do you call this?"

I don't have nothing to say. I don't know how the fuck I feel. I
can't shake that press on my back from his body, from the way his
arms wrapped me, held me in my place.

Bruce keeps stepping forward and I keep stepping back. Bruce's
backed me into Devil's stall. In front of me, Bruce. Behind me,
Devil. My heart goes runaway hoofbeats in my chest, bam bam bam.

"What now?" Bruce asks, like he's not running the show.

What now is what I want to know, too. Like I'm not even thinking about it, I reach down and pick that carrot out of the straw. My
head near those goddamn devil hoofs and I don't even care, 'cause
everything's upside down anyway and maybe a kick to the head will
right it. But Devil don't kick, he just waits 'til I get that carrot

toward his lips, and then he takes it between his soft lips and bites it dainty, like he's saving some for me.

———

A WHOLE WEEK goes by and no Bruce. Devil and I got some kind of truce going—I bring him couple a carrots and a bit of oats, and he lets me do what I got to. Lunging, currying, cleaning the stall around them slamslam hooves.

I do my best, 'cause the truth is I don't really want to hump feed bags down at that store. The truth is, I'm coming to like them fat mares and long-legged colts. If Bruce is pissed, if he's going to fire me, I wish he'd hurry up and do it. Instead, I'm watching for him all the time, waiting for his thin shadow, that tobacco smell. Sometimes at night, in my cot above the foaling barn, I think of Bruce's chest up against my back. Them shivers in my belly. Fear. Fear, and something else I don't like to think about.

I'm running this circle in my head and Devil's snorting over my shoulder. Not thinking, I rub my hand over the soft spot on his nose. Skin's real velvet there, and he shoves against my palm without opening his mouth. Maybe I'm coming to like this Devil a bit, too. Not being so afraid of him, at least.

I get Devil inside the pasture and unclip his lead. Used to be, I'd stand outside the fence to unhook him. Didn't want to be in there with him. But now, I give him a kind of pat on the shoulder, sending him on his way. Then he takes off, those big hooves spitting up blades of grass. Tail like a kite out there. He's glory and glory, no matter how you like him.

Devil hauls down the length of the fence, snorting. Runs past the little house where Bruce lives. I never been there, but now my feet are walking that way like they know where they're going. I'm still inside the damn fence with the damn horse, but it's like my feet don't know that. They're just going and going. When I get to the other side, near where Devil's tearing out the grass with them big teeth, he raises his head at me. Got a mouthful of greens coloring his slobber. Makes me want to laugh, but I just hop the fence, head toward Bruce's porch.

It's a bitty house. Bittier when you get close as I am. Front door's open, which seems like as good reason as any to cross the front porch and knock on the door frame.

"Bruce? It's me."

I lean my head around the door jamb, look into the kitchen. Bruce leans back in the chair. Jeans. No shirt. His horse-working muscles under his chest skin and his arm skin. I have to look away, like I just came on him naked.

"Sorry," I say.

There's a stud book cracked open on his front porch chair. Devil's on the cover, looking mean as hell, his coat oil-slicked to show his muscles. I need to get off this porch, back to them mares and foals, away from the picture of Bruce, of Devil, but my feet are stuck solid. Nailed like horseshoes to this wood porch.

Inside, Bruce doesn't say nothing.

I can't help it. I peek back in. He's got his arms behind his head, leaning back. Them eyes doping somewhere else. Out the window, like. He doesn't move. And I can't move.

I don't know, we stay like that for a long time before I get it. Soon as I do get it though, my feet start across the door jamb and onto that kitchen floor. See, what I get is that he's waiting for me. Just like he waits for them horses. Sitting still until we ain't scared no more. Until we want what he's got so badly, it kicks that fear down somewhere inside where we can't feel it.

I'm six shuffs across his kitchen floor and thinking how I wish he'd look at me. And how I wish he wouldn't, 'cause then I'd be stuck again. Him not looking means I can get right up close to him. I stop in front of his knees, smelling him all cigs and hay and horse. My head goes down until I'm looking at his work boots, the back of my neck open to the air.

For all the ways his body is still, his feet are moving his work boots on the floor. Just little tap-taps against the wood. Not obvious like me. But I like to know he's got some fear in him, too. Makes it okay for me to hold my hand out flat in the air between us.

Bruce looks at me finally. Looks and looks until I'm near to going away. And then he puts his lips on my palm. Rests 'em there like the Dev does sometimes.

"What took you so long?" he says against my hand. His lips aren't soft as Dev's, but they make them shivers in my belly all the same.

I can't answer. It's just me, standing, standing.

"Are you afraid of me?" Bruce asks my palm. His voice same lowlow as mine when I talk to Devil.

I swallow to keep the shivers from coming out when I answer. "I might be."

"Good," he says, just like the first time I met him. "You ought to be."

He raises his head and I have to put my hands on both sides of his head like he's some yearling needs a halter. Soft hair and the sharp sides of his glasses in my palms when he stands. Face to face and I don't know what to do with lips and teeth, mine or his, but they're doing their own thing together. Like our mouths is smarter than we are.

And if that's true, then our bodies is smarter than we are, too. Pressed together. Feet to feet, both of our feet still now, but our hands going all over. Bruce is all hay-tossing, horse-riding muscles tucked inside that baby-soft skin, pale and warm as straw.

Bruce puts his fingers on my belt buckle. The clang of metal starting to unbuckle, that's what undoes me.

"Wait," I say. My heart goes runaway hoofbeats in my chest, bam bam bam. "Wait, wait." You're alone long enough, you put up a damn lot of fences. Now, I can't find my way out of them. It's not like Dev's pasture, where I can just hoof my way over. I got to find a gate to go through. I close my eyes, let my hands still at my sides.

Behind my eyelids, the sound of Bruce leaving. Step-step-step of cowboy boots on the wooden floor.

It's all the gate I'm needing, that sound of him moving away. I swing open my eyes, ready to tell him what I'm fearing.

He just puts the front door shut and snaps the lock. He's got a grin like I never seen, teeth as big as Dev's. But, somehow, not making me afraid.

This time, it's me that undoes my own buckle. I undo Bruce's, too. And when he leads me into his bitty bedroom, you know I don't toss my head. I just follow. Even when he drops his hand from mine to pull his jeans the rest of the way off, I follow. This is my gate. There's nowhere else to go.

Bruce's cock is just like maybe I dreamed he was, if I'd admit to dreaming. Long and curved like Dev's neck that he was stroking the first time I met him. When I put my lips around his cock, it don't taste like I dreamed though. Maybe 'cause I didn't dare dream this far. Maybe it's still not happening, this sweet haystalk of him inside my mouth. His hands tangled in my hair, holding me, not holding me. My lungs trying to breathe through it all. My heart trying to slow down its gallop.

When Bruce pulls me up, meets his lips with mine, he's taken off his glasses. Without that pane in front, his eyes are just as smart, but they lose that sweet Jersey cow. They're all horse. They're all Dev's when he gets a whiff of something he wants.

I don't have time to get feared though, 'cause he is putting me down on his bitty bed, climbing over top of me. He takes me in his mouth, so gentle at first I almost can't feel nothing but warm and wet. Then his tongue and teeth on me, roping me in. Lots I want to say, but my body's doing the talking. My hips buck up off the bed in time to Bruce's mouth. His lips slide up and down me, perfect fit. We're doing some kind of gallop together, something I never seen or felt or even knew.

Fast as that, Bruce moves his mouth to the inside of my thigh. Down, down. His tongue against the inside of me, opening that dark gate. His tongue entering and leaving, entering and leaving. I'm saying things I don't think I ought to be saying, but it's like them words been stuck somewhere inside me and now there's no stopping them.

Them words make Bruce sit up. He puts my knees up against my chest. Heart's hoofing so hard I can't hear nothing but them beats in my chest.

He takes the tip of his cock and swings me open, slow and careful, and my heart goes quiet. Bruce waits there, just the tip of him inside me, looking at me, until I want what he's got so badly, I have to ask for it. My low, low voice asking please, please.

This time, when he backs me to the bed, same as he backed me between him and Dev that day, this time I ain't afraid. Everything that was afraid in me is gone somewhere I don't know. And it's all pleasure, all us moving in tandem, equal. Don't matter who's on top. Who's on bottom.

He comes first, quiet, just shudders and the smell of sun-hay everywhere. His brown eyes doping on me. He slows to a walk, softening cock still inside me. Up and down slow. Up and down. The beat of him is all that matters.

When I come, it's like Dev's tail, spraying out away from me into the air. Glory and glory, no matter how you look at it.

After, Bruce puts his hands all over me, all in it, like he wants to hold on all of me. And I let him. I let him halter me with those fingers of his. I'll let him lead me anywhere he wants me to go.

# Hard Lessons

**TERESA NOELLE ROBERTS**

WEST TEXAS, 1893

L YDIE SYKES SAT in her empty schoolhouse, trying to focus on a pupil's essay on "My New Puppy," trying not to think about Gus, and not being too successful at either attempt.

She'd never told anyone in Dry Branch about Gus, not wanting to see the pity in their eyes: Poor Miss Sykes—about to be married back in Philadelphia and her fiancé gets run down by an omnibus.

She tried not to focus on the past sorrow, didn't want others to either. And the last thing she wanted was for her lady friends in Dry Branch to start trying to set her up with every bachelor in the area. Better they thought of her as a shy maiden-lady teacher, twenty-eight and never been kissed (or hadn't particularly enjoyed it if she had been.)

If only they knew! Then again, if her friends in Dry Branch knew the whole truth about Gus—that they hadn't been waiting for the wedding night like a proper young couple should, that they'd been misbehaving in every way they could imagine that couldn't get her with child—they'd be shocked, even if, or especially if, they'd been just as bad themselves with their own sweethearts. And if they'd known one of the favorite games was Gus pretending to be a naughty schoolboy and her spanking him until he spent in her lap and she spent from the sheer joy of reducing him to a quivering mass of flesh in that particular way—well, she'd be out of a job for sure, and the only other offer she'd get would be from Madame Flora's House of Pleasure.

Just thinking about Gus and their wicked games made her feel warm inside.

No, hot, despite the sorrow that clung to those memories. Something about Gus had turned her into a wanton, wild creature, a fallen woman in the guise of a proper schoolteacher—and she'd loved it, and loved him for it. Since he'd died, she'd never met a man who made her feel even the warm, comfortable way a nice young lady ought to feel with her beau, let alone like that.

Mostly it didn't matter. Mostly she was happy with her work, her tidy little house and garden, her friends, her spinster's inevitable tabby cat.

But sometimes, like today, her whole body ached with loneliness and longing and she wished she could feel that lusty way again. She didn't expect that to happen, though. Not if she couldn't even use her memories and her hands that used to be so good at touching her own secret places and Gus's to bring herself to pleasure.

It hadn't worked when she'd tried, and she'd tried a lot. That part of her was dead with Gus.

Which didn't keep her hand from settling in her lap, her legs from easing apart, as if maybe the sheer wickedness of touching herself in the schoolhouse might help.

Someone knocked at the door. A child who'd forgotten something, most likely—the little ones, especially, were always forgetting hats or lunch pails or jackets. She jumped into a more decorous position and sung out, "Come in," trying to sound more cheerful than she felt.

And a cowboy blew into her schoolhouse on a cloud of dusty fall wind, hat in his hand, boots polished to a sheen.

Lydie looked up and liked what she saw.

More than liked it, if she were being honest. He was tall, lanky, with a tanned, austere face that appealed to her immediately and gray-blue eyes that had to focus off the horizon to meet hers. He wore a baggy suit—his Sunday-go-to-meeting best for this meeting with the schoolmarm—but she could see, just from his posture, his walk, that he'd be more comfortable in dungarees and chaps, a pullover shirt and a vest, with a scarf rather than a tie around his neck. He had an air of calm that seemed to contain all the heat of a Texas summer, and for the first time in five years, she felt a shiver of real desire, sparked by a real person, in her loins. Watching him come undone with lust would be like watching a glorious sunset transform the dry, monotone landscape.

"Ma'am, I wanted to find out if it's too late to enroll in school?"

Her heart sank.

He was married. Of course.

The West was full of single men—part of the reason her family had encouraged her to take a job in Texas after Gus died, although she'd seen it mostly as escape from the weight of memories—but the first one she fancied had to be married with children. (She scolded herself it wouldn't be right to hope he was widowed.) "How old is your child?" she asked.

He flushed under his leathery tan. "Ain't got a child, ma'am. It's for me. Name's Will Franklin, ma'am, and I'm a hand for Mr. Drake's ranch outside of town. He tells me I got a good shot at being foreman when old Ned retires, but I need to learn readin' and writin' and figurin'. So I guess I gotta go to school."

She looked at the tall figure, tried to imagine him seated next to a seven-year-old. Tried not to chuckle.

Failed miserably.

"I'm serious, ma'am. World's changed, and I've got to change with it. Seemed once like all a man needed to know was ropin' and ridin' and how to spot good cattle, but I need some book learnin' if I want to get anywhere and be able to support a family someday."

She nodded. "What you want isn't funny at all. It's commendable." She watched him, saw comprehension, realized that his vocabulary was larger than his speech patterns and lack of education might suggest. "But you have to admit the idea of a grown man in with the littlest children, chanting nursery rhymes, is comical. You wouldn't even be able to fit your . . . your limbs under the desk properly. I think private tutoring would be best, don't you?"

"Might be wisest, ma'am. Can't see me keeping a straight face readin' about Fluffy Bunny and his friends."

As soon as she said it, she'd realized she was putting herself in temptation's way. This wasn't Gus, whom she'd loved, who'd loved her. This was a hard man, a cowboy. No telling what he might do.

No telling what she might do, if he gave her any encouragement.

Gus had been the one with the sense to find ways other than the obvious to satisfy their hunger for each other. If it had been left up to her, she'd have risked pregnancy and scandal to get his prick inside her traitorous quim.

A traitorous quim that was very much awake again at the worst possible time, when she'd just offered private tutoring—potentially scandalous even if they did nothing improper—to a man who made her knees weak and her drawers damp without doing anything but look at her.

Well, Lydie, she told herself, this is either the most foolish thing you've ever done in your life or the cleverest.

---

AFTER A WINTER of tutoring, however, it seemed that it was neither, and Lydie couldn't make up her mind whether that was a good thing or a bad one. Oh, Will Franklin could definitely make her melt with a glance of his pale eyes, but that was all he had done through long months of bimonthly tutoring sessions—look at her. If anything, he was even more careful than she was to be decorous. He was the one who suggested that when the weather permitted, they sit on the porch, and otherwise perch in the front parlor near the window instead of in the more comfortable kitchen. "Gotta do this all public," he said. "Otherwise, folks'll be fixin' to marry us off by Christmas."

Lydie mentally marked the date. Not that she necessarily dreamed of marrying him—although the more time she spent with the affable cowboy, the more she thought her heart as well as her body was thawing again and maybe a spinster's life wasn't for her after all—but she definitely wanted to do the sort of things with him that nice young ladies who'd gone to the Philadelphia Teachers' College were only supposed to do once they were married. But it gave her a deadline of sorts.

He'd missed the deadline by about four months. Of course, he hadn't known he had it.

On the other hand, he did know he had a lesson today at ten, and he'd missed that, too.

Lydie glanced at the parlor clock. Almost eleven—well past time.

She should be used to it by now. Clocks and watches weren't part of Will's life. Cattle didn't care about ten-past-four or half-past-ten. They knew eating time, sleeping time, milling-around time, and milking time, and cowboys followed suit.

Lydie had made it quite clear, though, that she expected promptness, that it was as necessary as reading and writing to the new life Will hoped to build for himself. Overall, he'd been improving, showing up, if not at 10:00 A.M. on the dot, then close enough to it to show Lydie he was making an effort.

But this was a fine spring morning. Like the children who came to her one-room school, he'd probably been taking his time coming into town, not planning to be late, but not in that much of a hurry to get into town either, when things both more urgent and more pleasurable needed doing outdoors at the Drake ranch.

Lydie always hated smacking her younger pupils' bottoms for tardiness. The older children, on the other hand, were another story. They knew why schooling was important, knew that grown-ups who couldn't read and write and do basic arithmetic got cheated at the store, by their bosses, by the tax collector. When reason didn't work, nothing made an impression like a good over-the-knee spanking, humiliating them in front of their friends. The humiliation factor even worked on the biggest boys, although she had to resort to leaning them against a desk and smacking them with a paddle, since having someone who was nearly a man grown in such intimate contact with her was likely to cause talk.

Right now, she was tempted to smack Will.

Actually, she was tempted to lay him across her lap and give him a sound, bare-bottomed thrashing, feeling his body pressed against her, but that was another story altogether.

Damnation, the man was attractive! Everything about him, from his lazy drawl that masked a keen, observant mind, to his long, hard hands, to the crinkles at the corners of cool eyes the changeable color of water. And his legs. And the lines of his back as he moved. And God help her, his bottom. Not the kind of thing a woman was supposed to notice on a man and not the thing you would notice in his town clothes, which didn't fit his lanky frame well. But she'd run into him a few times when he'd come to town to run an errand for Mr. Drake, still in his dungarees and sometimes his chaps, and then Lydie couldn't help notice the high, sweet shape of his bottom, and sometimes the even more dangerous sweet shape, the outline of his prick hugged by denim, as if while riding into town he'd been thinking . . . well, the sort of things she tended to think about him.

The things she was thinking now. How he'd look naked, all lean hard muscles and long hard cock. How he'd feel in her mouth, how he might taste. How he'd feel thrusting into her after warming her up with his beautiful, callused hands, his tongue.

Just thinking about Will Franklin that way made her want to touch herself. It would probably just make her crazier, unable to gain release, but at least she'd be able to pretend her own small hands were his big, work-hardened ones.

Must be so nice to be a man, she thought—all a man needed is a few minutes' privacy to open his fly and whip out his member.

Women's clothes were much too complicated, and much as she lusted after Will, it would hardly do for him to learn of her interest by finding her with skirts askew and drawers around her ankles, frigging herself.

But there was another way, a trick she'd learned as a young girl, still so innocent she was only dimly aware that it was naughty, a trick that, once upon a time, had allowed her to spend and still compose herself quickly. She hadn't even tried in so long she wasn't sure if she remembered how, but she was desperate to try.

Lydie drew the dark green drapes against prying eyes, then pressed herself against the corner of the walnut side table and rolled her hips in a slow circle, grinding her pearl and cunny against the hard surface.

Remembered straddling Gus, rubbing herself like this against his hard prick, both of them wanting to take it further, but not daring to.

Imagined doing it to Will Franklin. Only he would dare, him with his knowing eyes and shy smile that was really a sly smile, and she wouldn't be able to stop him because God save her she wouldn't want to.

His prick inside her cunny. Fucking her.

Just thinking those wicked words made her clench up.

And afterward, of course, she would have to pretend to be indignant. Just pretending, in a way that he, too, would know was pretending, so he could drawl, "How can I make it up to you, ma'am?"

"Well, you've been a very bad boy," she'd say. "And you know what happens to bad boys in my classroom." And she would get him over her lap and paddle his delicious bottom.

It would probably sting her hand at least as much as it would him. That had happened with Gus, and he'd been a clerk in a bank, already running a bit toward respectable stoutness. A man hardened by hours of riding a day would have a firm, muscular bottom, which might be difficult to redden, but would feel delightful to touch and caress.

The question was would he take his "punishment" and enjoy it, rubbing himself against her, gasping in pained pleasure until he spent again or at least grew inspired for more fucking? Or would he decide to turn the tables on her, wriggle out of her grasp as he surely could, then spank *her*? Either idea, her body informed her, had merit.

It might be delightful to melt under his hand like that. But more so, she thought, to see him wither, see all his defenses break down.

And at the image of that big, strong cowboy whimpering—but still spending—in her lap, Lydie stiffened, bit her lip, but still cried out as she came for the first time in five years.

She returned to herself to find Will standing behind her, hat in hand as he had been the first time she'd laid eyes on him. Only this time the hat was attempting to hide, and instead drawing attention to, the fact that he'd not only seen what she'd been doing, but had enjoyed the show.

Since it was a little late to attempt the cat's trick of pretending nothing ordinary was going on as it perched on the kitchen table eating the chicken, Lydie figured she had two choices. She could break down in a whimpering mass of humiliation or she could go on the offensive. The expression on Will's handsome face— fascinated, yet embarrassed—made her opt for the latter.

"First you're late and then you don't knock. Your manners are slipping, Mr. Franklin. This is not a barn, and I am not a cow."

"I'm sorry, ma'am. I knocked and I called out, thought I heard you saying something and reckoned it was 'Come in.' I am . . ." He paused and took a deep breath before continuing. ". . . powerful sorry I caught you at a bad moment, Miss Sykes."

Lydie felt almost sad about the way he said Miss Sykes. Not that he'd ever called her Lydie to her face—part of the way they'd both been holding on to propriety with tooth and claw—but it had reached a point where she could tell he thought of her that way, just as she thought of him as Will. Now he was being as painfully polite, in his drawling cowboy way, as he'd been when they first met.

And that just made her more frustrated.

"I accept your apology. However, you're still almost an hour late. We've had this problem before, Mr. Franklin, and I've been very lenient with you. I expect you haven't done your homework, either."

He hung his head, scuffed one booted toe against the other foot like a little boy caught in misbehavior. "Calving season, ma'am. Whenever I had a minute's peace, I was catchin' a little sleep."

Then he grinned at her, a grin with nothing of the little boy in it—pure grown man and pure wickedness, so it sent a flash of fire into Lydie's sex. "At least I may have some sweeter dreams when I catch those catnaps from now on. I know it wasn't right for me to keep watchin' you, but it sure was a pretty sight."

"That's enough!" She had to do something, do something to hide just how much his words, and the thought of him watching, inflamed her.

Or maybe to reveal it, but on her own terms.

She took a step closer to Will, then again. Improperly close, close enough to smell the scent of leather and sagebrush and dust and horse that clung to him even when he was dressed up for town. Close enough to touch him. Which she did, roughly, grabbing his collar so it popped open, yanking his head forward as she'd do to one of the larger and rowdier teenage boys in her class so she could glare into his eyes. "You've been a very bad student, Mr. Franklin. Tardiness, rudeness, failure to study—and spying on your teacher. Do you know what I do to naughty students?"

"You thrash 'em," Will said. " 'Specially the big boys. They say in town you're pretty kind to the little tykes, but hard on the older fellas." There was nothing but respect in his voice, respect and a little awe, and underneath it, desire. He'd dropped his hat when she'd grabbed him, so she knew about the desire for certain. His baggy trousers were tenting in the most inspirational way.

"That's because the older boys ought to know better, and more so a grown man. Don't you agree, Mr. Franklin?" She couldn't resist putting her hand on his throat as she spoke, just where the collar button had popped open, as if to make a point, stake a claim.

His skin was hot under her fingers, hot as chili peppers, hot as fever, and she could feel the blood pulsing in his throat.

It was the first time she'd ever touched him.

He could shake her off any time, could snap her like a twig, if he had a mind. And that should have frightened her, knowing she was playing with danger, but instead it made her feel powerful, excited.

For an instant, they both froze, her hand on his throat, his eyes, wide enough so they looked almost black, fixed on hers. He looked at her like she was . . . well, Lydie didn't rightly know what would make a man like Will Franklin stare with such a combination of fear, fascination, and pure want, but she knew the look made her wet.

The impasse ended with Will saying, in a whiskey-rough, graveled voice, "Reckon as I've earned myself a good whupping, Miss Sykes ma'am. I ain't . . . I mean haven't . . . exactly been a model student."

She took a deep breath. Should she push it or should she not?

She decided to push it. From most people's points of view, they were on the way to hell in a handcart already.

They might as well enjoy the ride in style.

"Very well, Will." She used the first name as if he were one of her bratty students, felt a daring thrill as it passed her lips for the first time under such curious circumstances. "It's good that you admit your failings, but you've been very bad. Strip down. I don't want anything protecting you from a good spanking."

As he obeyed, she removed her navy wool skirt, leaving her shirtwaist in place because her hands were too shaky to deal with all the buttons. Petticoats were much easier to wash than skirts if, as she certainly suspected at this point, Will shared Gus's predilections. And it just felt naughtier.

It was almost impossible to keep her stern demeanor once she saw Will stripped down to skin. He was such a contrast to Gus, the only other man she'd seen naked, and while she'd seen Gus through the eyes of love, she had to admit her dead fiancé couldn't hold a candle to this handsome, hard-bodied Texan. Long and lean everywhere except his prick, which was just plain long, and she had a feeling wasn't even fully aroused yet.

He took a few steps toward her.

Lydie gulped.

She had to take control of the situation, make it play out her way, or they would simply be two naked people about to do something regrettable. Undoubtedly wonderful in the short run, but regrettable in the long run, especially if she ended up with child.

She sat down in an armless side chair, a small, prissy, straight-backed thing barely scaled to her, let along to someone like Will, but the best option she had. "Over my knees," she ordered. "Now."

He obeyed without question, without hesitation—with nothing but a jaunty bob of his hardening prick.

For about a second, the utter ridiculousness of the scene struck Lydie more than anything else. Will was too big and lanky to fit into her lap easily, and his long legs—just as sculpted as she'd imagined, but a milky white, even fairer than she was, in stark contrast to his tanned face and forearms—were liable to kick over some ornament or another, and lean though he was, he seemed heavier than Gus. She was afraid she was going to start laughing too hard to go through with it.

Then she let herself touch Will's ass—just touch it, not even spank—and she was both lost and found.

Perfect. Hot, velveted steel.

Just like his cock must be. She could feel it pulsing against, even through layers of flannel and muslin petticoats.

Yes, that firm bottom would sting her hand. But she didn't care.

She raised up, began to spank.

To her delight, he said, "You've sure got hard hands for a little lady!"

"And I'm just getting started."

At first, Will seemed determined to take it like a man, without sound, without squirming, but before long, he was mewling and bucking against her lap as his bottom grew hotter and redder.

"That must be starting to get tender," she purred, stopping the spanking to caress his warm ass. She hoped so, anyway. Her hand certainly was.

"A bit."

"Do you promise to be on time and get your homework done in future?"

"I'll try, ma'am. But cattle don't keep to a clock too well."

She cupped his bottom, daringly slipped a finger between his cheeks to caress the tender, wrinkled opening there. Gus would never let her play there (although he liked doing it to her), but Will made a strange, strangled noise and pushed back, seeking more contact.

While she did that with one hand, reveling in his reaction, in the way he was rubbing himself against her, frantic with pleasure, frantic to find release, she groped with the other hand until she found a book on the table next to her.

Her palm was sore. Time to resort to tools—and it seemed fitting to use the sensational novel she'd been using to improve Will's reading. (H. Rider Haggard's tales of African adventure were more to a grown man's taste than the advanced *McGuffey Reader*, and not much more challenging to read.)

A thwack with the book.

He shied away, but there was nowhere to go except burrowing deeper into her lap, pressing his stiff prick against her.

She teased more at his arsehole until he began to writhe again.

Another thwack.

And so on until he stiffened, barked a few words he'd never used in Lydie's presence, and spent. She could feel the warmth of his seed soaking into her petticoats, and grinned. "Well, Will, you've made a mess now. I'm going to have to wash these myself—can't very well send them out."

She grinned a little wider as he slid off her lap and burrowed under her layers of petticoat.

"But you've found . . . a fine way . . . to make amends. . ."

The feel of his tongue and lips, warm and wet and velvety, caressing her through the already drenched fine cambric of her drawers made her insane, made her buck in the chair and pant and drive her fingernails into his hard-muscled shoulders.

Made her peak, and shatter into shards like a slate dropped on a tile floor.

Brought forth tears she hadn't known she needed to shed, and laughter she didn't know was bottled up inside her.

And through the whole storm of emotion, Will stayed on the floor at her feet, his arms around her waist, his head against her thigh, muttering something that didn't even make sense, but still comforted her, the kind of calming sound he'd probably murmur to soothe a spooked horse.

Finally, that passed, and she looked for a handkerchief and couldn't find one. Will solemnly reached into the pocket of his discarded pants, pulled out his.

With it came a couple of folded sheets of paper with Will's careful writing on them.

"You lied." Lydie exclaimed. "You did do your homework."

"Of course. That foreman's job is mine, but I want to be ready for it. And I want you to be happy with me, ma'am."

She felt like she ought to say, "For heaven's sake, call me Lydie," after what they'd just done. But she liked the sound of "ma'am" off his lips.

"But when I was so late and then . . . saw things I shouldn't have, I figured you'd be spitting mad at me anyway and I couldn't resist. Mr. Drake's nephew—his sister's boy Silas—was complaining the other day about how strict you are when a student doesn't do homework, and how hard you hit and . . . well, ma'am, I've fancied you since I first met you but that notion just put me right over the moon. Don't know why. I hated getting thrashed as a boy, but I do love the idea of a pretty lady doing it to me. Especially one I look up to as much as you. "

She couldn't help herself. She giggled, and confessed, "And I was thinking of this very thing when you caught me. I don't like spanking children, except that it makes them behave for a while, but doing it to a grown man—to you—that's a different story."

Will pulled out from under her skirts, changed position so he was on one knee. "This ain't . . . isn't, I mean . . . how I aimed to do this. Figured I'd wait until I got the first pay from the new job and buy a ring and do it proper. But that was before, and now I don't want to wait. We like each other—knew that a long time ago. We suit each other in the ways we're peculiar, and we know stuff 'bout each other that only married folks really ought to know. And thanks to you, I'll have a better job soon and a house on the ranch to go with it—old Ned's rheumatism got worse over the winter and he's moving to El Paso to live with his sister around the end of the month. Would you marry me . . . ma'am?"

A proposal was the last thing Lydie expected, but the more she thought about it, the more sense it made. They did "suit each other," so well that they weren't likely to keep their hands to themselves anymore, and in a town the size of Dry Branch, they'd be a scandal in no time. And she could imagine far worse things than waking up every morning next to a long, lean, sweet-natured cowboy who had a secret yearning to be spanked. "Well, you did say the townsfolk would expect us married by Christmas, and that's long past. Can't keep them waiting much longer. How's the Fourth of July?" She bent over him, cupped one hand around his still-hot ass. "I promise we'll have fireworks before then."

And then she kissed her naughty cowboy—so much better than a "naughty schoolboy"—for the first time.

# When the Rancher Needs a Loan

ANDREA DALE

S HEA HEARD A truck door slam
outside. She tried to swallow, her mouth dry, and she smoothed her
hands over her jeans. They weren't her best ones, but they were the
cleanest, because she'd changed into them after seeing to the herd
in the north field.

She'd even spritzed on a little perfume to counteract the eau de
cow that clung to her, because she hadn't had time to take a shower.

Might as well take the bull by the horns. She opened the front
door and met Bill on the porch.

"Morning, Shea," he said, touching his hat. On someone else, a
cowboy hat and a suit might have looked silly, but Bill had some
sort of Bobby Ewing thing going, and it just worked.

"Morning. Would you like some iced tea, or should we just get
started?"

"Tea sounds mighty tempting, but let's wait 'til afterward. I'm
sure we'll have things to talk about."

She nodded. The porch was swept, a braided rug in front of the
door. Inside, she'd neatened up, and even put out a china bowl that
her aunt in Cleveland had sent her years ago. She never displayed
it because she was afraid one of the dogs would knock it over. But
it looked fancy, like she had a little wealth.

Not a lot, but just enough to show she could keep things nice.

It was a fine line to walk when you were trying to get a loan from the bank so you could build a new irrigation system.

They agreed she'd drive, and she was glad she'd hosed off the truck and vacuumed inside. It might be seventeen years old and beat to all hell because it was a farm truck, but it ran well.

If Bill noticed the cracks in the vinyl seat held together with duct tape, or the fact that the radio knob had been replaced with a binder clip, he made no comment.

Didn't that make her look resourceful, anyway?

She drove him to all three fields, briefly explaining the different types of cattle, the way she moved them around so she didn't burn out any of the land, and how she'd expanded the herds over the past five years. She talked about the cattle industry, too, even though she figured a banker in the middle of ranching country would know exactly what the industry was doing.

When they swung back by the house, she talked about how it was paid off, even the second mortgage her parents had gotten so she could go to college. She deliberately mentioned college, that she'd double-majored in business and animal husbandry, to show she really did know what the hell she was doing.

They got out of the truck and walked the pens, the low of the cattle a backdrop to their discussion. In truth, throughout the whole tour, Bill didn't say much. He asked some sharp questions, and they managed a little small talk—hell, they'd known each other for years, and the town wasn't what you'd call large—but otherwise he made no comments.

The horse barn smelled of sweet hay and stinky manure, despite the fact that the stalls had been shoveled out that morning.

They paused there, and she tossed him a bottle of water from the small fridge. Then she regarded him, seeing him in a way she'd never exactly seen him in all the years she'd known him.

His sandy hair, streaked lighter by the sun, had never fully been tamed; the bank manager despaired, but there was nothing he could do. His eyes could change from pale blue to a flinty green when he got emotional, like when Gabe Mitchell, after too many drinks at the Sip 'n' Feed, had insulted Barbie Granger, and Bill had told him to apologize. Gabe had refused, and Bill had knocked him flat with a single punch.

Shea knew Bill could ride circles around half the men in town and always won the strongman at the county fair. He'd strip off his shirt to do it, too, and his biceps and back muscles would ripple as he tipped the heavy mallet back and then hauled it down on the target, no question that he'd make that bell ring.

Like most of the women in town, Shea always made sure she was present for that spectacle.

She knew that, despite all the positives she'd shown him, the loan was a long shot. Truth be told, she was breaking even—just. She wasn't losing, but she wasn't gaining, either. She was confident the renovations would benefit the ranch, but she had to convince the bank—which mean convincing Bill—that the money the upgrades would bring in would be more than enough for her to pay the loan back.

And Shea was willing to do whatever it took to convince him.

Anything.

Bill had courted her for years, and she'd resisted him for years. They were friends, but the sexual tension was always there, bubbling under the surface like the natural hot springs over in Bakers Falls.

Which is why, before she'd even opened the door that morning, she'd unbuttoned her softest flannel shirt so a vee of shadow showed between her breasts, and she'd slicked her lips with a little gloss, and now she stood, lounging against a stall door and wondering what Bill was thinking.

"You've got a fine establishment here, Shea," he said finally. "You've done really well for yourself, and you've presented the bank with a well-thought-out application."

Her stomach knotted. She clearly heard the "but" coming.

"But," he said. "It might sound funny for a bank to say so, but we're a little concerned about some of your methods."

"What do you mean?" she managed.

"You're pretty much still ranching the way your parents did. You seem unwilling to try anything new, and while not jumping on every trend is smart, it's still good to keep up with progress. We think you need to diversify. Try something new once in a while."

"In what way?"

He was right, of course. She did do things pretty much the way her parents had, because her parents had been successful at it and she respected that. She'd upgraded to computers—college had made it clear how important that was—and kept any other technology reasonably current, but she still believed in tradition.

If it ain't broke, she didn't see the point in trying to fix it.

Bill pulled a sheet of paper from his clipboard and held it out to her. "I wrote up a list of suggestions."

She didn't take the page from him. "I can't," she said. "I don't have the available finances to make any big changes. If you give me the loan, after I upgrade the irrigation system, things will be better. . . ."

He shook his head. "We need more assurance that you're willing to try new things," he said. He held out the paper again. "Just read it."

Reluctantly, she took it from him, and scanned the list.

Her cheeks flamed when she processed what it said.

At the same time, arousal stirred inside her. Beneath her soft flannel shirt, her nipples hardened. Beneath the second-best pair of jeans, her cunt clenched.

She'd told herself she'd do anything for the loan. This, though . . .

Bill took off his hat and set it on a hay bale. He ran a hand through his hair, then crossed his arms over his impressive chest and waited.

He had big hands. She shivered.

Could she do it? Could she handle it?

"This is what it will take to get the loan?" she asked. "The bank will finance, period?"

"Yes ma'am." His voice was calm, but his eyes had gone a little green, and something glinted in them.

She looked down at the list again, not able to face what she saw in his expression. How long had he been thinking about this? How long had he fantasized? Had these specific, kinky fantasies?

About *her*?

She had to go through with it. She needed this loan, damn it.

And there was no denying that, as appalled as she was, her body was reacting, betraying her.

Shea looked Bill in the eye. "I'll do it."

A smile toyed at the edges of his mouth. "I figured you might." As quick as a flash, the hint of a smile was gone. "Strip. Slowly."

He'd want a show, wouldn't he? Shea wasn't shy about her body, but neither was she the type to jump up on a bar and shake her half-naked booty, no matter how soused she got. Well, she'd just have to do the best she could.

Moistening her lower lip with the tip of her tongue, she slowly unbuttoned her flannel shirt and drew it over her shoulders. She supposed she should do some sort of tease, dropping it and raising it before she removed it, but she didn't really know how and she'd probably look silly. Better to go with what she could handle.

Beneath the flannel she wore a plain white cotton tank, probably a man's one because it had been cheaper. She'd washed it so many times that it fitted her like a second skin, molded to her slender body.

And it was obvious that she was aroused.

Her breasts were small and high, and she rarely bothered with a bra unless she was going to do some hard labor that might necessitate a little more protection.

Now, her nipples stuck out like silver studs on a belt, the areolae darkly apparent beneath the thin fabric.

So far, Bill hadn't changed his position, lounging against the hay bales with his arms crossed negligently across his chest. At the sight of her hard, beaded nubs, his nostrils flared, and his gaze darkened.

Shea shivered even as her body reacted, a thrill of pleasure tightening her stomach.

There wasn't much of a graceful way to take off her boots, but she turned around before she bent over, wiggling her ass in a provocative manner as she pulled off her scuffed red leather footwear.

Still with her back to him, she popped the button of her jeans and drew the zipper down, the rasp mingling with her nervous—and excited—breath. Slowly she turned back, slid the jeans down over her hips.

Her panties were plain old cotton Jockey for Her, although in an unlike-her blush pink because that's all the store had when she'd run out of her last stash. A quick glance at Bill showed her he wasn't disapproving—if the bulge in his pants was any indication.

She kicked off the jeans, gathered all her courage, and stripped out of the T-shirt and panties.

And waited. She trembled under his stare, but not from fear. It was like he was touching her with his gaze, caressing her.

Finally, he said, "Put your boots back on."

She didn't try to be sexy; she just yanked them on. She straightened, waiting for his next instructions.

Now he moved, finally. A long length of leather reins was in his hands, even though Shea hadn't seen where it had been hanging or when Bill had grabbed it. He told her to hold her arms out, cross her wrists, and she obeyed, mouth dry, pussy wet.

When he finished, Shea tested the bindings. She'd learned to tie knots practically before she could walk.

She knew just how helpless she was.

The fact that he was fully dressed while she was naked and bound wasn't lost on her. He led her over to a row of saddles and now, finally, he touched her. Without warning, he picked her up and draped her over one of the saddles. Her toes barely touched the ground; she dangled, pivoted perfectly over the oiled leather.

What was going to happen next had been detailed on the paper he'd given her. She clenched in anticipation.

He made her wait. Left her hanging there until, without realizing, she started to relax.

When his hand connected with her bare, vulnerable ass for the first time, she didn't make a sound. The stinging smack knocked the sound right out of her.

He set up a steady rhythm, his hand slapping against the tender curve of her butt. Her flesh heated even as her pussy followed suit. The sting increased at the same rate as the pressure on her clit.

Without warning he switched to something else, another implement, hard and flat. Through the haze of pain and pleasure, Shea tried to figure out what it was. The back of a curry comb?

At any moment he could turn it over, hit her with the metal bristles. At that realization she twisted, squirmed. Whether she was trying to get away or trying to rub herself against the saddle, she didn't know. Didn't care. The flaming heat of her ass and the thought of what might happen drove her beyond rational thought, and Bill's soft laughter made things only worse.

He stopped, leaving her with the sound of her harsh breaths and the throbbing of her butt cheeks, which she imagined were as red as her boots. The mental image made her face flush just as red, even as her cunt fluttered and clenched around nothing.

What was he going to do to her next? She couldn't remember what the paper had said. It was all a blur. There was nothing outside her pain and heat and wetness and growing desperate need for release.

She jumped when he rested his big hand against the curve of her ass. When he raked the curry comb across her sensitized flesh, she shrieked, kicking her feet, so close to coming that she thought she would die.

Bill lifted her off the saddle, carried her—because her legs weren't working properly—a few feet away. She understood why a moment later, when he hooked her bound wrists over a convenient hook in a ceiling beam. She couldn't remember why the hook was there. She didn't care.

"Spread your legs," he said.

She did her best, but apparently it wasn't enough. He used the handle of a whip to nudge her thighs farther apart.

Oh God oh God, was he going to use that on her? She didn't think she'd be able to take the pain. But when he'd gotten her into a position that pleased him, he didn't move the whip handle away.

Moved it farther up her thighs.

Shea flushed with humiliation and stimulation as Bill nudged the handle between her pussy lips. Worked it gradually up inside her. With excruciating slowness, stuffed her full of braided leather.

Her legs were too far apart, her feet not firmly on the ground, so she couldn't rock against it with any real force. When he twisted it inside her, she tried to grind against it, but she couldn't gain any purchase.

She wouldn't beg. So help her, she wouldn't beg. But he kept her teetering on the edge, drawing the damnable thing most of the way out, then pressing it back up inside her, teasing her until she sobbed from need.

Then he flicked the end of the whip, lashing it against her nipples.

Shea screamed, her cunt convulsing around the whip handle as she came.

The next thing she knew, Bill was draping the whip around her neck, so she could feel the leather against her flesh and smell her juices coating the handle.

He hauled her up, his hands on her sore ass making her wince before he drove into her and drove all thought from her mind again. She swung, helpless, forced to let him take control of her body as he thrust her against him, taking his pleasure even as he gave her pleasure.

She came again, and on her heels, he followed.

⎯⎯∞⎯⎯

SHEA LET BILL drive the truck back to the house, so she could brace herself on the seat, not quite letting her sore ass fully press down.

When she got out of the truck, he said, "So I'll pick up some steaks for tonight?"

"As long as you're grilling," she said.

She watched him drive away. She'd been the one to come up with the sexy loan-officer-coerces-rancher-who-needs-a-loan scenario, but she'd had no idea her husband harbored such kinky fantasies.

Slipping her hands into the back pockets of her jeans, she swore she could feel the heat of her reddened flesh against her fingers.

As she went inside to pour herself a glass of iced tea, she couldn't stop grinning.

# Pistol Packin' Mamas

DAVID SHAW

T HE BROAD-SHOULDERED young man wearing a fringed deerskin shirt and white Stetson was leaning casually against the deck rail of the *Queen Charlotte*, watching the Indiana shoreline steadily passing to the beat of the riverboat's stern-wheel. A spur-fitted riding boot rested casually on the lowest of the rail bars, the man's slumped attitude suggesting no more than a casual interest in the summer greenery and sun-speckled ripples. It would have seemed an entirely peaceful scene, save for the butt of the Colt Navy revolver protruding from a well-worn leather holster at the man's right hip. That, and the way his head and eyes seemed never to be entirely at rest. Somehow he seemed both relaxed and yet never quite relaxed enough to be taken by surprise.

If any bystanders had reached the same conclusion, they would have been correct. And indeed there were bystanders, two of them, both female and both looking quite intently at the cowboy from the corner of a deck house a few paces away. Each of them would have been surprised to learn that he was well aware of their presence. As indeed they were surprised, and then in equal measure disconcerted and discomforted when he suddenly turned toward them and doffed his hat in a respectful bow.

"Ladies."

"Oh my!"

The one that responded first was somewhere into the middle years of her third decade, her features strong yet well proportioned, with tresses of ginger hair underneath a saucy blue hat and a body that would have needed a powerful stallion to carry it swiftly and, the cowboy instantly thought, a strong man to do it full justice. Junoesque was the word which came to mind. And he was well aware that no one aboard the *Queen Charlotte* would have looked at his cowpuncher clothes and believed that such a word could exist in his vocabulary. Not that he needed to consult any dictionary in forming a instant opinion of what he'd like to do with the redhead's lush bosom and generous hips.

Then the second woman spoke up. "I'm sorry if we seemed rude, but my sister-in-law had an idea she'd seen your face in a newspaper sketch. With a hat and shirt like the one you're wearing now."

The cowboy turned toward the speaker and bowed again. She was perhaps three or four years younger, hatless, slimmer, her long blond hair piled on top of her head and secured at the peak with a tortoise shell, falling away into two ponytails secured behind her graceful neck by black ribbons and then flowing out free and loose past her shoulders.

"Ma'am, it does seems my moniker has been mentioned some in your Eastern papers. That is if the name you had in mind is Jake Jefferson Jackson, 'cause that's what'd be printed on my calling cards, if'n I had any."

Both of the interlopers gasped as he proudly introduced himself. In fact the copper nob was so surprised she twitched as if jabbed with a pin.

"The gunfighter! I knew I was right. Oh, I've read so much about you, Mr. Jackson. In Mr. Buntline's stories. Why, you're mentioned in the same breath as Buffalo Bill and Wyatt Earp."

Jake smiled, revealing an excellent set of white teeth in his handsome face. He spoke slowly, as if savoring every word.

"Well, now, a man couldn't want for better company than to be named with than those two gen'l'men. But to be right truthful, old

Ned sometimes draws it on too strong by a chain and a quarter. I could say more but I'm kind of shy about shouting the odds in front of strangers."

"Strangers? Oh, I'm so sorry Mr. Jackson," the older woman answered. "I'm Clara Butler and this is my friend, Georgina Tasker."

The cowboy showed the unabashed grace of a true caballero as he kissed each presented hand in turn. And an equal lack of embarrassment in eyeing the hands he didn't raise to his lips.

"Well, ladies, you've plumb disappointed me enough to make a rattlesnake cry salt tears. Here I was thinking I'd fallen down a gold mine and it turns out you're both wearing golden rings already. I guess Mr. Butler and Mr. Tasker are going to be showing up hot footed real soon, and all ready to whip my hide for trying to cut out the best-looking pair of fillies ever to step on the deck of this mobile tea kettle."

Clara blushed as she answered, "Oh no, Edward and Eric have gone ahead to Pittsburgh to look at a business there they may be buying as partners. We would have gone with them, but there was a last-minute problem in boarding our children, so we've had to follow on the next boat."

Jake made a great play of being astonished: "You gals have family! Why if that ain't the biggest surprise I've had since Ready Money Mary O'Cready hit me over the head with her bed warmer, and me never even suspecting she ever had the need of that kind of implement at her place."

Georgina and Clara broke out into a fit of giggles, very unladylike but very attractive giggles. Jake laughed, too, as he replaced the hat over his neatly trimmed blond hair. Underneath it was the developing thought that these eastern females had a style and easy confidence about them that was like nothing he'd seen before in women—not married ones, anyway. Maybe some of those stretchers he'd heard about eastern goings-on hadn't been so stretched out after all. Well, he'd soon enough find out in the big city.

"Why, the pair of you are just such natural belles of the ball I figured you were hardly old enough to be excused Sunday School, let alone figuring on taking your own tackers to one. Ain't that something? Well, I guess I'll watch the skies tonight and have myself a wish on a falling star the gals they find for me in New York are something like as admirable as you ladies—though I won't be denying I'll be adding a postscript that they're not married."

Georgina stared at him curiously. "What girls, Mr. Jackson?"

"Why, Mrs. Tasker, every time you talk about Mr. Jackson I'm figuring to turn around fast and see who's looking behind me. I'd take it kindly if you'd call me Jake. As for them gals, there's a gentleman in New York, name of Samuel W. Loftus, who's sent me letters saying he's a mind to do a stage show there, the same kind of a show that Ned Buntline persuaded Buffalo Bill his'self to do, 'til they parted brass rags."

"*Scouts of the Prairie*," Clara said. "I've heard of that. Why, it was a huge success. It packed the theaters everywhere it went."

"Well, Mrs. Butler, I guess we've been hearing the same story, so that's why I'm here, a simple ranch hand aiming to stash a few dollars away in his poke while he can."

Clara smiled. "Jake, please call me Clara. And can I ask how it came about that a simple cowpuncher ended up in so many gunfights? Some of the people who write about you suggest that you fell into bad company."

The cowboy gave her smile for smile. Only this time his handsome face was somehow not nearly so friendly. Neither were his eyes.

"Clara, what they write about me I can't hardly help. But along the trail there's been some hombres who've called me a few names to my face." Jake patted the butt of his Colt. "Can't quite recall how many at the moment, but I guess I could always get old Betsy out and count the notches again, if'n you was curious."

Clara blanched, her face stricken: "Oh Lord, Jake, Mr. Jackson, forgive me. Insulting you in any way was the furthest thing from my mind. Please let me apologize."

Jake took off his hat and bowed again before answering.

"Miss Clara, I wouldn't be dreaming of asking a lady of your quality for any such thing. I guess I'm as nervous as a shepherd at a rodeo myself in being honored by the presence of two such beautiful women and I misspoke. I beg your pardon."

"Oh, granted, Jake, completely granted. I made a fool of myself."

While mea culpas were being exchanged, Georgina's vivid blue eyes had become fastened on the Navy Colt. Indeed, aimed at it as if they were weapons themselves, with an obvious glint of excitement lurking in their depths.

"Mr. . . . Jake, is that really the pistol you used to kill all those men with?"

"It surely is, Georgina. I'd like to show it to you, but folks might start getting nervous if'n I was to clear leather out here in the open. Why the fellow up there at the big wheel might take on such a turn we'd end up ploughing a stretch of riverbank with those big blades back there. Tell you what, ladies, I'm traveling in a private cabin on the Texas deck, cabin number one, all paid for by Mr. Samuel W. Loftus of New York, and plumb comfortable it is, too. Step inside for a powwow to pass away the time, why don'tcha? I'll show you my six shooter and tell you all about those gals in New York."

Jake wasn't sure of what reaction his bold suggestion might get, but Clara did as he thought she might, blushing, putting a hand to her mouth to stifle a startled laugh, then looking sideways at her friend. Georgina was less-visibly surprised, though her lips twitched, and Jake could have sworn the gleam in her eyes grew even more intense.

"Why, Mr. Jackson," she breathed slowly. "I could almost think you were trying to pen us up inside your corral."

Jake grinned, put on his hat again at a rakish angle, and leaned forward to whisper gently into her delicate, pearl-decorated ear.

"Well, Georgina, you know what happens to wild mares in a corral, I guess. They surely get to buck a lot. But when Jake Jefferson Jackson is breaking them in they damn near buck themselves right out of their hides. And I never yet met a lady who didn't think it was the best thing that ever happened to her."

Georgina had heard what he said. Clara had a very good notion of what he'd said because her friend looked as shocked as if a skunk had suddenly run up inside her skirts. Both of the respectable married ladies quivered as if the *Queen Charlotte* had indeed run aground at full speed and shaken the decking underneath their feet. Especially Clara, despite all the ballast she had stowed away in her expansive curves. As for their eyes, well, Jake had never seen any pop out so much since a string of mules in Laramie had gotten themselves a smell of a circus camel.

"See you later, gals. And I've got a bottle of sipping whisky in the cabin I'd surely like your opinion on. Stirs the corpuscles up and loosens corsets, too, so they say. 'Bye."

The last thing Jake saw before he turned away was a back view of the two women facing out over the deck rail, heads close together and two pairs of shoulders heaving with emotion. What emotion Jake couldn't have exactly sworn to, not on a Bible leastways, but if it had been a pair of Comanche squaws he was studying instead of white women, he would have said for certain the pair of them were nigh on choking with laughter. Of course squaws usually needed to be liquored up to laugh that much. But given half a chance he could soon fill that want—as well as any others that might come along.

Jake went up the steps to the Texas deck two at a time, grinning and happy. Sure, he'd already figured out that he was probably going to be on the losing side in this encounter but at least he'd played his cards hard and fast. Better yet, he'd enjoyed the game. Even better, he was halfway convinced that if either of the eastern wives had been on her own she'd have let herself be sweet talked into dancing the mattress polka underneath him.

Why all these easterners, male and female, they all seemed to think the West was some kind of a romantic place, a Camelot just a crossing away over the Missouri, with cowboys as knights on horseback. Except those of them that had actually ridden the trail along the North Platte long enough to find that the real West was a howling wilderness of half-assed towns full of dirty shacks and dirt poor people. Oh sure, one day it might become a fine place to live, but right now the West had one appalling shortage—women. While in the East there were cities with millions of sassy spankers like Georgina and Clara high stepping around in them, all seemingly ready to go weak at the knees at the sight of a Stetson, Levi's, and a six shooter.

A thought brought to mind a shortage that did exist in the eastern states, a shortage of ill-intentioned ranchers looking out with cocked firearms for Jake Jefferson Jackson on account of their wandering livestock, which had somehow ended up with his brand on them. There was also a power of husbands clear through to the Rockies just as eager to plug him for the same reason. Nope, it'd take a team of oxen to drag Mrs. Jackson's son Jake west of Saint Louis again. New York and a tasty young widow with a fat portfolio of railroad stock would settle this wandering cowhand down just fine.

Inside his cabin Jake poured some water in a basin, washed his hands and face, removed his boots, and carefully opened a small box marked DR. POWER'S FRENCH PREVENTATIVES. Out of the box he took two of the rubber sheaths packed inside and carefully examined them. Freshly bought at a barber's shop in Saint Louis, he expected them to be in good condition, but the new-fangled rubbers aged quickly. Another problem with living way out in the West was now made worse by the newly introduced Comstock laws, which made it a federal offense to send contraceptives through the post. Maybe the U.S. government figured the Comstock nonsense was the quickest way to populate pioneer territories.

Jake piled up the pillows on the cabin's double bed and spread a horse blanket on top of the coverlet. Not only did the blanket protect the fancy coverlet, it gave off a stallion smell that had often proved remarkable results in certain ladies he had come to know in the past—in the biblical sense of the word. But when he stretched out and relaxed on top of the blanket his attention was almost fully taken up by the ribbon-bound bundle of papers in his hand. It was the script for the stage show that Sam Loftus had sent him, and Jake was set on having it engraved word perfect on his mind by the time he reached New York. Yet before he settled down to reading he got up again, set out three glasses on the table and a bottle of Maker's Mark whiskey. He poured a measure into one of the glasses, then shrugged and filled the other two glasses as a libation to the gods of luck and love and lust. And if they were not on his side then he'd stoically salute fate's power by drinking all three shots himself.

Taking one glass back to the bed, Jake lay down again and began muttering the lines as he read through them. He'd turned over three pages when the .36 seemed to flow from the holster into his hand with hardly a flicker of movement. He looked up to see Georgina and Clara almost jammed together in their rush to get through the cabin door and get it closed behind them. A man might have thought the pair were seeking shelter from a sudden storm—until he saw the apprehension on their faces, as if the shelter was underneath a solitary tree with lightning flashing through the sky.

Jake's smile showed more teeth than a he-wolf baying underneath a full moon, and he lifted up the gun until the muzzle pointed at the cabin roof.

"Hello, ladies. Sit yourself down and have a drink. They're already poured."

The two women stood with their backs to the door, staring around them at the luxurious cabin and then at Jake. Clara seemed as nervous as a young miss at her first church social dance, while Georgina's cheeks were flushed and her pert bosom betrayed more hard breathing than she'd acquired merely from climbing the steps to the upper deck. Jake chuckled and took a sip from his glass.

"Okay, so which one of you dared the other to come and visit a stranger in his cabin? For my money, it was Georgina."

She stared back at him, then gave an unexpected ghost of a smile. "Why me?"

"Because of my gun. Because you want to handle something

that's killed a heap of men. Don't get fussed about it, there's a lot of gals like you. One of these years mebbe you'll all get together and start your own civil war with your menfolk—or maybe just ignore them altogether. Doesn't matter to me, as long as you're here. As for Clara, she's pure female through and through. You like men, don'tcha, Clara? And men surely like you. So if this is the only chance you're ever going to get to have a gallop with another man riding you, why not pick a right handsome cowboy, right?"

Clara's cheeks were turning as red as a prairie sunset. "I think we'd better go, Georgina."

"Ah, that might be a problem." Jake lowered the barrel of the Colt and squinted down it toward them. "See here, gals, this pistol is loaded and cocked and on a hair trigger. Just one twitch and off it goes. Only I wouldn't want you to have the idea I'm threatening to shoot you. The truth is, this pistol is as harmless as a toothless snake. I'm too far East to risk shooting people. So there's nothing in the chambers but black powder for show. If I was to pull this trigger there'd only be a big bang and a power of smoke and sparks."

Georgina's breathing was apparently becoming even harder as she stared down the Colt's muzzle.

"I don't understand why you're telling us that."

"Because the wheelhouse is above this cabin. And if the captain or one of his officers heard a shot in here, why they'd naturally come running to investigate. And guess who they'd find here. Mrs. Butler and Mrs. Tasker together in a male passenger's cabin. Wouldn't that just cause some gossip on board this hooker? I should just about say so. Why, there's no telling how far that kind of talk could spread."

"Oh dear," Clara said slowly. "Oh dear."

Georgina only nodded, as if hearing nothing but what she'd expected: "Corralled. You've got us corralled. Just like I knew you would."

Jake nodded, too, affirming her statement. "Seems like that's the way of it." He put his hand down beside him on the blanket, the six shooter still in it. "Okay, girls. Over on the wash stand there's a bowl, a jug of water, soap, flannel, and a towel. Get them."

They both seemed surprised but did as he ordered. In the meantime Jake stood up, moved his pillows farther along the blanket, then lay down again with his feet out beyond the edge of the bed. Clara stood watching with the bowl in her hands and the towel over her shoulder, Georgina carrying the jug and flannel and soap.

"Wash my feet for me, ladies. Make them clean because you'll thank me for this later."

The women exchanged glances but knelt down. Or rather, Clara put the bowl down on the table and spread out her skirts before kneeling down. Then she took the bowl and jug and other things from Georgina and put them on the cabin floor before Georgina also rearranged her dress as she got down beside her friend. Jake smiled down the length of his body at them.

"Ready when you are, ladies."

It was Clara who began on his right foot, gently rubbing the soapy flannel under his sole and then over the top of his right foot. Jake wriggled with pleasure.

"That's nice, that's sure nice. I was figuring to tell you ladies about those gals in New York, wasn't I . . . sure was. Hmm, that's right Clara, every one of those toes and in between them."

Georgina's eyes were growing wider to match the growing bulge in Jake's Levi's. Her elbow jabbed against Clara's arm, and Clara looked up in turn, her eyes showing the same gleam as on first seeing the drawn Colt. Jake laid his pistol down carefully on the blanket and moved his hand away from it a few inches.

"There's no hiding it, ladies, the touch and smell and sight of you pair of beauties surely has the South rising again. And mebbe also because Mr. Loftus has promised me a couple of chorus gals to come on stage with me, dressed up as saloon dancers. Only wearing a sight less, judging from some fancy daguerreotypes he's sent me. Seems like they're hardly even planning on keeping their underwear on. Looks to me like there'll be a riot in the theater before I get to do anything—shucks, that's a good feeling. Okay, Georgina, your turn."

The blonde took the flannel from Clara and carefully resoaped it before wiping the material over his left foot. Jake admired the way Georgina made a pretense of trying not to look at his half-cocked cock, yet kept glancing at it with quick looks from under her lowered face, sneaky looks that were both somehow coy and sultry at the same time. Clara had a different style. As she toweled his other foot dry, she was staring at his groin with the undivided attention of a town drunk watching a bottle of whiskey being uncorked.

"Kiss the bottom of my foot, Clara. Then start sucking my toes, nice and gentle, all along the line."

Jake gave a gentle moan of pleasure as she went to work with a will. Georgina glanced sideways at her companion's obedient behavior and the tips of her ears went pink. But she picked up the towel and applied it as thoroughly to the foot in front of her as Clara had done—and even more quickly. Then she crouched lower and put her lips against Jake's sole.

"Mmm, yes." The cowboy tilted his head back and grunted with pleasure as two mouths sucked and nibbled on his toes. "Now that is some pleasuring—yes, sirree. But now I want you fine belles to help me out a little here. See, I got to thinking about these girls on the stage and how they come out wearing these pink tights on their legs. So I figured maybe I could tease the men folk in the audience by covering everything else up with ponchos."

Jake lifted his head: "Hey, wait up with the toes and pay attention here. You gals listening to me, now."

"Yes, Jake," Georgina answered quickly and Clara nodded.

"Okay, now I want you to help me put on a little production here. Only I don't have any pink tights. But in that chest over there are two ponchos and two Mexican hats I bought them along special in case I couldn't find what I wanted in New York. You two are going to model them for me. But first of all you'll take off everything you're wearing now. And while you're doing that I'll be watching the door to make sure both of you keeps on this side of it."

The two females glanced at each other with furtive eyes, as if each was afraid of revealing her emotions.

"Come on, ladies, come on. Bowl and jug back on the sideboard and then dump all that fancy gear you women have to carry around. Turn everything loose for a while. Just leave your shoes on and put on the ponchos and hats. And have another shot of firewater as you pass the table if'n you feel like it."

Clara snorted with what seemed gallows humor. "That's an invitation I badly need."

They stood up, Clara first, reaching out to take the water-filled bowl from Georgina's hands, and then the jug before her friend got to her feet. The utensils went back on the sideboard and Clara poured another glass of whiskey, sharing the shot with Georgina in one quick gulp apiece and two gasps of—what—satisfaction or disbelief at the speed things were happening? Or a joint summoning up of courage? The boat's steam whistle blew a long shriek overhead, and during it Georgina said something to Clara that made the bigger girl glance involuntarily toward Jake with her hand to her mouth, the knuckles showing white.

He had a good idea of what had been said: "She's right, Clara, you will be making a noise like that yourself pretty soon."

"Oh God," Clara said. "I've gone mad. I must have gone mad." But she allowed Georgina to take her arm and pull her into the corner of the cabin.

It took iron concentration for Jake not to move his head or his eyes toward the rustling of material and muttered snatches of conversation occurring just out of his line of sight. There were reasons to keep them averted though. The personal one was that he liked to spread his pleasures out as long as possible. The business one was that he wanted to see the girls in their ponchos for the first time the way an audience would see them. If they looked as good as he thought they would—well, maybe the idea would work in a theater.

The problem was that it seemed to take an age before both dresses were removed and corsets were unlaced, although Jake knew to the second when Clara's was loosened because of her explosive gasp of relief. Yet even that seemed only an opening movement in the discarding of chemises and petticoats and bustles and God alone knew what else. And then there were the astonished mutters and gasps of disbelief as both of the women put on the ponchos and looked at themselves in the mirror

Only after what seemed like an eternity did he hear Georgina speak in a quavering voice, "We're ready, Jake."

"Fine, ladies, fine. I'm going to close my eyes now. I want you to stand in front of me at the end of the bed and tell when I can take a look."

Jake shut his eyes with confidence. There was no way either Clara or Georgina could leave the cabin now. Even so, his palm still rested lightly on the butt of the pistol. There were clicking sounds on the wooden deck, the delicate clicking sounds of female shoes, the only items of everyday dress either of the married women had left. Excitement raced through his veins stronger and more potent than any liquor could have done.

It was Georgina's voice again, on a quivering note. "Ready."

He looked. Both of them were standing straight up, side by side. On each woman's head was a black felt hat, of the style worn by wealthy Mexican women when out riding, flat topped, narrow brimmed, with narrow chin cords hanging loose.

Jack's eyes dropped lower. Both of the ponchos were made of thin white linen with gold and red edging, cut so that they hung deeper front and back than at the sides. The V shape of Georgina's reached a point just above her knees, the top of the poncho was close around her graceful neck, and under the thin material the shape of her breasts stood out clearly enough for the nipples to be visible. So were the bright blue stars gleaming in the band of shadow under the hat brim.

"God!"

The cowboy could not believe the sight of Georgina's legs. No wonder women had to keep them covered up lest men should go mad with lust—women with legs as long and as incredibly beautifully shaped as hers, anyway.

Jake swung his eyes toward Clara. And said the same word again, but with even deeper resonance. If Georgina's pose was enough to grab the attention of an entire audience of men the seminaked Clara was in a fit state to start a stampede onto the stage. Like her friend, Clara's arms were down by her side, because lifting them also meant lifting up the bottom of the poncho. But where Georgina could at least have brought her hands up to her shoulders and still have been within an inch of decency, Clara's linen figleaf needed to go barely a handspan higher to lift the veil on her secret valley. Her hipbones held firmly in the poncho's grip, Clara's face was deeply flushed—and in between—in between was a pair of trembling cahoonas big enough to keep all three of them afloat if the riverboat sank.

"Sweet Jesus," Jake said in stunned admiration. "Clara, your tits are so big a man could stake out a claim on them under the Homesteading Act." The big woman gaped at him. "I'll tell you something else, even from here I can see that you're as excited as a saloon hostess on pay night."

Clara twitched, stared down at the hard nipples standing out underneath the poncho, and instinctively raised her hands to cover them. Before yelping and dropping them again as she realized what else was happening—but not before Jake had caught a glimpse of the ginger patch of hair revealed by the lifted poncho.

"That was just what I wanted, Clara. If I can get one of the girls to reach up for some reason while's she's dressed like that the boys in the theater will get a real thrill. Although I guess not as big as the one I just had."

Clara shook her head as if she'd been hit with a club. "This can't be happening. I can't be letting some strange man see me naked."

"Don't fret about it, I'll find a way to convince you. I'll say something else for you, Clara, you're legs are fine, too, even compared to the splendiferous set of pins standing next to you." It was true. They were sturdier and wider than Georgina's but every smooth contour was just as attractive.

"In fact, I can't quite make my mind up which pair I'm going to slip my hand in between first."

Georgina took a step back, apparently took a deep breath, and moved forward again.

"Corralled. He's got us corralled." It was hardly more than whisper, directed at Clara.

"Yes," the older one answered huskily.

"Hey, ladies, don't be upset with me," Jack protested. "I swear I've never seen anything like the pair of you standing there the way you are. Why, you're more rousing than an entire corps of Army buglers. If'n I could, I'd take the pair of you to New York and have you in the show. You'd be the biggest sensation ever, I deClara. You'd have dukes and senators drinking champagne right out of your shoes. Come over here and we'll talk about it some more. One of you on each side of the bed."

They edged toward him like nervous fillies. Wide eyed, a little fearful, yet compelled to advance by a mixture of curiosity and desire neither could deny. The same emotions that must have had bought them into his cabin in the first place. It occurred to Jake that Eric and Edward might be enterprising businessmen but far from enterprising enough in their home lives. Something he'd soon find out.

"Georgina, you go over to the left. That's it, stand close. Clara, over on the right and step up."

The two women faced each other over his body, looking at each other and then down at the cowboy as Jake savoured the sight of every delectable inch of flesh quivering within his reach. Then he stretched out his right hand, slowly, and tickled the back of Clara's knee. She took a deep breath and shivered. When the movement eventually reached the points of her breasts, it had magnified to a degree that had Jake shivering as well.

"Okay, gals, you can haul my pants off. I guess they won't be needed for a while. And then you can go back to what you were doing before with my toes."

Clara giggled into her raised hands and the tip of Georgina's tongue flickered for the space of a heartbeat between her white teeth like a rattlesnake's warning. Jake lifted the Navy .36 and pointed the muzzle upward again. In a hurried response the bed creaked as two more bodies knelt down on it. With immense satisfaction he watched the pair of ace-high lovelies quickly unfastening his belt and pulling it apart. Georgina's tongue appeared between her teeth again as she concentrated on undoing the top button of his Levi's. Not an easy task because the pressure on it was increasing. Something that had to do with Clara's palm gently rubbing against the next buttons down. What stirred to life underneath her hand made her lift her head in surprise and turn it to gape at the cowboy.

"Now look what you've done, Clara," Georgina complained, still struggling to loosen the Levi's.

The young, blonde femme laid her hand flat on Jake's stomach and slid it underneath the top of the Levi's. Then she maneuvered the hand to push the side of it against his iron-hard pecker, moving it the right and from below the line of buttons. "Quick, Clara, undo him now," she demanded.

Clara bent her flushed face to the task and quickly loosened his pants. Two pairs of hands caught hold of the top of the garment and hauled them down—but only a few inches before the movement stopped and the eastern matrons looked with slack-jawed amazement at what they'd uncovered.

"Oh God, Georgina," Clara moaned in shock. "It belongs in a cage. In a zoo. Or is it Eric who's lacking? I'm confused."

Georgina took hold of the base of Jake's erection and gently waved it around as though testing to see if it might fall off in her hand. "No, it's huge compared to Edward's as well. I think he's made more like a stallion than a man."

Clara took a full handful of what was protruding above Georgina's grip and shuddered in a delicious tremor. "Oh God, you're right. Neither of us could handle this."

"But you are handling it, girls," Jake pointed out. "And it's rude to talk about me as if I wasn't here."

Georgina chuckled and gave him another of her sultry glances, this one pitched high enough to just slide out from underneath the brim of her hat. "But you are here, Jake. All of you. That's the problem." With one hand still gripping the base of his stand, the other crept in between his thighs and he felt her soft fingers stroking his balls. "Yes, you're all here, I'm sure of it now."

"Hmmm . . ." He stirred in pleasure at her touch. "Come on, ladies, do as you're told. Off with those pants and then stand up."

The delicious duo seemed reluctant to abandon their examination of the finer points of Jake's manhood. But they obeyed. The Levi's were pulled clear and thrown aside, the action fast enough to set enough flesh heaving around underneath the ponchos for Jake to feel like blowing bubbles and whispering "coochie-coo."

"Okay, Clara, you stand at the end of the bed and push your hat back behind your head. Georgina, you stand behind her." The straying wives showed puzzled expressions but did as they were bid.

"Clara, down on your knees. In the middle, up against both my feet."

She obeyed and stared at the column of flesh curving back over his stomach, her lips tightly pressed together. Jake slid down the bed an inch or so, setting the column swinging, and pressed his soles against the soft mounds underneath the white linen. Clara grunted and wriggled forward on her knees, staring at Jake's face before bending her head to lick his toes.

"Okay, Georgina, get down behind Clara, reach around, grab her tits and rub them against my feet."

Clara's head bobbed up again as sharply as a cork bobbing to the surface with a hooked fish attached to it. "What!"

Jake lifted up the pistol and ostentatiously thumbed back the hammer. Georgian looked at it, shrugged her shoulders just as ostentatiously, and went down on her knees behind Georgina. The redhead swung her head from side to side as if not believing what her ears were telling her about the movement at her back. Then Georgina leaned forward and whispered calming words in Clara's ear at the same moment her arms were moving around underneath her friend's and stealing in below the poncho. Clara squealed, gasped, and shivered as her partner in sin took a firm grip on her maternal assets. Whatever Clara's shock, it had no effect in reducing the big-titted woman's lust because Jake could feel the firmness of her nipples as Georgina moved them backward and forward and up and down against his soles.

"Pull the poncho up, Clara. I want to see your tits while Georgina's shaking them around for you."

Clara's hands seemed to be trembling almost as much as her breasts as she hauled up the sheet of linen between their two bodies. The layers of linen bunched up around Clara's mouth as her hands uncovered two mounds of virginal white flesh overflowing Georgina's restraining fingers.

"Oh, sweet Jesus!"

Clara moaned, her popping brown eyes growing ever wider as her maid of honor began to rub the newly exposed nipples against Jake's feet again, still as hard as unripened plums and surrounded by circles of brown skin large enough to serve hotcakes on. The cowboy began singing softly, joyfully, beating out the time with a two-fingered grip on his tower of masculine power.

> She wouldn't call for sherry; she wouldn't call for beer;
> She wouldn't call for cham, because she knew 'twould make
>    her queer;
> She wouldn't call for brandy, rum, or anything they'd got;
> She only called for cock: hot! hot! hot!

Georgina was staring over Clara's shoulder at Jake's shaft as if it was a rearing rattlesnake, yet she seemed to have picked up on the same swaying movement because her own body was writhing against her friend's spine. Clara's eyes were fastened on Jake's every movement as she snorted into the pushed-up poncho material with all the ladylike demureness of a drowning pig.

"Right, ladies, would one of you like to have her velvet smoothed down before we start?" Jake grinned and waggled his tongue between his lips.

"What? What do you mean?" Georgina asked. "You mean—you mean put your thing into one of us?"

He pushed himself up on his elbows for a better look at their faces. "There's another hand to deal first, gals. Where I lick your honeypots out for you."

Georgina wasn't fooling or hanging back, he was certain. The expression on her face was of genuine puzzlement. She really didn't know what he was talking about. Neither did Clara, he was just as sure. Jake's questions about Eric and Edward had been completely answered. He sighed, stood up, held the Colt by the barrel and butt and presented it to Clara.

"Be a good girl and hold this very carefully while we have ourselves a little demonstration here." Clara gaped at him and took hold of the pistol with both hands as if it were a piece of priceless glass.

"Good girl."

Jake lay down on the bed again, in reverse direction, his head close to the end where his feet had been.

"Right, Georgina, put your knees on either side of my head. And don't be scared. There's no biting allowed. But hang onto your hat."

His last glimpse before his eyes were covered by Georgina's poncho was of two pairs of puzzled eyes staring down at him. He reached up underneath the linen to take hold of the blonde's waist, positioning her body. He heard Georgina gasp as his ears brushed against the insides of her thighs. A sound followed by a much louder gasp as his tongue laid a snail track of saliva along her slit. Georgina shuddered against his hands, in surprise, in shock. His tongue moved again, tracing the same path, more slowly, more gently. She made more sounds of surprise, but his contact on the soft body was enough to let him know that the eastern ma'am was relaxing. Relaxing enough to lower herself closer to his probing tongue.

Jake would have chuckled if he could. This was the kind of rodeo ride that could earn a man an awful lot of good loving and home-cooked meals if he knew how to do it right. And Jake Jefferson Jackson knew exactly how to do it. If there was a woman he couldn't lift up to heaven on the tip of his tongue he hadn't met her yet.

Georgina was certainly no challenge at all. When he reached up to play with her perky tits, she grabbed hold of his hands and pressed them against her nipples as she wriggled frantically above him. Jake wished he could see her face—even more, he wished he could see Clara's face as she stood there holding the Colt and watching her respectable married friend bouncing around on a man's face with a head of steam building up inside her hotter than the boat's boiler. When he held two fingers up to Georgina's face she immediately sucked on them. And then they were sucked again, and Jake was sure the second time they had been inside Clara's mouth. God, she must be stamping the floor with impatience to join in!

Jake pursed his lips into an O, put them over Georgina's button, and blew out a great laugh at the same moment as he began finger fucking her. His rider's hands instantly leapt into action, her legs locked like iron bars, and somewhere above him he heard a partly muffled screech. It wasn't until Jake slid out from underneath Georgina's sprawling weight that he could see he'd just done something new to a woman. Whether or not Mrs. Tasker ever talked through her hat, she could honestly say now she'd had an orgasm through one. She'd used the stage prop to stifle her scream of ecstasy and the hat appeared to be ruined for life. So did Georgina, but it was a passing illusion. She moaned, dropped the hat to dangle on its cords, twisted around, and threw herself on top of Jake, pressing her lips passionately against his. The old black magic had worked again.

Not only on Georgina, either. Clara was still holding the Colt but only with her left hand. The right one was out of sight underneath the poncho and her face was as hot as a sacrificial virgin feeling the first blast of a dragon's breath. But there was nothing virginal about the way her ample body was responding to her own stimulation. And when Jake stretched out his hand, she desperately grabbed it and put it where hers had been. Jake laughed and entered her with the same two fingers he'd just used on Georgina. Curling them up into the top of her snatch was like tickling a trout. Clara sagged at the knees and bit on her forearm to stifle her cries. Georgina leapt up and quick-wittedly took the six shooter from her adulterous accomplice before it fell.

Jake rose, too, taking his hand from Clara's body. He grabbed her shoulders and pushed her toward the dressing table. The mirror above the dressing table showed their two reflections side by side. He pulled up her poncho to reveal her breasts again, dragged the loose material back over her shoulders, bit down on a fold to keep it clear of Clara's bouncers, and then grabbed hold of both wobbling jugs with all the passion of a pilgrim entering the promised land. Clara's face stared back at him from the mirror with slack-jawed incredulity as she rubbed her backside against his erection. Another face appeared in the mirror.

"Are you having a good time, Mr. Jackson?" Georgina asked, almost as coolly as if she was serving him tea after church.

"Happy as a darkie in a melon patch, ma'am. All I need now is a rubber. There's one on the table there. Take another for yourself. And put that pistol down on the bed. It's not loaded anyway. But I am, and not with blanks. So get down on your knees, girls. I'm sure you can figure out what to do, as long as you both keep your mouths open."

He stared into the mirror again, at the fringe of his deerskin hoisted up to his waist and at the two heads bobbing up and down on his cock, copper haired and blond, both taking polite turns at blowing a tune on the pink piccolo and then rolling a rubber down it. The pair of them had a lot to learn about prick pleasuring before they got off at Pittsburgh. But he was a patient teacher—sometimes. Not now though. He reached down, grabbed Clara's ear, and hauled her to her feet.

"Bend over!"

Small bottles were knocked off the table as Clara rested her forearms in front of the mirror and stared into it, her tits almost touching the polished wood. She saw her own face, her own shameless nakedness, and then a glimpse of the huge male organ moving in behind to split her apart. She groaned and Georgina's fingers clamped lightly over her lips.

"Quiet, honey, quiet!"

Jake positioned his tip between the juicy lips and plunged forward, just as the screech of the *Queen Charlotte*'s steam whistle blasted through the cabin again. The cowboy reared up on his toes and yelped with laughter and pleasure as he began giving Mrs. Clara Butler a fucking she'd never forget.

# Angel to a Cowboy

**LANEY CAIRO**

EMERGENCY ROOM TRIAGE was mad, completely insane, but Rhonda was past caring about the chaos. She'd stopped caring about the confusion, noise, and mess some time the previous year. She'd seen it all.

"When did the pain start?" Rhonda asked the young woman on the other side of the security screen, who was retching into one of the plastic bags provided for the purpose. "Have you had a fever? Noticed a rash?"

The woman retched again, and Rhonda shrugged and typed "3" into the urgency box on the electronic assessment form. "Take a seat, you should be seen within an hour. Next."

The injured and sick people waiting to be seen weren't actually looking at her or trying to get her attention, for a change. They were all peering through the glass to the forecourt of the ER, where ambulances parked, and Rhonda could hear a commotion.

She slapped the buzzer to call a security guard to the forecourt, and pushed herself up out of the plastic chair, her legs sticking to the worn plastic through her pantyhose.

She didn't need to shove her way through the press of sick and wounded; there was a side entrance to her cubicle that led out to the forecourt through the ambulance access doors.

"Well I'll be . . ." she said.

There was a horse in the forecourt, shaggy and filthy, with a man slumped forward across the saddle and onto the horse's withers, hand clamped over one shoulder, blood seeping through the caked-on dirt.

"Two!" Rhonda called over her shoulder, to the rapidly swelling group of Emergency Room staff.

"Hey there," she said to the man, moving the battered Stetson that covered his face so she could see him better. His face was bristled with stubble, smeared with dirt, but he opened his eyes when she touched his face.

"Hey, sweetie," she said. "How about you get off the horse, and let me look at your shoulder?"

He grunted, the dirt creasing around his smile.

"I'd be dead then?" he said, voice a drawl of midwestern accent. "You'd be my own angel?"

"I'm a nurse," Rhonda said. "Think you can slide off the horse?"

"If you're going to catch me, darlin', I can do anything," the cowboy said, and he slung his far leg over the back of the horse and dropped to his feet in front of Rhonda, his hand still clamped tightly over his left shoulder.

He was unbelievably filthy, stinking of sweat and horse shit and unbrushed teeth, but so were most of the people that fronted at Emergency, so Rhonda breathed through her mouth and steadied the cowboy with both of her hands.

"There you go," she said, as an orderly trundled a gurney across to her. "How about you sit down on this, and I'll take you indoors and someone can have a look at your shoulder."

"You won't leave me?" the cowboy asked, and his left hand curled around Rhonda's wrist.

Rhonda lifted her eyes for a moment, and the other nurse, Terri, nodded at her. Terri could cope with the mess in triage.

"I'll stay with you," Rhonda said.

The cowboy kept hold of Rhonda's wrist, and his eyes were fixed on her as the orderly wheeled the trolley through the sliding doors, to the staging area for Emergency.

"I'm Deputy Sheriff Edwin B. Daniels," he said. "And I ain't never seen a woman as fine as you, darlin'. Figures I'd have to go to heaven to see an angel."

"I'm Rhonda, and I don't think you're dead," Rhonda said. "I think you're in Los Angeles. Where are you from, Deputy Sheriff Edwin B. Daniels?"

"Osceola, Missouri," Edwin B. Daniels said, and the orderly wheeled the gurney into a cubicle that was still littered with medical packaging and the mess from the previous occupant.

"I need to look at your shoulder, see what's wrong with it," Rhonda said. "So you'll have to let go of my hand."

"Apologies, Miss Rhonda," Edwin B. Daniels said, and Rhonda shook her hand as she reached for a pair of latex gloves from the box mounted on the wall. "Though, if I'm dead, surely a scratch like this don't matter."

Rhonda smiled at Edwin. She really loved the mad ones, they were never dull. One time, a guy in a suit of armor had walked into the ER, having broken an arm jousting. He'd insisted they all call him Sir Bedivere.

"Does it hurt?" she asked as she began to unbutton Edwin's flannel shirt. "Can you let me see it, please?"

Edwin was three-baths-dirty, with the kind of filth matted into his chest hair that took years to generate and days to remove, but he let her ease his shirt open and pull the blood-caked material away from the wound.

It was a gunshot wound, ragged and messy, but still only superficial. There were no in-and-out points; it looked like the bullet had merely grazed the surface of the shoulder, tearing at the flesh but not breaking any bones.

Edwin hissed when Rhonda squeezed a small bottle of normal saline over the wound, but made no other complaint, not even when she picked over the flesh with forceps.

"It's not a serious wound," Rhonda said. "So you can decide what you want done to it. If you've got health insurance, or can afford to pay for your care, you can get a doctor to have a look at it, perhaps even have a graft put over the top of it. If you can't afford that, I can stitch the edges together for you, at minimal cost." She had to report the wound to the police, too, but prior experience told her that if she mentioned that, the patient would be out of the door in an instant, untreated and unbilled.

"I've got money," Edwin said, feeling around in his jeans pockets with his right hand, and pulling out a small purse. There were three small coins in it, gleaming gold. "I've got legal tender, honestly come by, not like some other folk."

Rhonda looked in the purse, then at Edwin. She knew a little about coins, and they were Indian Heads, worth thousands each, more than enough to pay for a stitch job.

"You must be thinking I'm not a civilized man," Edwin said while Rhonda set up a sterile field and unwrapped a suture kit onto it. "I'm not usually unwashed, but I've been chasing that outlaw Jesse Woodson James for days, and ain't had the chance to bathe."

"Would you like a wash?" Rhonda asked, looking up from pulling on sterile gloves. "I can get you some warm water and soap, and you can fix yourself up."

"That'd be right kind of you, Miss Rhonda," Edwin said. "Perhaps you could check on my horse, too?"

"When I've fixed your shoulder," Rhonda said, picking up plastic forceps and soaking the gauze in sterilizing solution. "This'll sting."

Edwin hissed again when Rhonda cleaned his wound, but didn't flinch at the suturing. "Dr. Lewis don't have hands like yours, Angel," Edwin said.

Rhonda smoothed the sterile dressing over the wound and smiled at Edwin. He was a very attractive man, under his dirt, and his gentle manners touched her.

"I'll get you a basin and a towel," she said. "And I'll have someone check on the horse."

She bundled the trolley of used supplies away, out of the cubicle, and took in a bowl of warm water, a bar of soap, and toothbrush and toothpaste.

She left Edwin washing his hands and face and trekked tiredly across the ER to the nursing station. "He's worried about his horse," she said to the ward clerk. "Can you check get security to check on the horse?"

The ward clerk crossed her arms and leaned back smugly in her chair. "I can tell you that the horse started eating the roses out the front, so someone caught it and tied it up in the ambulance bay. Your cowboy might want to check out of Hotel Healthcare in a hurry, before someone bills him for the roses as well as his care."

"Thanks," Rhonda said, levering herself away from the counter where the ward clerk sat.

She opened the cubicle curtains and peered in.

Edwin was sitting on the edge of the bed, his filth-caked jeans around his ankles, washing his groin.

"Sorry," she said. "I'll wait outside."

Edwin looked up at her, his eyes twinkling, and he was really hot without the grime on his face. Scrubbed clean and shaven, he'd be a hunk.

"You could stay," Edwin said, and he held out a hand to her, his skin clean apart from around his nails.

She had to smile, he really was adorable.

"I can't," she said, but she was tempted enough not to just close the curtains and walk away.

"You'd be doing me a favor, Angel," Edwin said.

It was stupid, but it had been so long since anyone had called her Angel, and even longer since someone had wanted her, and she was so tired and frazzled. She flicked the "procedure in cubicle" light on, to stop anyone from walking in on them and stepped closer. It wouldn't hurt to watch him.

His cock was thick and long, and she couldn't remember the last time she'd seen an uncut man. The German tourist with the burns, that was right. Edwin stroked himself one-handed, and she took hold of the other one, where he was still reaching out for her.

"Come here, Angel," he said, his voice low and rough. "Let me touch you."

The scent of soap overlaid the sweat and horse, even his breath was soapy, and she had to giggle at the idea of him brushing his teeth with soap.

He let go of his cock and lifted a hand to her uniform, pressing against the blue cotton, cupping her breast, making her ache. God, if that was what one touch felt like . . .

His hand squeezed her breast gently, and his eyes were just as gentle when she lifted her gaze from his hand.

"Let me . . ." she said, and he lifted his hand enough for her to unzip her nurse's uniform down to her waist.

She owned decent underwear, but she certainly wasn't going to wear it to work, though Edwin didn't seem put off by the sagging cotton of her bra. If anything, his other hand, which was stroking his cock, worked harder, the slide of skin on skin suddenly loud over the background din of the ER.

She reached behind herself and unclipped her bra through the back of her uniform, then pulled it forward so it slid off her breasts.

"Sweet Lord," Edwin murmured, and he ran his fingertips over the fullness of one breast, then dipped his fingers into her cleavage before sliding them across the other breast to brush over a nipple.

Rhonda was so fucking turned on that it felt like her nipple was wired directly to her clit, making her ache inside.

She curled her hand around Edwin's cock, covering his fingers and squeezing, and Edwin leaned forward and nuzzled whiskery lips over her nipple, his eyes closed and a look of bliss on his face.

"Sit back," she said.

Edwin slid back on the gurney, pushing his jeans lower, and Rhonda hitched her uniform up and reached for her crotch. She had pantyhose on, support hose to stop her legs from aching, but she could always buy another pair. Her fingers snagged on the tough lycra hose, and she tore the crotch of her pantyhose out, the fabric rending and Edwin gasping.

It took a moment to check the brakes were on the gurney, then Rhonda clambered up and knelt over Edwin. Her underwear was wet when she gripped the edge of the crotch and pushed it aside, exposing her cunt, and she didn't think she'd ever been so hot before.

"Edwin B. Daniels," she whispered. "You might just be the sexiest man I've ever met."

The first brush of the head of his cock against her labia made them both moan, and the gurney squeaked a little. She knew the gurney could take their combined weight, she'd clambered over enough patients during emergencies. She just hoped the brakes would hold this time.

Edwin's head lolled against the upright back of the gurney, his mouth open and eyes closed, and the head of his cock eased into her body. "Angel," he gasped, and she worked herself down his length, her lycra-clad knees settling beside his body, her hands pushing his shirt all the way open then bracing against his chest.

She rocked forward, grinding her clit against his pubic bone, then grinding back, steady rock, and his hands settled on her hips, over her bunched-up uniform.

It was delicious, feeling how hard he was, watching the delight slip across his face, his breath quickening, his hands tightening on her flesh, hard enough to mark.

Rhonda's cunt burned, the heat building with each grind, his cock hard enough and thick enough to be pushing against all the right places inside her, until she was moaning and Edwin was groaning and rocking, too, pushing deeper and deeper inside her.

She came, painfully intense waves rushing through her, making her cunt clamp around Edwin's cock, so she had to close her eyes and try not to scream.

Edwin came just as she was finishing, hot, slippery come flooding her cunt, soaking into her underwear, and she slumped forward against his chest, his hand stroking the back of her neck.

He crooned quietly, humming to her, until she extricated herself from his arms, lifting herself off his softening cock, letting him slip out of her reluctantly.

Her legs were wobbly when she clambered down off the gurney, and she wasn't quite able to meet Edwin's gaze while she settled her underwear and did her bra back up, then smoothed her uniform down.

Edwin pulled his jeans up and buttoned the fly, then swung his legs over the edge of the gurney.

"Mighty appreciative for that, Angel," he said, and he took out his purse and opened it. "Here's a dollar for the doctoring, and a dollar for you," he said, pressing two gold coins into her hand. "You can buy yourself some more clothes, since I ruined those ones."

Rhonda glanced down and grimaced. Not only was she rumpled, but there was dirt smudged over the front of her uniform where he'd touched her.

"Oh," she said. "But I'm not a . . ."

"A whore?" Edwin said, buttoning his shirt up and jamming his hat back on his head. "No, you're an angel. Think you can show me where my horse is tethered?"

They walked back out through the ER, through the whirl of activity, of shouted instructions and crowded gurneys, but Edwin's eyes stayed on Rhonda's face, making her acutely aware that her cheeks were flushed and her skin glowing.

The horse was tied up to the fence, beside an ambulance, and Edwin loosened the reins and slung himself up into the saddle.

He lifted his hat to Rhonda, his smile a warm secret, then dug his boots into his horse, urging the animal forward.

"Good-bye, Angel," he called out over his shoulder, and Rhonda stood in the forecourt, beside the ambulances, and watched Deputy Sheriff Edwin B. Daniels ride off into the darkness.

Terri slung her arm around Rhonda's shoulder and said, "You get some fucking weird ones, don't you?"

"I think he was really a cowboy," Rhonda said.

---

SHE PAID HIS medical bill with her credit card. He had left her with two gold Indian Head coins, his lucky bullet, and the conviction that her job was rewarding. It wasn't everyone that got to be an angel to a cowboy.

# Ace in the Hole

**M. CHRISTIAN**

THE MAN WITH Many Names rode high—and hard—in the saddle.

Two days out from Laredo. Two days till Bad Water. The sky was so blue it hurt. No clouds. Damned little breeze. His horse kicked sullen clouds of dust. The range was frozen in dry, still air. A few sagebrush. A few scattered dumps of stone. This was his home—just as a sod house was some folks', just as the high mountains were others, and wigwams were for certain Indians. He rode steadily through a hot, dry day, miles from nothing, perfectly at home.

Or shoulda been. Fact was, the tall, hard man in the serape, bruised old Stetson, silver spurs, and comfortable old saddle, wasn't all that much at home. Maybe it was the hot, beating sun, maybe the lingering bite of sagebrush, the blue hurting sky. Maybe because of that certain crop of stones, maybe that one bird's high, long song. Maybe that lone tree, leafless and baking in the hot sun.

Whatever the cause, the man sometimes called Diego, Dan, Jesus, Burt, Colt, or many others, rode high—and very, very *hard*—in the saddle.

He wanted to play.

It didn't show up on any maps—not that there were that many maps of that particular stretch of dirt anyway—just a junction between two ridges. It was a slightly raised vee with its back up to the wind and a few more dead trees. A tumbleweed did just that. Still, Hole-in-the-Wall offered much to a tall, hard man in the saddle: more than dirt, the strong sky, tepid wind, cacti, and a horse.

The Man with Many Names tied his nameless horse to the hitching post and started toward the door. Hole-in-the-Wall was just a little more than its namesake—whitewashed adobe, a cracked and buckling rough-shod roof. Two windows covered by limp and faded blankets. A cracked and empty trough. A pair of swinging doors.

Diego, Dan, Jesus, Burt, Colt . . . lit a dark cheroot with a single explosion of a sulfur match off his silver belt buckle before pushing through the doors. Right hand on the butt of his sidearm, naturally.

He entered listening, since he knew he'd be blind against the awful ink inside. He walked in and listened for *those* noises: the skidding of a chair being roughly pushed back, the quick jingling of coins in a pocket as someone stood up, the metal snap of a hammer getting cocked—as well as the absence of noise: the sudden cession of talk that meant he was suddenly way, way too interesting.

One wall was a bar, and Pedro, Jesus (the only thing the two of them had in common), Che, Raul, or sometimes Bean was polishing a fogged glass with a dry towel, his massive body like a tanned redwood and his hands like a wooden Indian's. The rest of the place was three tables and four men. One old Mexican rocking back and forth in a slice of hard sunlight leaking through one of the blanket-covered windows. Two at one of the tables, eyes sizing him up over fans of dirty cards for craziness, the law, or something to prove. They were like the dead trees and the dry, dusty air: common as the dumps of rock and the cacti. They were very much a part of the Man with Many Name's home, the range.

When they figured him for someone who wouldn't draw unless drawn on, they went back to their game.

"Whiskey," the Man said to the Bartender. Pedro, Jesus, Che, Raul, Bean coughed once, reached under the bar for the bottle, uncorked it with the two remaining teeth in his head, and poured a good hefty shot.

The Man downed it in one swallow. The fire of it was almost cool down his throat, against breathing in hot dust. Almost. It kicked somewhere below his ribs like a horse. He pushed the glass back calmly, "Another."

After "another" was nothing but dull roarings in his belly, the Man turned back to the room.

The old Mexican still rocked, the white beam of sunlight flashing across the colored blanket in his lap.

One of the men, a tall, sandy-haired range hand with great curls of mustache, threw down his cards in exhausted resolution, nodded to the dealer, picked up his guns (which had been hooked around the back of the chair), and left through the swinging doors, the sunlight of his passing showing on the dirty floor.

The Man walked over to the table and stood there just long enough to catch the Dealer's attention.

"You up for a game, Mister?" the Dealer said.

The Man with Many Names just nodded, once, hard—and took up the empty seat.

"Man's a conversationalist," the Dealer said, "I like that." He started to shuffle, fast but not too fast—the sign of either an excellent card player who knew enough to not be flashy or just a good card player.

"The man who just left was a chatterer. Chatted up with the sun and down with its set. Frankly, sir, I think I would prefer your company. A lot more can be said with silence."

The Man with Many Names nodded and indicated the cards.

"See, you don't have to say anything. I know just what you want." The Dealer flipped cards. "Game's stud. Five card."

The Man smiled and scooped up his cards, fanned them, looked them over, took a dollar coin out of his pocket and flipped it onto the table.

"Even lets his money do most of the talking—" said the Dealer, smiling even broader, flipping his own coins onto the table.

———∞———

THERE WERE NO clocks in Hole-in-the-Wall. Too easy to break. Too expensive. And no one cared. At a certain time the old Mexican got up out of his rocking chair and started lighting lamps.

Their game only paused while the old man hobbled over and lit the lantern on the wall next to their table.

The Dealer looked at the Man over his cards. Over his own cards, the Man did the same. Many have said that you can learn a lot about a person by the way he plays a game. The Man with Many Names looked at the Dealer and saw a medium man. Flaming hair. Irish parents—yet his skin was warned by a yellowish tan that spoke of many summers on the range. He had a full, firm mouth that grinned broad (which was often) and surprisingly straight teeth. His eyes sparkled and danced in the setting sun, then in the lamplight. His shoulders were straight and broad, and rolled down to corded arms and hard hands.

Now, the Dealer, he looked at the Man and just grinned his grin. "What's the stakes then this time?" he said.

The Man just nodded again, indicating the Dealer.

"High stakes, pardner. Very high stakes." The Dealer shuffled, keeping his eyes down and hooded. He shuffled for a surprisingly short time—and that grin again—before flipping cards at the Man.

The game was playful and in earnest. No one there was really watching, but if the old Mexican or the Bartender with Many Names did, they would have seen them flip and raise, discard and fold with a kind of tense earnestness: the Man with Many Names attacking, bluffing with his craggy, carved face, staring at the Dealer with eyes the chill of rifle barrels. He nodded for cards, flipped others down—all with gunslinger reflexes.

Now the Dealer, he was dancing and darting this way and that, ducking out of the way of those sighting eyes, moving just a bit too fast for The Man's craggy perceptions.

Around ten—though there were no clocks—they faced each other over the last hand. They both knew what was at stake, they both braced themselves, they both eyed the other over their cards.

"Okay, let's see them," the Dealer said, kicking a bit back in his rickety chair and twirling a toothpick in his mouth. "Let's see what you got."

A straight.

The Man with Many Names nodded his nod that said many things. In this case it said, *Let's see yours, then.*

Three aces and a king.

This time, it was the Man with Many Names who smiled wide and broad.

<hr>

THERE WAS A full moon that night. The corral next to Hole-in-the-Wall was ghost lit with pale white light. The ponies swished their tails, pawed the ground, and ignored the two men who opened their gate, came inside and went to one corner.

In the glaring moonlight they moved through the corral, drawn by something—naturally—unspoken. The Dealer started to say something, but a hard look from the Man silenced him. To add something to the command, the Man took a dusty black (or blue, hard to tell in the silvery moonlight) bandanna and carefully balled it up and slowly, forcefully, shoved it into his mouth with two fingers.

The Dealer looked up at him with eyes lost in moonlight as the Man took him firmly by the shoulders and turned him toward a corner of the corral.

The Man was an almost invisible heaviness behind the Dealer, who could feel him there, his knees against the backs of his thighs.

A pair of range-chapped hands appeared from behind him and guided the Dealer's own less-rough fingers to the fence.

The Man breathed on the back of the Dealer's neck, and the Dealer smelled cheap whisky, dust and—something else—an animal beyond the wild things in the hills, beyond the ponies. The hands left his own and dropped to the Dealer's slight paunch, and grabbed him firm and hard, hugging him with hands used to fighting, shooting, and riding. The Man squeezed him hard—and the Dealer responded with a deep thunderous groan, feeling himself start to get tight in his britches. It was like a fire was being built up behind him, its warmth spreading through him, igniting all of him—especially his cock.

The Man with Many Names played, for a moment, with the Dealer's simple iron belt-buckle before undoing it and pulling his dungarees quickly to his knees.

The night was warm. The Dealer was *hot*; he didn't feel the breeze at all. He didn't smell anything at all except for the heavy smell of a rutting man. He didn't feel anything (including the rough wood of the fencing) except for the strong hands of the man reaching around for him, his cock.

The Dealer was long and strong, and the Man found himself holding what could have been a man's wrist. The Man smiled even more and kissed the back of the Dealer's neck.

The Dealer was also grinning as he slowly bent away from the Man to rest his burly forearms on the fence.

The Dealer's pale moon was almost white in the other moon's light. His legs were strong, like the trunks of trees, and his ass was two globes of tight muscle, surprisingly soft to the Man's touch. He had a narrow band of hair, like a tail, that ran from the base of his spine to the apples of his balls. His asshole was a wedding ring of soft pink.

The Man with Many Names dropped his own pants with a jingling of buckle and spurs. His own long, thick cock was straining against him for the touch of a hand, lips, for something. . . .

Slowly, carefully, pulling back against his lust but pushing forward nonetheless, the Man eased himself forward, to rest his uncut length on the seam of the Dealer's crack. Slowly, again, he worked himself back and forth along the hairy valley, never quite pulling back far enough to enter him on the next stroke.

To let the Dealer feel exactly what he was facing, the Man with Many Names put his hand calmly down on top of his cock, pressing down with his palm. Bent under him, the Dealer gave a shuddering moan at feeling exactly how long and hard and strong the Man's cock was. He found himself nodding encouragement.

But not yet. First the Man licked and sucked two of his fingers, getting them good and wet. Then he pulled a little more and eased his cock down to where his smooth head was jangling against the Dealer's warm, hairy balls. Then he slowly started to circle the other man's asshole with his wet fingers—hypnotizing his asshole to open up for him.

It was distracting, but pleasing, when he felt the Dealer's hand circle around his cock and start to milk him with smooth, sure strokes.

After just a little teasing, the Dealer's asshole swallowed his fingers, pulling them deep and warm inside. Not that anyone could have seen, save that big silver moon and those two ponies, but the Man smiled big and broad once more.

Again he pulled back, inching his cock from the Dealer's soft fingers till he was almost a pace away from him. In that white light of the full moon, the Dealer's ass was pale and hard, his puckered asshole like a pair of pursed lips. Running a hard hand down the crack of the Dealer's ass and touching his asshole with a strong finger, the Man carefully took two steps forward and put the head of his cock to those special lips.

Below him, head almost touching the fence, the Dealer mumbled something like, "—man's gotta do what a man's—" through the gag, ending in a low moan as the Man with Many Names carefully slipped his cock into his asshole.

The Dealer stiffened, his moan arcing up to a slight squeal as the Man inched his cock into him.

Warm. Tight. The Man resisted the fucking instinct with everything he had. Rather, with the patience earned from long days on the range, he slowly eased his cock out a bit, then back in a bit: inching with inches 'til before the Dealer knew it, he *was* getting fucked with the full length of the Man's muscular cock.

With each long stroke, the Dealer grunted, moaned, and squealed with maybe pain but definitely pleasure, eventually blowing out the handkerchief with one explosive sigh. Caught up in it, he reached between his own legs and started to furiously pump his own cock, feeling the muscles in his ass start to milk the Man.

The ponies, rather than being spooked, moved closer till one of them, a tall palomino, snorted warm horse breath on the back of the Man's neck.

They came, one not soon after the other. First, the Dealer, jetting come into the dirt and dust of the corral, feeling his knees start to give with release. The Man went next as the Dealer started to fall under him—his own silvery come splattering on the back of the dealer's shirt.

They both sat down in the dirt and heaved and panted and smiled, smiled, smiled.

After a point, the Man with Many Names looked down at the Dealer's pants, still wrapped around his knees. In the moonlight, the Ace was like a plate of fine china. "You could have won," he said, nodding to the card the Dealer then pocketed.

"I did," said the Dealer.

# A Dying Breed

RAKELLE VALENCIA

H E STILL WORE a six-gun at his thin hips, which I had hoped wasn't loaded but knew better, and was packing a rifle in his scabbard for riding the mountainous terrain of grizzly and cougar. He rode a big horse that towered above all others on the working dude ranch. But that didn't make the beast pretty. It was a throwback to foundation lines, proving its ancient lineage with a roman nose, thick-boned, heavy-haired legs, a goose rump that tucked under itself, and an attitude to match its ugliness. The mustang-looking gelding must have been a grade or crossbred, because of its height. Somewhere in the woodpile was a thoroughbred, perhaps a remount turned loose by the cavalry after the Civil War eons ago, to help replenish the government with hardy, tall stock that was lost in the battle against brothers.

The fellow never said much. He was the last of generations before him to wrangle for, and stock-manage this ranch. I think he resented the ranch being turned into a tourist trap under new ownership, which of course he would never say. But the gelding said enough for the both of them by rolling his eyes to show their whites, grinding his teeth, and flattening his ears to his neck with the approach of folks whose company the large workin' bay didn't enjoy.

I'd been to the B Lazy U Ranch before, taking part in the myriad of events and clinics that the ranch had to offer over the years, so I was accustomed to Snowdin's crankiness and standoffishness when it came to people. It hadn't scared me away from him, as I supposed he'd meant it to. He was a hell of a horseman. And I had watched Snowdin intently each and every time I was on the ranch, hoping to glean just a smidge of what he had going on with those mustangs he broke and rode.

The genuine cowboy was a dying breed. His skills were learned partly from the life he grew to know and partly from survival, but mostly from the teachings of the horse. His was a way of being— just *being*, in a human society so rushed in *doing*. If there was one thing I had learned from Snowdin on the rare occasions that he had graced the lot of us "dudes" with his infinite wisdom, it was that horses wanted to *be*, while humans wanted to *do*. And that was why the two didn't understand each other well.

I had mulled that piece of psychobabble bullshit over and over, trying to comprehend its true meaning, until all I got were erotic dreams of Snowdin laying next to me naked and satiated. Our sticky, exhausted bodies were warmed by the sun somewhere on one of those rock outcrops I had viewed from the vast vista surrounding the ranch. Then we were miraculously in the hot tub on the back deck of one of those private log cabins, tongues entwined as his hard-on pressed between us with urgency until he picked me up to place me on the side of the tub and thrust his prick fully into me.

He slapped his chinks, or short-chaps, with his coiled rope and almost ran a feral herd of crossbred Mustangs over me as I stood in their path lost in reverie. I sidestepped in time to avoid the deadly collision that a stampede could cause. Snowdin grinned as he loped after the dozen or so scrubby tails of those horses, tipping his Stetson in my direction.

The agenda at the ranch for the week was an advanced learning of colt starting by readying a usin' or workin' horse, and perfecting horse-roping skills, which are clearly different from calf or steer roping techniques. This week was a private, invitation-only clinic. And,

I think, a week for the ranch to take a breather from the hoards of citified people with their overexuberant children.

Both horse and rider had to be up to the level that would be presented in an on-the-job training clinic. And with the ranch so empty, each guest received their own small cabin with all of the amenities like that hot tub on the back deck, a king-size bed, fully stocked kitchenette, fireplace, and the works. Something I would have never been able to afford normally. I had always stayed up in the long house in a one-room bedroom with a small bathroom, shared cafeteria dining, and a large, boisterous common room for relaxing by an immense fireplace.

My coveted invitation had arrived in the mail months ago. I had immediately called to confirm a reservation for my quarter horse mare and myself. I was looking forward to it immensely. Except that the instructor this time would be Snowdin. Snowdin whom they had kept away from the paying guests most of the time. Snowdin with his tough attitude and intimidating persona that would have a person packing for home, spitting mad, or crying like a babe before the week was out. Snowdin who was one of the last real cowboys; the kind that cared more for the horses than the people, that he knew would surely screw them all up.

I screamed out, awakening in the early hours at dawn. My top sheet was crumpled and the bottom one was soaked from sweat. I had slept lightly, alone in my cabin. In half-sleep, I had always dreamed. This dream, like most, was fading fast from my memory, but my body still felt its effects. He had lunged into me. His muscled, rangy body had hovered over mine until my fingernails raked reddened stripes along his back forcing him down upon me and into me.

I pulled the rumpled sheet over my still-moist, naked, chilled body and reached a hand between my legs. I was surprised to find how wet my pussy was; after all, it was only a dream. Too early to bother my horse in a corral of other four-legged guests, I slid my fingers through creamy folds, trailing the self-made lubricant to my clit, encompassing the swollen ridge of the clit shaft. My thighs spread

apart. My legs flattened against the mattress. I shoved two well-
known digits from my left hand into my cunt while furiously mas-
saging my clit and shaft in tiny circles using my right hand fingers.

An orgasm was fast growing. It was building faster than any I had
recently been accustomed to. My pelvis jerked toward my hands. My
ass and thighs lurched from the mattress as my heels dug the fitted sheet for support. This time, I bit my lower lip in stifling that
carnal scream as waves of orgasm overtook my body until I shuddered in relief and basked in the aftershocks. My mouth filled with
the metallic taint of blood from my teeth's scoring.

---

THERE WERE ONLY three invited for the session, just two rugged
men and myself. I had recognized both of them from a distance.
They were from down Texas way, one a ranch owner and the other
a manager. The ranch manager had studied almost exclusively with
Joe Wolters of the famous Four Sixes—better know as the Sixes.

The ranch owner had traveled to hound out information and
skills from Ray Hunt and Buck Brannaman, two world-class natural horsemanship clinicians that had privileged our generations
with teaching their diminishing art of horse-breaking/gentling
and handling.

I had ridden in clinics put on by each of those famous cowboys.
But then I would go home with my retread quarter horse mare to
a small New England pasture, over-full with a dozen, practically
useless, rehab equines, to struggle alone with the concepts and
experiences of the clinic even after I was sure I hadn't ingested a
mere tenth of what those cowboys had tried to get through to me.
In short, I lacked the working-ranch background of the two good
ol' boys participating, and felt totally outclassed.

In greeting my mare, I ran my hand lightly over her silky hide,
noticing that her summer coat was shedding out. She turned to look
at me and offered her hooves for inspection. She was shod on the

front, and I continually checked for lodged stones from the hard-pack that we weren't accustomed to. I fed and watered her, then left for a shower and a cup of steaming coffee.

The streams of water beat upon my body in harsh rivulets. I turned to rest my forehead against the shower wall, allowing my shoulders to be pelted until they were red. I bent forward to feel the heat penetrating my lower back, then decided I had better get serious. But the soap felt too good sliding along my stomach, breasts, and thighs. I paid special attention to my pussy and then my anus, both becoming alert and electrified. I scrubbed shampoo into my short-cropped hair quickly, raked at my face with a cloth, then gathered my Mach III razor and shaving cream. Pits, legs, twat, ass. It was all so regimented. I caressed gel into a thick lather over my lips and through my crevice then removed the stubble of hair growth until I was smooth all over. The electric tingling became inescapable.

I reached for my toiletries bag where I had packed a few, small necessities. The red, streamlined silicon dildo stared up at me with its one eye, while the shorter, purple butt plug appeared to be quietly awaiting attention. I yanked both novelties and a travel-sized jar of Hand Job from the bag, profusely lubricating the silicon items.

That's when I thought of him. This time it hadn't started with a dream; something I could blame my subconscious for and not feel responsible. This time I envisioned his hands as my eyes closed. A callused palm clenched my ass cheek before a long finger dove into my crack and began rimming my puckered hole. He would push his stiff dick into my cunt much like the red silicon dong, while tormenting my butt-hole in preparation for invasion.

As he fucked me, the callused pad of his pointer finger would continue to rim, intermittently seeking the release of my tight sphincter. His mouth would come down on mine at the same time he would shove his finger into my back hole. Snowdin. Drenching my face under the relentless shower streams, I ruthlessly teased and fucked both holes to exhaustion.

My legs felt like rubber as I headed toward the corrals, sipping hot coffee from a travel mug. Setting the mug on the nearest post, I managed to get my mare double-cinched under her buckaroo saddle. The forty-pound saddle was mostly rough out with a little bit of basket weave tooling on the rounded skirt behind the seat The base model was named the Ninety-eight Wade. McCall had made it in 1998 during a time when the natural horsemanship fad had flared. Thick leather sat on an old-timey wade tree, which seemed to be comfortable for most horses from ponies to drafts. I hadn't found one horse yet who balked because of the Ninety-eight Wade.

Instead of trying to be in vogue, I had acquired the equipment because it was specifically made to aid in breaking or gentling horses. I checked my cinches again, tugged across at my wrapped coils of hanging rope, then hung the mare's breast plate and bridle off of the post horn on the left side.

Taking up my momentarily abandoned coffee cup, I led my mare in her Double Diamond rope halter, with a twelve-foot lead and popper, to the round pen where we were to gather.

Snowdin was already in the pen warming up his horse in a spade bit. Their movements floated as if they were one, with no discernible cues between the two in making changes, turns, gaits, or collection. A pencil-thin bosal hung across the bridge of the big bay's nose. A leather latigo thong tied from the center of the bosal up to the animal's forelock held it away from the two bony ridges, signifying the last steps in spade bit training, the ancient art of the vaqueros. The spade bit was rarely to be touched, and if ever needed, it was to be used with complete *feel*, a sensitivity so great that its like reading each others' minds—the true language of the horse. The bit itself, especially in the wrong hands, could be most cruel, with its long shanks, high port, and spoonlike top that was made to fit exactly to the roof of an individual horse's mouth, sometimes hiding a cricket or a roller beneath.

Many cowboys didn't understand the use of the spade bit and hadn't had the patience for the years it took to make a finished spade bit horse. There were very few horses left at this level and very few true horsemen who could get them there. I continued watching Snowdin and the beast of a horse, this time seeing the beauty and majesty of both, dancing as one with movements that seemed impossible to ask of either human or equine. Together, though, they made most anything appear possible.

He knew I was staring with my mouth ajar like some dumb kid seeing a pony at the county fair for the first time. I turned away, swigged the last of my coffee, stowed the cup on the ground against a fence post, and proceeded rigging my mare's breast plate, then bridling her into a simple breaking headstall with a snaffle bit, slobber straps, and a twenty-two-foot Mecate (pronounced "McCarty" after the American cowboy obliterated it in the misunderstanding of Spanish-Mexicans, sometime in the thirty-year heyday of cowboys and cattle drives).

I had never moved the mare into a bosal, or even imagined her as a finished spade bit horse. Maybe I worried that my hands were not good enough, not light enough, or that I didn't have the education to help either one of us progress. We were both safe in the equipment we had, and we did work off of *feel* together, not the old kick and pull.

She lowered her head and took the bit. Before buckling the throatlatch, I undid the knot on her hand-tied rope halter and slid it down over her nose then through her mouth, around the bit, on top of her tongue, and out. I always loved that trick. Checking my cinches once again, I then mounted from the ground.

Snowdin was leaning a forearm on his post horn while his gelding stood perfectly steady in the middle of the pen. He was now staring at me. "Well, looks like you're ready," he said. "Bring her on in and we'll get started."

I peered around expecting the other two participants, but they weren't near.

"I can run a rank one in for you. Nothing like getting your feet totally soaked, not just wet." He chuckled to himself. It didn't sound sinister at all. Maybe there was hope for this New England girl yet.

My mare and I warmed up at a slow jog as I shook a loop into my rope and swung it on either side of her and over her ears. Snowdin exited through the adjacent chutes to retrieve an unbroke horse. Feral, was more like it. They weren't truly wild horses. The ranch had bought mustangs to run in with their own, but these were ranch-raised horses, fed on hay and cow-cake in the winter if needed. The big difference between these horses and our domestic-raised animals was that from birth to three or four years old human hands never coddled the feral ranch horses.

Snowdin was right. He ran in a rank one. The blue roan, roman-nosed stud colt snorted and stopped on its forehand just inside the gate to the round pen. He lined me up in both eyes, which is a bad deal. The prey animal had plans to act as a predator. Flight or fight. This one would fight. His eyes were ringed white with sclera, proving that maybe there was some Appaloosa in his breeding. He sniffed the air, scenting my mare. I couldn't help but think he was planning to get rid of me so that he could claim my refined quarter horse mare for his own.

I was hit with the jitters and froze a moment. The stud colt threw his head in an arc in the air, then lifted his front end off of the ground only a foot or so. It was enough to declare intent, if not an outright challenge. My mare shook me out of my stupor by tucking her nose into her bridle and arching her back in collection, ready and waiting for my actions.

Slapping my chinks with waxed coils, I jogged to the side of the colt and sent him off in flight. He was young. He was boastful. But I wouldn't let him make good on a bad attitude. I swung my loop in a Hoolihan which is a backhanded, back-assward throw created only for horse catching. It worked. I'm not sure I had wanted it to. I mean I wasn't expecting it to. The colt was rank enough to try to haul me out of my saddle via the rope, and I had never been great at the Hoolihan, since it is the hardest of throws.

The loop sailed high and wide to float down over that colt's head like a parachute. As an ingrained reaction, I jerked in the slack and coiled it into my left hand about the same time this thousand-pound colt decided *he* had *me* on the end of a rope. The blue roan took off at a fast lope around the sixty-foot diameter pen, spitting dirt out from under his hooves. My responsive little mare swung her forehand over fast to avoid getting socked in the neck and head with the waxed rope. She kept spinning on her hind end until I asked her to lurch forward from those powerful, square hindquarters to get in front of the colt and put a stop to this high-speed merry-go-round.

The colt spun back. I sucked in some more slack, keeping my mare in pace with him but not close enough to make him think we were pushing. I put the speed on, bringing the mare in toward the middle again to position her at his side. He was making my sleek little mare into a hairy carnival ride.

There was no time to think. I reacted to the colt's every action, constantly attempting to get one up on him and take over controlling the action. Within ten minutes, which seemed like days of eternity, I had the colt slow enough and close enough that I could snub his nose short to my post horn had I wanted to. But that would seem cruel to the animal, and senseless, since he would then be trapped and have no other option but to fight.

My mare effectively blocked him to a stop, nose to tail. That's when I dallied my rope around that post horn, giving the colt enough slack to free up his legs and stretch his neck. I stepped my quarter horse's rump over and pushed her nose to his rump to tell him he could move forward. When he snagged at the end of the shortened rope, he reared and pawed the air impressively. We pulled him down to the side and began again in asking for this nose to tail dance.

This time he lunged at us with his lips peeled back; newer, mature front teeth gleamed in the wakening sun. I didn't know if he were coming for me, or my mare. It didn't matter. We were in this together; we were one. I backhanded the animal in the mouth and readied on the rope for his recoil. The loop tightened about his neck. He hopped forward, stiff-legged, to release the bite of it, finding out by accident, for the first time, that *release was reward*.

For all the fight that was in him, he was smart. Horses inherently moved away from pressure, always seeking calm and comfort; release is reward. Inherently he knew that. That might have been the Appaloosa heritage coming out, the breed was known to be quick. The colt decided that he might want to renegotiate the terms of our new relationship, so he tentatively yielded his hindquarters as my mare pushed through.

That was his awakening. He changed quickly from there to where I could fashion a halter from my rope and slip it over his nose, halter-breaking him easily. By the end of our session he could yield his hind end deep beneath him and walk over his front, away from me, yet not leaving me. I reached out for him, asking permission of him to meet my touch. It seemed like a wait before he reached back to me, acquiescing to be rubbed on his sweaty forehead, between his eyes, and scratched along his short, thick neck.

Release was reward. We were done for the day.

---

SNOWDIN RAN THE next colt in for one of the Texas cowboys, as I left the round pen leading the blue roan in halter. After I turned the blue colt loose in a small corral, the mare and I returned wearily to the pen to watch the two cowboys' techniques in handling unbroke colts. Snowdin was already hollering advice to the fellow in the pen who had to drop his coils or else become hopelessly and dangerously wound inside of them. Snowdin moved his bay into the pen to hold the feral colt away from the Texas boy as he climbed off of his horse and gathered his gritty coils from the dirt.

The day ended with no serious injuries. It was counted as a good day. The four of us walked our sweaty horses in hand back to the corral to unsaddle and rub them down. The two Texas cowboys were done first, inviting Snowdin and myself for beers at one of the

cabins. "Be along in a bit," Snowdin replied. "Gotta check feed
bunks and water tanks." I didn't think I needed to reply. I wasn't
all that sure I was totally welcome as an equal.

Snowdin ran his powerful yet sensitive hands over his gelding's
hide, checking for girth-galls and saddle sores, and had to smack the
nasty gelding in the side of the mouth for rolling back his eyes at
my mare and trying to take a bite out of her. He then led the rough-
looking gelding to a separate corral to turn him loose for the night.

He followed me into the tack room where I stowed my gear last.
Trapping me against the wall by blocking my exit with a long,
rangy arm at the height of my ear, palm flat against wood, he said,
"You make a hell of a ranch hand. Don't let those Texas boys intim-
idate you." His green eyes stared into my own until I felt flustered
and looked down, stabbing my toe at unseen dirt on the floor.

Snowdin lifted my chin with a crooked pointer finger. "You're
also one of the best looking hands I've ever seen." He kissed me then.
His semidry lips caressed mine as gently and expertly as he rode that
raw-boned horse of his.

I ducked beneath his arm and scurried to my own cabin, retriev-
ing my travel mug on the way. I didn't want him to guess how I had
been recently feeling about him.

Several hours later, Snowdin was at my door, standing one step
lower, on the decking. He was wearing clean clothes and smelled
like shaving cream. His western-yoked shirt sported pearly white
snaps down the front and was tucked into newer Wranglers. He
looked like he was wearing his Sunday-go-to-meeting outfit.
"Didn't see you at Tom's cabin." He paused. "Look, I came to apologize. I was out of line—"

Without letting him finish his words, I twisted the top of his
shirt in my fist and kissed him with vehemence. In exigency, his
large hands engulfed my waist to pull me closer. His tongue beck-
oned at my lips. I opened my mouth to receive him, entwining my
tongue with his in a furious manner. He yanked my clean sweatshirt
slightly up as he moved me backward into the cabin and slammed

the door with his booted foot. Snowdin's hands were now hot on my flesh, practically singeing a path to my naked breasts.

I gave him one huge shove, his back hitting against the hardwood door, then ripped open those snaps with a sound that made my eardrums hum. He was as insistent, taking my baggy, comfortable sweatshirt off over my head and discarding it to the floor. Palms engulfed my pert breasts. Stiffening nipples tried to leak through his fingers only to be pinched in exquisite torment. Snowdin's mouth covered mine once again as his hands played on the flesh of my torso. I plucked at the ripening, flatter nipples of his chest and explored his muscular pectorals, which were in contrast to his lanky body and thin, almost delicate, waistline.

Unbuckling his conservative leather belt and ripping open his Wranglers, I found no underwear to inhibit his hardened prick from springing forth. I grasped the shaft slightly behind the tip and had Snowdin moaning into my mouth. I jerked his jeans below his rounded, firm buttocks and fingered the fuzz of his ass cheeks in a light, teasing manner.

He returned the favor by hauling my Wranglers and panties to my knees, then stepping one booted foot between my thighs to escort the pair to the floor, where I easily stepped barefooted, out of them.

My small hand firmly slid the length of his shaft to its base, pressuring the skin to move with it, making the head of his dick appear more reddened and taut. His balls hung low and heavy for a few strokes. I balanced the weight of them in my other palm while jerking him. He thrust into my hand. The head of his prick hit my belly. And his testicles began to tighten toward his body.

I gasped into his mouth as his callused fingers dove into my crease of creamy wetness and plunged directly into my cunt. I was shocked at the speed and audacity with which he took me, until I realized I was wanting more than fingers fumbling in my twat.

As if he read my mind, his hands were on my hips, turning my back to the door as he lifted me with ease and drove me down onto his cock. The door supported a portion of my weight and balance.

My arms flung around his neck, one hand tangled its fingers into his short brown wavy hair, knocking his Stetson to the floor.

Snowdin fucked me up against the door with power and grace. He fucked me until an orgasm unexpectedly ripped through my body, clenching my eyes shut and making me grip all the more onto him. Then he fucked me further. Sweat began to moisten the back of his shirt and his face showed the strain of containing the force of his own body, so I bit his bottom lip, letting him know that this was no gentleman's girlie fuck. He took that as permission and thrust harder, plunging into me, and knocking my body against that damned hardwood door.

He felt so good filling me. A second orgasm built to a crescendo. "Come, damn you! Come!" I hollered at him as my head lolled back and forth on the door.

That's when I felt it. He gave another heaving lunge then tensed his entire body as spurt after gooey spurt shot warm and thick into me. His cock throbbed and pulsed. His teeth were gritted. And he made short grunting sounds of bestial pleasure.

I came again. This time my muscles seized his hard-on and milked it with every convulsing wave. I was sure I would nearly pass out from the involuntary effort of my body. I ripped at his tangled hair in my fingers and clawed at his soaked shirt, raking him until my needs were satiated.

We slid to the floor in a single heap. His mouth on mine, exploring more slowly and sensually this time. Snowdin slid a hand between us and played with my clitoris, driving me mad at the same time that I noticed he was still as hard as one of those rock outcrops.

The wood floor and braided rug chafed my ass and bony shoulder blades as he humped and pumped within me while strumming my clit to another tremendous orgasm. Sweat beaded on his forehead. Moisture glistened in the dusting of hair on his pecs. He was close once again. And so was I. Snowdin let out a sound like a raging bull, as my own tuneless bawl accompanied him when we simultaneously came.

He stayed within me, as his dick grew soft, wrapping his arms behind me, and padding my shoulders from the harsh floor all too late. Snowdin smiled at me. I could tell he was holding back laughter or some remark.

"What?" I asked with a bit more venom than I had intended.

"Nothing," he said.

"It's got to be something."

"Mmm . . . you are something."

I shoved at his chest. "I've got to get off of this floor. I need a shower. You'll let yourself out, won't you?"

———◦◦◦———

A CHILL ROLLED in from the higher altitudes, pressing on summer's end and threatening an early fall. The morning dew sat thick on the ground as if it had thawed from a frost. I wrapped a silk neckerchief double around my scrawny neck and tied it into a square knot consisting of four smaller squares. The knot, symbolizing the four elements, and the silk tie were both traditional gear known as a cowboy's turtleneck. The visor of my New England–style baseball cap was drawn low over my brow. My shoulders hunched inside of the lightweight Carhart jacket I threw on over my long-sleeve button-down, with a white, conservative, short-sleeve T-shirt beneath that, and, thankfully, a padded bra providing for a minor bit of warmth where it counted.

I shivered atop my mare as the Texas cowboys and Snowdin approached at a swift jog from the barns. "Catch as catch can," Snowdin bellowed, sitting deep in his saddle to drop his gelding onto its hind end and effecting a sliding stop while the other two dwindled their mounts to a walk before completing a halt.

"That means, each of you will rope your colts from yesterday out of the remuda over in the north corral." He was smiling that smile again. And there was no way anyone could actually be that happy this early in the morning.

I shook out a good-sized loop and started warming up my shoulder, being more sore than usual. My mare had stood steady for the moments of creaking and moaning and groaning that my body had done. The colder weather must have had me stiff. Eventually I made my way over to the north corral to find the blue roan, no friendlier today than yesterday, that is, until a loop dangled from his neck. Once caught the rugged colt became docile as a lamb, allowing me to approach with my mare at a sidepass to tie on the rope halter I was carrying strung to the back of my saddle.

The day flew by quickly after that as we checked our work from yesterday, then dismounted to struggle at sacking out and desensitizing the colts from the ground in preparation for saddling.

I felt exhausted as I untacked my mare and rubbed her down, making sure she had enough feed and water for the evening. Avoiding the men, I dragged myself to the cabin, tossed a sandwich together, then padded out to the back deck. That hot tub looked awful inviting. I flipped the top off to check the temperature. Steam rose, fogging my sight of the distant mountains. Kicking off my boots and shedding my outer layers, I stepped in and sunk down in 103-degree water.

Tight muscles went lax as scabbed abrasions stung. I turned on the jets and lost myself in a cocoon of mist.

Approximately an hour later, I heard banging at the front door. My half-sleep broken, I stepped out, slammed down the tub's cover and dripped through the cabin first for a towel, then to the door.

"I see you were expecting me," he said.

Damn, he was cocky. But I supposed that came with the self-confidence of being one of the best at something, at anything. Snowdin leaned against the side of the doorway, waiting. "Well, can I come in?" he asked.

It was all too easy. It was too easy for him, and too easy for me. I stepped out of his way in some sort of silent invitation. Was he using me? Had he used others this same way, in this same cabin? Was I using him? What would the end of the week bring?

He kissed me as he closed the door, then brought his lanky arms around me in a warm hug. When our lips parted he still held me. "God, I think I've fallen for you," he said.

I pressed my hand to his lips. "Don't. Don't say anything," I said.

Snowdin released me to tug the towel tucked at the center of my chest. It fell away. "Let's get you out of those wet clothes," he said in a husky voice that cracked as if he were going through puberty. He licked his lips and cleared his throat, recognizing the breaking of his own voice.

I reached to untie his neckerchief, sliding the slick silk from his collar. I took hold of both his wrists and brought them together, wrapping the silk like a rope, restraining the tall cowboy. He didn't resist. He simply stared into my eyes like a lost puppy, and cracked a grin across his slanted lips.

My hands went behind my back to release the clasp on the sodden bra then I pushed down my sopping panties to step out of them, leaving both on the rug at the door as I moved Snowdin into the bedroom by the tails of the tied silk.

Shoving him to the bed, I straddled him to hook his wrists around the log post on the opposite side of the headboard. He reached with his tongue and mouth for one of my nipples. A stroke of warmth caught me off guard. I moved back and sat on his thighs, popping a trophy buckle that I hadn't seen him wear before, and grappling with the rivet of his Wranglers then the zipper.

I stepped off, like dismounting a horse, went to the end of the bed, removed his boots and socks and tugged his jeans by the bottom of each pant leg. He made it easy, lifting and swiveling his hips this way and that. As the jeans were loosed, the contents of his pockets emptied onto my floor. I heard a couple of heavy thunks, his pocket watch and penknife, no doubt. The jeans and trophy buckle followed as I released them from my grip.

Crawling catlike from the end of the bed up the length of his thighs, I shoved the tenting shirttails out of the way, then licked from the base of his prick to the tip before looking him directly in the eyes. "Is this what you want? Is this all you showed up for?" I wrapped my mouth around the tip of his dick, cutting off any response with the sharp intake of his breath.

"Two can play at this. This is what I want. This is what I'll take." I dangled my tits in his face until he sucked them, until he nipped and bit at my nipples, until my cunt gushed with its wetness and I could no longer withhold from wanton needs.

I suspended my twat over his hard-on while grasping the shaft. Using the tip, I spread cream from my hole to my clit, exquisitely stroking with live, hard, hot skin before impaling myself.

Snowdin gasped, his body bucking in shudders. I rode him up and down at varying speeds while running my fingertips in little circles over my clit, spreading my lips wide every few strokes so that he could get a good look. He licked his lips, straining his neck forward, off of the pillows, and pulled on his tied wrists for balance as he began thrusting to meet my rhythm.

The implosion building was going to be immense. I kept holding off, hoping it would grow a little larger, and a bit larger on top of that. The holding off was creating a greater urgency. With a loud growl, Snowdin began pulsating his load into me. The sound of his release drove me over the edge with an upsurge of orgasm. My pace slowed. My fingers stilled themselves. I fell forward onto Snowdin, my head against his chest. I heard his thumping heart as I felt my own pulsing blood course through my pussy.

I was done. Finished. Satiated by one orgasm alone, and slowly drifting into a light post-fuck nap.

With his tied arms wrapped snugly about my body, Snowdin whispered into my ear. "I've had a crush on you since the first time you showed up at this ranch several years ago. That first year, you rode one of the outfit's horses, a bald paint. He was cagey but I sensed the two of you would get along. He didn't want to be a hooker-horse and you weren't in it for just a ride. I was always watching and, I'll admit, nervous about that horse. He'd thrown or spun out from under quite a few other riders. But you were different. You cared about what was under you. You wanted to work with him as a team within a partnership, having a relationship beyond toting your ass around the mountainous trails. You were good for him. And he left here with the former owner's daughter, finding another soul mate in her." He paused. "And that's just about the most I've said at one time in ten years or so." His long arms squeezed me tighter before he continued. "All I really needed to say was that I think I love you."

I feigned sleep until it became real. This had been an unexpected turnaround and I wasn't prepared.

In the morning, I woke alone. Snowdin had left, although I didn't know how he would have gotten out of the knotted neckerchief imprisoning his wrists. My muscles felt slack, resisting any fine motor coordination. Sloppily dressed, I headed out to feed my mare before starting the shower and coffee ritual. I wondered if that famed freshly fucked look showed on my face, and was glad that no one else came by to feed while I was.

We saddled our colts for the first time by noon, then let them "live with their saddles" as we broke for lunch. The afternoon session was a chance for each of us to use a flag off of our horses in moving and directing the newly saddled colts. There was some hopping and one incident of outright bucking, but the colts got their stickiness out of them before we had all finished. Snowdin rode his big spade bit horse in to check our work at day's end. He pronounced that the colts looked ready to ride tomorrow, after the usual preflight checks of course.

Before quitting for the evening, Snowdin expected each of us to climb the rails of the round pen and teach the colts to "pick up at the fence," allowing them to see us from above and to get used to having weight and sound and motion in and around the saddle atop them. Then he rode his tall, ugly horse toward the barns to unsaddle and turn him out.

That night, I expected Snowdin to show up at my door. I sat at a small dinner table hacking a steak and chasing corn around my plate with the fork in trepidation of his arrival. He never came

around. I went to bed half relieved and half mourning the fact that
I didn't have him here with me. Sleep was elusive.

Day four we rode in the round pen by afternoon with Snowdin
flagging the colts from his raw-boned horse. We had accomplished
a lot in a short morning to get to that point. And that first ride was
like any first ride, indescribable.

But that night, there was still no Snowdin at my door.

On day five, in the morning, we accustomed the colts to snaffle
bits and headstalls teaching them to yield to the slight pressure in
their mouths. A quick colt, like my blue roan, moved on just the
suggestion of pressure, and would already promise to be lighter than
my workin' mare. After lunch, we took our colts out to trail cattle
in the mountains, using all of their gaits and gently swinging the
tail end of our ropes off of their sides.

At day's end we all turned out our newly broke colts into the
remuda permanently, where they would come off of welfare from
now on and have a job for a living, making them solid four-legged
citizens. It was a graduation of sorts and should have been a happy
moment in praise of our own job well done. But it was also saying
good-bye. And somehow, I just didn't want to say good-bye at the
end of this clinic.

The knock at my door was barely a whisper. I opened it and said,
"Come in," closing the heavy door behind him.

"I said some foolish things the other night. Maybe you hadn't
even heard them. You did fall asleep awful fast." He chuckled but
it sounded as if it came from nervousness. "Anyway, if you had and
didn't wish to respond, I don't blame you. I'm just a cowboy and
that's all I'll ever be. . . . It's good that you're headed out in the
morning." He nodded, agreeing with himself. "You probably have
a big ol' life in New England that misses you." He paused for a
moment. I thought I saw an aching in those green eyes. "You probably have someone who misses you. I hope I wasn't out of line."

I threw my arms around his neck and kissed him with every
ounce of passion and every ounce of myself that I could put into one

kiss. I felt a tear glistening in each eye. Would I lose him? Or could I convince him that he was all I wanted, all I had ever wanted?

Snowdin wrapped his arms about my waist and lifted me off of my feet.

My legs swung easily to entrap him, and he carried me to the bedroom.

Clothes were torn off in haste and tossed about the room. We wrestled on the bed, feeding our hungry mouths each and every part of each other's body that we had missed these last nights, until finally resting in a sixty-nine position.

My thighs hugged his ears as his tongue sunk into my cunt, his lips suckling and humming against my nether lips. I had difficulty concentrating as I slurped the underside of his prick, lathed his balls in saliva, and traveled farther to rim his puckered hole.

My half-packed bag was at the end of the bed where I easily reached the red, silicon dildo and jar of waxy lube. The dildo, swathed in slippery goo, was ready for action. I held it away until deep-throating his cock, driving him to the edge. With a waxy finger, I probed his puckered hole for release. It pulsated a little with my first invasions, then seemed to suckle like a hungry calf, grabbing hold and angry about having to let go.

Snowdin drove two fingers deep inside me as his teeth clenched onto my swollen clit. I jerked in response and came. His dick jumped in my mouth.

When Snowdin began slowly thrusting with determination to get off, I used the head of the dong to circle and tease his asshole. He moaned, which sent shivers through my recovering twat. I lightly plunged the little head through his sphincter and back out, in an abbreviated rhythm.

"God. Oh, God." He grabbed his shaft and drew his engorged penis from my mouth. "I'm gonna blow. Oh, God."

He looked bewildered. He looked straight at my tits. I nodded. "Go ahead." Slithering so he could, his large palms wrapped my breasts on either side of his dick. He thrust once, twice, and then hollered incoherently. I shoved the silicon dildo home at that same time. Snowdin jumped and humped and pumped, spewing cum over my belly, smacking ropey cream all the way to my crotch.

"Wha . . . wha . . . what the hell—" he stuttered to a stunned stop as he arched and turned, and gingerly withdrew the dildo from his ass.

"Any cowboy of mine is going to have to be able to take it, if he wants to dish it out."

"Any cowboy of yours is gonna want to hog-tie you and get you married quick, even if it has to be at a shotgun ceremony."

"If that's your proposal, I accept."

# Two Visions

CONNIE WILKINS

FAR BEHIND HIM, beyond peaks scoured to bare stone by wind and ice, prairie grasses would be rippling under the August sun. That green-brown sea dotted by herds of elk and buffalo might once have been an Eden in its own way, Isaac reckoned, though lately the snakes had been getting mighty thick on the ground. He shifted in the saddle, trying to ease the nagging pain of the knife-slash across his ribs.

No denying that he'd been as bad as many, throwing in with a low-life bunch of rustlers and cutthroats, driving horses he knew were mostly stolen up through Montana toward Canada's Northwest Territory. A thirst for danger and eternal movement still gripped him a decade and more since the War had scorched away the New Hampshire farm boy he'd once been. Still, while the plan to sell the horses through a shifty dealer to the newly formed Canadian Mounted Police hadn't bothered him much, some scrap of the conscience he'd been raised with had kicked in when it came to stealing horses from the Crow and Blackfeet for a few cents worth of rotgut whiskey. So a week ago he'd cut loose from the outfit.

Got himself cut up in the process, too. All he'd taken with him was his old horse Ulysses, crossbred from a Morgan mare and a Clydesdale sire back in New Hampshire, and a pack pony loaded with his fair share of the provisions. Well, those, and a sack of cash that didn't come near what he'd put into the venture. Whether it was the money, or suspicion that he might talk too much, a couple of his ex-partners had caught up with him at the Fort Benton settlement on the upper Missouri. He'd got away with no more than a knife wound only thanks to the uproar when a fight in Keno Bill's gambling house burst out into the street.

Four days later and a hundred miles northwest, Isaac shifted again in the saddle. Ulysses twitched an enquiring ear, knowing they'd been stopped longer than normal, feeling his rider's unsteadiness, maybe even smelling the inflammation that had set in where the jagged knife slash had opened an older scar left by a bayonet at Gettysburg. Likely he sensed, too, the haze of fever that clouded Isaac's mind from time to time.

Just two or three more days, and they'd be in Kalispell on the far side of the Rocky Mountains. Isaac figured a mining town that size would have some kind of doctor who would fix him up. He could make it that far. If his old cronies still had a mind for pursuit, they'd figure he'd headed toward Bozeman, and be traveling south themselves asking after a tall redheaded rider on the biggest horse in the Territory. He didn't reckon they'd take the time, though, with two hundred horses to be driven north before winter set in, and the outfit short-handed already.

He urged Ulysses onward and upward. It might be summer still back on the prairie, but here where the Marias Pass Trail crossed a mountain meadow, snowflakes were beginning to swirl on the wind. At the edge of a rocky outcrop, a family of mountain goats munched on brown pods of lupines that had bloomed blue as the sky a few short weeks ago, and then rushed to finish their procreative duty in the short, harsh growing season that was their lot.

Ulysses picked up his pace, knowing as well as Isaac that they'd better reach some shelter from the rising wind before nightfall. Bands of thick forest stretched up from narrow valleys in places, even so near a mile high as this was; at the crest of the next rise the trail sloped downward, then leveled off across a wide plateau, and on the far side Isaac could see a dark green mass of lodgepole pine and spruce. The snow was coming heavier. He pulled his hat brim down low to shield his eyes and hunched inside his buffalo-hide coat, trusting Ulysses to make their way for a while.

Isaac's thoughts drifted, from weariness and fever. He should have headed back to Bozeman after all. There was that fancy whorehouse, where the Madam had a soft spot for "boys" wounded in the War . . . a mighty fine soft spot indeed, as he recalled. . . .

Ulysses stopped so short that Isaac grabbed at the saddle horn to keep from pitching forward. For a moment he thought his eyes had gone blurry, then saw that snow had furred the rocks and scrub brush around them. As his head cleared, he noted marks just visible ahead where someone else had come up from the valley and joined this trail, recently enough that their tracks weren't yet quite covered. Two horses, and the drag marks of a loaded Indian travois; that meant a buck and his squaw. Only a squaw pulled a travois behind her. A good sign, on the whole; an Indian with his woman wouldn't be out looking for trouble.

An Indian family wouldn't be likely to spook Ulysses, either, but the big horse was sniffing and snorting, and the pack pony began to squeal and lurch against the lead rope. Isaac went for his rifle before he even saw the dark snow-speckled bear rear up two hundred feet ahead of them, taller than a man, shaking its huge head. Two smaller mounds of fur lit out toward the trees not too far off. A mother grizzly with her cubs, likely rooting for wildflower bulbs to fatten them up for the fast-approaching winter. Nothing could be more dangerous, and now she was down on all fours and barreling toward them.

Ulysses stood firm, but the pony was thrashing in such terror that Isaac couldn't get good aim. He drew his knife, twisted in the saddle, felt his wound flare with gut-searing pain, and slashed the lead rope. The bear wouldn't pursue a running horse, especially one as big as Ulysses. Isaac gave the signal, and leaned forward as his mount took off, but his ribs screamed with agony, and a dark mist seemed to rise before his eyes even as his whole body slipped downward.

The last thing he heard, before darkness swallowed him up, was a high-pitched yell like some unearthly war cry, "Kyai-yo, Kyai-yo!" rising and falling and speeding toward him from the dark fringe of the forest.

ISAAC WOKE TO the warm scent of a woman. Something covered his eyes, and his wrists were bound at his sides so he couldn't reach out, but he knew the woman was there even before her long hair brushed across his naked chest. She seemed to be adjusting some poultice or bandage on his wounded ribs.

As memory seeped back he recalled the snow, and the tracks of an Indian couple on the trail. An Indian buck would have long hair, as well, but still he had no doubt that a woman was tending him, a woman whose soft hair smelled faintly of pleasant herbs and whose body gave off a musky essence of desire recently fulfilled. Isaac, in his roving life, had found all too few opportunities to indulge in the pleasures of the flesh, but he'd made the most of those that came his way, and he knew better than many the scent of a well-fucked cunt.

So who else was with them? His lack of vision sharpened other faculties. There'd been many a time when sensing his surroundings without benefit of sight had been a matter of life and death; this might well be one of them. He cast around the room, sure by the very feel of the air that it was a room with walls rather than the interior of a buffalo-hide lodge, but he found no trace of another presence. Just as well, though, not to let on that he was awake yet.

The woman moved away. He heard her putting wood on a fire, and could swear that the blaze was contained in a fireplace with a chimney. Definitely a cabin of some sort, though little spurts of wind from the storm outside, rain now instead of snow, made their way through chinks here and there. Surely she couldn't be alone in here with him, but who would choose to be outside in that weather? And who had been fucking her? While he could catch no distinct scent of a man in rut, he wasn't familiar with any but his own and might not notice. Still . . . could she have been pleasuring herself?

At the visions conjured by such a thought, Isaac's pulse speeded up and tension seized his groin. A hand kneading a full breast . . . another working vigorously along slippery folds and over the hard little peak an experienced whore had displayed when he'd shown an inclination to learn . . . long hair thrashing from side to side as the moment of bliss pounded closer . . . moans, cries. . . . Isaac's own flesh burned, and his cock raised itself without restraint to surge upward.

Without restraint? All at once Isaac realized that he was entirely naked, and mere seconds later he heard a soft chuckle and the sound of the woman returning. Her hair brushed his chest again, then stroked lightly along his torso toward his loins. If she put her hands on him, there would be no way to play at being still asleep! Or, if she didn't, how would he stand it?

She did keep her hands to herself, only sweeping her hair deliberately back and forth across his thrusting cock, muttering a few words in a laughing tone when he jerked uncontrollably. The language of the Blackfeet, he thought, as much as he could think of anything beyond his own pulsing need. It had been a very long time since Bozeman, and even longer before that since the carnal delights of Cody, Wyoming.

Then she leaned again over his chest, and face, and he jerked more from being startled than from lust when she said, in slightly accented English, "Such a fine bighorn we have here, though he is surely no sheep!" Her hand did slide across his cock-head, very lightly, and a gasp escaped him. The cloth covering his eyes was jerked off in a movement so sudden he couldn't get his eyes closed before he was staring into other eyes, dark, but not Indian-black, with a look of the green-brown depths of a woodland stream.

She smiled, full lips curving, white teeth bright in contrast to skin just a shade too coppery-dark to owe its hue solely to the sun.

"Well, awake at last! I will loose your hands if you promise not to pull the covering from your wound." He nodded dumbly, and felt her soft hair brush now against his cheek as she bent to unfasten the leather strips binding his hands to the sides of a crude bedstead. The face so close above his had the smooth, soft curves of youth, made lovelier still by the elegant arch of high cheekbones. A 'breed, Isaac thought, and noted the red highlights in her hair, too bright to come only from the fire and the little oil lantern on the floor beside them.

His own lantern! That small luxury had been wrapped in the bundle carried by the pack pony. A memory of the bear flooded back, of pain, and shock, and the slide from the saddle into unconsciousness.

"My horses!" he cried out, straining to sit up, feeling pain begin again across his ribs, though muted from its former intensity. "Ulysses!"

The woman pressed him down with strong, slender hands. "The Great Bear Horse is unharmed," she assured him, "though he turned to challenge the charging Kyai-yo when you fell to the ground. Even a she-grizzly would think better of chancing those great hooves! Na'-toki Okan', who speaks to bears, rode to save you, but found it harder to calm your horse than to send Kyai-yo away. The pack horse, too, is safe."

Isaac fell back, strength drained. She propped him up a bit with his buffalo-hide coat as a pillow, and pulled a blanket he recognized as his own over the lower half of his body. Lust enough remained to twitch his cock from time to time as he watched her lithe body, free of a white woman's cumbersome underpinnings, move beneath her soft deerskin tunic.

"Na'toki Okan'?" he asked. "Your man?"

"Two Visions, in the white man's tongue. Or Two Medicines, they might say. Na'toki Okan' is a great shaman, but living in a world when the time for great shamans will soon be past. He has seen this himself, in dreams, and would know it even if he were not a seer."

An old medicine man, Isaac thought, with a frisky, young wife.

All the more likely that she had been pleasuring herself. Such possibilities! And such danger. He had never knowingly poached on another man's territory when it came to women, but if she kept on as she'd begun he'd be hard pressed to resist.

He turned his head to search the cabin. It was small, a single room built of logs chinked with moss, one slit of a window boarded over now, a doorway masked from the inside by a heavy buffalo robe. Likely built by a trapper who might return when winter was fully back and animal pelts thick enough to command high prices. There seemed to be nowhere here an old Indian could be concealed.

"Where is Two Visions now?" he asked, deciding not to try to get his tongue around the Blackfeet words, though he had learned enough for basic trading during his months in Montana.

"Na'toki Okan' does not like the hard lodges of the white man." She rapped her knuckles against the log wall for emphasis. "Dreams do not travel so easily through the wood. I have set up his proper lodge of buffalo hide nearby, but he will come soon to check on your wound. He is a great healer as well as a seer. Kyai-yo did you a good turn, causing you to fall where you did."

Considering that his fever seemed to be gone and his wound somewhat improved, Isaac thought that she might be right, however much he would rather not feel beholden to the husband of this seductive woman. "Then I will thank the bear, but from as safe a distance as ever I can manage," he said, and watched her eyes light with laughter. How much more than a healed wound might he yet thank the grizzly for?

"But I should thank Two Visions even more, and I would thank you as well if I knew what name to call you," he said.

"I am Sinopah'ki," she said. "Fox Woman. And what of you?"

"Sinopah'ki," he repeated, finding the word smooth on his tongue, a sigh of pleasure as it flowed through his mouth. A wind gust a little stronger than the rest slid into the cabin, sounding like an echo of his voice. "Folks generally call me Red, but my given name is Isaac. Isaac Atkins."

"Ik'sisakwi." The word, followed by a bark of laughter, came in a husky voice Isaac had not heard before, and from the direction of the door. He swung his upper body around to look, wincing as his wound complained.

The man had slipped through the door with scarcely a sound and stood now inside, raindrops catching the light of the fire as they dripped from black braided hair even longer than the woman's. This was no ancient medicine man, but a lithe, smooth-skinned figure, lean of face and form, who seemed scarcely more than a youth until Isaac noticed the fine lines at the corners of his eyes. His voice was neither deep nor high, roughened, at a guess, by the smoke of many a fire and sacred pipe.

"Ik'sisakwi," the newcomer said again, and Isaac thought for a moment that it was an attempt to pronounce his name. Then, catching the sardonic cast of the Indian's expression, he remembered the meaning of the word, one learned in the course of trading with the Blackfeet. "Ik'sisakwi" was "meat." Likely a pun was intended, and not a complimentary one.

Isaac's chin lifted. He held the other's gaze in challenge even while saying to Sinopah'ki in a respectful tone, "Please tell Two Visions that I thank him for his kindness, and hold myself in his debt."

She said something quickly to her husband. He nodded in acknowledgment and came forward, then pulled back Isaac's blanket and lifted an edge of the wound's dressing to inspect it. Isaac watched his impassive face closely. A few words were spoken, translated by Sinopah'ki to the effect that the wound-poison had been nearly drawn out, and in another day Isaac's ribs could be bound securely enough that he might walk around, and possibly even ride a little.

Two Visions murmured directions to Sinopah'ki, who did his bidding with deft, graceful movements, fetching a skin bag of warm water and holding it open while he sprinkled dried herbs into it from a pouch at his belt. A low hum rose from his throat, a chant without words, or none that Isaac could make out, and then he dipped a bit of soft deerskin into the water before holding it against the open wound.

Isaac managed to keep from flinching. He could have wished for more pain, in fact, as distraction, when his traitorous flesh reacted as though it were the woman touching him, and with seductive intent. The blanket still covered his loins, but he knew the wool was tenting above the thrust of his cock.

Two Visions glanced down at him from under lowered eyelids. There might have been a spark of amusement in his look, and even a trace of sympathy. He handed the deerskin to the woman. This did little to make matters better, but at least it removed some measure of ambiguity. Or did until the healer's hand came to rest on Isaac's bare shoulder.

"Nita'piwaksin," Two Visions said, squeezing the hard muscles there. This word, too, Isaac recognized. "True meat," meaning buffalo or antelope rather than insignificant game such as rabbits or squirrels. Sinopah'ki turned her flushed face away in embarrassment and did not offer to translate.

Two Visions ran his fingers along a ridge of old scar tissue stretching across Isaac's collarbone, much like the one beneath the newer slash across his ribs. His voice rose in a question, and now Sinopah'ki composed herself to explain, "You look to be a great warrior, and he asks how you came by your scars."

Isaac knew that recounting tales of brave exploits was an accepted custom among the Indians, but he had scarcely spoken of the War in a dozen years, and he wasn't about to start now. "Antietam," he said brusquely, raising a hand to his collarbone, "and Gettysburg," touching his side.

Two Visions cocked an eyebrow, then nodded. "Mr. Lincoln's War," he said, in clear English. Isaac wondered where the Indian had heard this, and from whose perspective, and, of more importance, how much English he did in fact understand. Best to make no assumptions, he decided.

Which was just as well, since the exchange that followed between

Two Visions and Sinopah'ki was entirely confusing. There was heat on both sides, and tension, interspersed with notes of such tenderness that Isaac felt obliged to turn away and study the log wall as though it had all his attention. He understood a few words: "meat" again, and "this one" and "your choice," but could make no general sense of them. Finally there was silence. He stole a glance, and looked away as fast as he could.

Two Visions was holding his woman in a close embrace, stroking her hair, moving his lips gently across her smooth face and then her neck and as far down toward her bosom as the deerskin tunic allowed. He inhaled deeply, as though consuming her warm essence, then let out a long, slow sigh. A few words passed between them, pleading on her part, weary on his, until he turned at last to slip out through the door almost as silently as he had come.

Sinopah'ki moved about in silence for a while, stoking the fire, preparing a meal for Isaac of dried buffalo meat stewed with berries, and tidying away her food packets into the folds of a painted parfleche. At last she came close to Isaac, bringing his own tin cup with a brew of herbs. When he had drunk it and handed back the cup, she pulled the blanket up above his shoulders, effectively trapping his arms beneath. He wanted to reach out, to ask questions, to know the cause of strain between wife and husband and his own part in it. When she touched a gentle finger to his hair, though, he lay still, watching her expressive face, waiting for whatever she might reveal.

"My father," Sinopah'ki said at last, "had hair of just such a red." Her hand moved to his face, stroking lightly across nose and cheekbones. "And the little dusting of"—she paused to search for the word—"of freckles, although yours are much fewer than his."

For a girl to liken you to her father should certainly be the death of lust, Isaac thought, but still felt a thrill of something between arousal and tenderness at her touch. He turned so that his mouth brushed her hand, not quite a kiss, but very nearly. She allowed the caress for a moment, then straightened and looked down at him with an expression he couldn't make out.

"Na'toki Okan' will dream on it," she said, then turned away, picked up a buffalo robe, and made for the door.

"Wait!" Isaac called. "You can't just leave it at that! What will he dream on?"

"On what I desire," she said, looking back over her shoulder. "And," with a sudden teasing smile and a deliberate twitch of sweetly curving hips, "what you desire as well."

Well, lust was certainly alive and kicking, Isaac thought, shifting his own hips. He had more thoughts to ponder on, and a glimmering of what he'd got himself into. Miz Grizzly Bear might yet have much to answer for.

Dream or no dream, could any man truly let another serve as stud to his woman, for the sake of producing a child resembling her father? The shaman might see in visions—hell, the way things were going in the West, Isaac could see it for himself without dreaming—that enough white blood for passing could be some advantage for future generations, but still, how could a man bear it? Why had he not filled her belly and then arms with babies before this?

But the herbal drink was making him drowsy, no doubt as intended. Isaac drifted into sleep without pondering further, and slept without any dreaming that stuck in his memory.

Two Visions woke him with a nudge next day, inspected his wound, applied an acrid-smelling ointment, and bound wrappings tightly around his midriff, all without speaking. Isaac understood his signing to get up, and managed it without groaning at his own stiffness.

Dressing was a challenge. Shirt and leather vest were easy enough, but trousers and boots were another matter, even if he sat back down on the bed. The Indian solved that problem by dropping to his knees, quite matter-of-fact in his movements, and helping Isaac into his garments. If he noted Isaac's flush of embarrassment at having a man kneeling before him when he was so nakedly exposed, politeness kept him from showing it, though there might have been a flicker of amusement in his eyes when he stood up again.

Isaac followed the lithe, graceful figure outside, conjectures flooding back. In the war he had known men who took comfort in each other in extremities, as well as a few girlish, mincing boys, the butt of cruel mockery, who proved braver than many a hulking braggart. He had also seen an Indian holy man, keeper of a ceremonial pipe, whose ambiguous mannerisms seemed to be accepted and, indeed, to heighten his role as shaman. If Two Visions were one of these, it might explain why his woman looked elsewhere. But no, the current of passion between them last night had been unmistakable, wiping out any doubts as to who had been fucking Sinopah'ki so well.

Isaac looked around for her, blinking in the unexpected sunshine. All traces of snow were gone. Then a whicker of welcome drove all else from his mind, and Ulysses' great head butted against him in greeting. Isaac could have done without a witness to his reunion with the horse who was as close to home and family as he had, and the only link to where he'd come from, but he stood in the shadow of the horse's bulk for a few moments of communication anyhow.

Two Visions watched with casual approval. Maybe the loyalty of a good horse was something to be chalked up in the credit column when choosing a sire for your children, Isaac thought resentfully. He longed for a chance at this man's woman with an ache that shook him when he thought of her, but he'd rather win her by challenge, in a good fight. He was strong enough, or would be in another few days, a bit taller than the Indian, and a good deal heavier in the muscle department. None of that mattered, though, next to the fact that this man had saved his life.

Isaac stepped away from Ulysses, who went back to cropping the spare tufts of grass sprouting here and there. The cabin and Indian tipi occupied a small clearing in the forest, with a narrow track leading away uphill, and another sloping down toward the sound of a fast mountain stream. Two Visions motioned him to follow and strode off downhill.

Sinopah'ki was working by the stream, bending aspen poles into a mound-shaped framework Isaac recognized as a sweat lodge.

When she saw them she ran to her husband and embraced him, until he pushed her gently away and, without another glance at Isaac, took off upstream at a steady lope.

She watched until he had disappeared among the trees before turning to Isaac with a hesitant smile. "Two Visions has dreamed," she said, "but does not yet know the meaning. He goes to a holy spot high on the mountain to seek understanding."

She resumed her work, and Isaac insisted on helping in spite of her protests. That it was squaw work among her people made no difference to him. His injury held him back somewhat, but soon they were laughing together, finding reasons for hands and shoulders and thighs to touch as they bent and bound the poles and hauled coverings of elk hide over the structure.

Sinopah'ki seemed to have a glow about her, an allure even beyond her obvious charms. Like a mare in heat, Isaac thought, or, she being named Fox Woman, a vixen. It might be his own heat that made him think so, but her lips and even her breasts looked fuller, and he was firmly persuaded that if Two Visions didn't hustle with finding that understanding, one way or another it would be too late.

By dusk Isaac had become grateful for the occasional nagging reminder of his slashed ribs. A sense of honor alone would have been poor defense against his impulse to press Sinopah'ki for more than brief touches and lingering looks. She was in the same boat, he guessed, and when she knelt before him to apply new ointment to his side and replace the bindings, her warm mouth so close to his crotch and the scent of desire rising from her made his cock leap and strain at his tight britches. What would be the harm? But when he thrust his fingers through her hair and tried to pull her face closer, she shook him off and retreated, and served his evening meal by a campfire outdoors.

Isaac stoked his own fire in the cabin that night, and was sorely tempted to stoke his fleshly fire as well, all the more so when he imagined Sinopah'ki doing something of the kind in her lonely tipi.

The herbal drink she had prepared for him this time must have been strong enough to stun a stallion, though, and he slept like a whole cabin of logs.

Two Visions had not returned by morning. When Isaac came outside he found that Sinopah'ki had managed to wrassle his heavy saddle up onto Ulysses' back, strap his rifle in its accustomed place, and was waiting with her own spotted pony. She handed him a pouch of pemmican, mounted, and swung toward the uphill trail.

"Are you strong enough to ride?" she called back, and of course he'd never have owned up to weakness even if he'd felt it. Astride Ulysses, Isaac had a firmer sense of his place in the world, as much as any wanderer could. Watching Sinopah'ki's slender back sway to the rhythm of the pony's haunches, he found a new sense, as well, of his possible place in the flow of life.

A scant mile up the way they emerged onto the plateau crossed by the Marias Pass Trail. Ulysses advanced with flared nostrils, but there were no foragers to be seen in the bright light of morning. Sinopah'ki, too, was watching for something, or someone, and looking often along a rocky ridge rising to the south, searching, Isaac was pretty sure, for a glimpse of Two Visions returning.

He had taken a different route, though, or purposely avoided them. When they returned to their camp in late afternoon, with a yearling elk Isaac had shot slung across Ulysses' withers, smoke rose from the fire circle down by the sweat lodge.

"Na'toki Okan' is there," Sinopah'ki said, staring long down the hill. She wrenched her attention back to the work at hand, helping to ease the elk to the ground and going about the squaw's business of preparing meat and hide for use. Isaac, once he'd skinned the carcass, went into the cabin to check on his wound. In spite of the day's exertion, the wrappings showed no bleeding, and the flesh beneath was only moderately tender to the touch. He rebound the strips by himself, and knew that he could, if he chose, journey on the next day with no further need of help. The thought was not as cheering as it might have been.

He must have dozed, because a knock on the door startled him awake. No one had bothered to knock since he'd been there. He looked out. Two Visions stood waiting, face averted, silent, motioning for Isaac to take the path to the sweat lodge. Isaac went, without question.

Beside the fire Sinopah'ki waited, flushed from dragging red-hot stones into the low structure. She stripped off her tunic and leggings, motioning for Isaac to undress as well. Her body already gleamed with sweat in the firelight, even more enticing than he had envisioned; if they were to be naked together, he thought, the answer Two Visions had found had damned well better be yes. He said nothing, though, following the woman's lead in a ritual he knew little of, except that men and women did not usually partake of it together.

He had to crawl to enter the hut, then turned as quickly as he could to watch Sinopah'ki enter. The only light was from the glowing rocks in the central pit, casting a red sheen over the curves of her breasts as she moved. Once inside she knelt, dipped a switch made from a buffalo's tail into a container of water, and sprinkled drops into the pit until clouds of steam rose around them, and their own sweat streamed and swirled and stung their eyes. Sinopah'ki's voice rose in a sound between chant and song. A prayer of purification, Isaac thought, and breathed his own prayer that he should still have some juices left in his body for other pursuits after this ritual was done.

A rush of cool air signaled the end. Sinopah'ki had thrown back the skins across the entrance, and now he followed the gleam of her sweaty buttocks into the outer firelight. Panting, they stood and ran together down to the stream's edge and into the rushing water, splashing each other like children until they had cooled enough to turn to pleasures not childlike at all.

They dried each other with blankets, laughter changing to wordless sounds of pleasure and discovery. Isaac fondled her breasts, the nipples rising hard under his fingers and then his tongue, and teeth, until she cried out. When he paused she cried out even louder, demanding more, but rubbing her steamy crotch against his thigh so hard and fast that he struggled to turn and get his cock into that glorious heat. She grasped his hand, though, pulling it to her damp slit, so he worked her flesh with a will, finding the taut nub that grew and quivered at his touch. Her own hand pumped him with such enthusiasm that if it was his seed she wanted, she was in danger of bringing it forth too soon, so with gasping directions he got her down onto the pile of skins and blankets.

All at once she rolled on top and straddled him, careful to put no pressure on his ribs. She rode him upright with a driving force that took his cock in to the hilt, slid back, drove forward again, and again, while his hips arched into her thrusts, until he fountained into her, lost in the searing joy of release and only faintly aware of her own keen cries of conquest.

Eventually, as the fire died down and the night cooled, they gathered themselves and their robes and returned to the cabin, where they played games more leisurely but no less sweet. When Sinopah'ki left at dawn, Isaac could still taste her juices, mixed with salty traces of his own.

The next day was the hardest. Isaac and Sinopah'ki, still flushed with pleasure, tried not to flaunt their satisfaction, while the impassivity of Two Visions couldn't mask his strain.

"Did he tell you about his vision?" Isaac asked, as he helped Sinopah'ki carry water from the stream.

"There were two such visions," she said, "but he does not speak of them, except when he first told me that he had seen a future with . . . with my child. I think he is still unsure of the other."

"Are you sure we have accomplished all you wish?" he asked. "Maybe again, tonight, for good measure. . . ."

"Na'toki Okan' is sure," she said with reluctant finality. "Much as I would wish it, I cannot cause him more pain." There was, Isaac knew, no arguing with that.

Perhaps Two Visions had not been so sure, after all. Late that night Isaac woke at a soft sound. The fire was entirely dark, and he could see nothing, but the scent of a woman was strong in his nostrils. A woman still in heat.

He started to sit up, but found his wrists once again tethered to the bed. There was a faint sound of breathing nearby. A hand stroked his face tentatively, lightly, then descended across his naked chest and belly, crossing his scarred ribs with the utmost delicacy.

Slowly, so slowly that he wanted to beg for more, long fingers drew teasing lines across his loins, down and then up his thighs, and around the swelling column of his cock. He was so ready he could have screamed by the time the hot, wet depths he longed for slid onto him and began to move in rhythmic demand. Fulfillment came hard, and swift, and intense, the spasming cunt gripping him like a clenching fist and drawing every drop from him, before slowly releasing and withdrawing. Before he could even catch his breath, he heard soft, retreating footsteps, and the door closing, and then he was alone.

Isaac slept long the next morning, and when he finally woke and ventured out, they were gone. He wasn't surprised. A circle in the grass showed where their lodge had been pitched, but the stones of their fire circle were already cold.

He could have tracked them, but it would have been an intrusion. Instead he packed up his gear, loaded the pony, saddled Ulysses, and rode uphill toward the mountain pass.

Pi'tamaken's Pass, the Blackfeet called it, Sinopah'ki had told him two days ago as they rode along the trail. Pi'tamaken, Running Eagle, the Woman Warrior of the Blackfeet, who had led many a raid on the Pend Oreille and Flathead Indians across this pass. Pi'-tamaken, whose woman had been the grandmother of Two Visions. Not a bad heritage, Isaac thought, for his children.

He rode on, still drawn to wander, though the wild places were dwindling as fast as the herds of buffalo. Sure as Shiloh the railroad would be next, slicing through Montana as it had everywhere else he'd been and left, bringing settlers and politicians and "morality," and then where would there be to move on to?

Well, he'd see what was on the other side of the Rockies, anyway, but he had a notion that by next summer his way would somehow take him back to the eastern slopes. He just might find a trace of two red-haired babies, one a shade lighter than the other, and let it be known that he would be there if needed, though never intruding, nor ever telling all he knew.

# The Branding of Miss Charlotte Babington

ANNA BLACK

"WHO IS THAT man, Mrs. Meriwether?"

Mrs. Meriwether turned in the direction Charlotte was looking. "Who?"

"The tall, dark-haired one."

Mrs. Meriwether narrowed her pale blue eyes. Charlotte suspected she was nearsighted. Then, when she saw to whom Charlotte was referring, she frowned.

"Nathan Henry Chandler." Her voice throbbed with disapproval. "I made it clear to Silas I didn't want him here but my husband possesses a rather forgiving nature."

"Why would Mr. Chandler require forgiveness?"

Mrs. Meriwether stared at Nathan as if he were something she had found crawling on her skin. "Nothing, I suppose. But it's well known that blood tells in the end."

"Blood? What do you mean?"

"He's a Chandler."

Charlotte gave her a perplexed look. Mrs. Meriwether smiled, but her smile did not reach her eyes.

"Of course. You're new to these parts. Nathan is the youngest of the Chandler clan." Mrs. Meriwether laughed sharply. "Clan. I should more likely say gang."

"Gang?"

"Thieves, murderers, and all-around a very bad lot."

Charlotte's eyes widened as she looked over at Nathan. "But if he's an outlaw, why is he not in jail?"

"I didn't say he was an outlaw. He fancies himself a rancher but he'll never be properly received by respectable folk. Lord knows where he got the money for those fancy clothes he's wearing, and who he thinks he's impressing by wearing them."

Mrs. Meriwether turned away from her hostile scrutiny of Nathan and looked over at Charlotte. Her eyes narrowed but this time with suspicion. "I must say I find it unbefitting of a woman who is soon to be married to display such improper awareness of another man. Especially someone like Nathan Chandler."

Charlotte's cheeks burned as much from Mrs. Meriwether's reprimand as from her insight. From the moment Charlotte had seen the darkly handsome man she now knew as Nathan Chandler, her awareness of him had been anything but proper.

"Your thoughts should only be on your husband-to-be," Mrs. Meriwether went on. "I gave this party to introduce you to society. You don't want to give the wrong impression now, do you, dear?"

"Yes, Mrs. Meriwether. I mean, no, Mrs. Meriwether. I don't want to give the wrong impression."

Since arriving in Montana, Charlotte had tried to not to give anyone the wrong impression and to keep her thoughts focused on the man who was to be her husband. But the more she learned about Isaac Smith the more she knew she did not want to be his wife.

She looked back at Nathan. "I was only curious about him."

Mrs. Meriwether smiled thinly at her. "Well, you know what they say. Curiosity killed the cat."

Charlotte quickly looked away. She made herself not look at Nathan and instead searched the parlor for Isaac. He was talking with a group of men she had learned were the leading citizens in the town. Mrs. Meriwether's husband, Silas, who was the town's marshal, was among them.

As for Isaac, not only was he the richest man in town he also owned one of the largest cattle ranches. Nearly forty years her senior, he was a big-boned man who, as a result of years of easy living, had gone to fat.

Feeling her eyes upon him, he glanced at her and, as she had under Mrs. Meriwether's scrutiny, Charlotte quickly looked away. She hoped Isaac would think she was being modest and not suspect that he in fact repelled her.

As she turned her head she found herself looking straight into the broad chest of Nathan Henry Chandler. She gasped and looked up.

His dark blue eyes, she now saw, matched the cravat he wore with his black frock coat and vest. His white shirt glowed against his sun-bronzed face. He was clean shaven, unlike most of the men, but he wore his chestnut-colored hair long enough that it brushed along his wide shoulders.

"Miss Charlotte Babington."

"Yes. And you are?" She knew perfectly well who he was but she did not want him to know she had been asking about him.

"Nathan Henry."

It did not go unnoticed by her that he neglected to provide his last name.

"It's a pleasure to meet you, Mr. —?" And she lifted a brow. She had no intention of calling him by his Christian name for that would not be proper.

"Chandler." Something flickered in his eyes, almost as if he were cringing.

She smiled. "Mr. Chandler. A pleasure."

The tightening around his eyes disappeared. Now there was something else. A predatory appraisal of her that made Charlotte feel both anxious and thrilled.

"And is it, Miss Babington?" he asked

"Is it what?"

"A pleasure to meet me?"

"Why, yes. Of course it is."

Nathan eyes gazed keenly into hers. "Can't say I much abide people who don't mean what they say."

"Are you accusing me of not meaning what I say?"

"Not saying that at all. Just saying I don't much care for people
who yap just to hear themselves talk."

"I was being polite, Mr. Chandler. Something one does in civilized
company. Which, I suspect, you probably are not accustomed to."

She hadn't meant to say that but he was trying to needle her for
some reason. She just wanted to give as good as she was getting.

Nathan glanced around at the other guests. "Reckon you could
say that. Never had much use for 'civilized' company."

"Then what are you doing here?"

"Came to see you, Miss Charlotte Babington."

His gaze slammed into her as if he had suddenly pushed her up
against a wall. And then, as bold as sin, he looked her up and down,
and as he did, his gaze was so intimate that her breasts swelled as if
he were licking them with his tongue, and her nipples tightened as
if he were sucking them with his lips, and the cleft between her
thighs quivered as if he were stroking the soft wet folds with his
fingers.

She knew she should be outraged by his bold scrutiny of her but
instead she felt rash and wild. As rash and wild as the lust she saw
burning in his eyes.

"Charlotte." Isaac sidled next to her. He slipped a beefy arm
around her waist and tugged her hard against his thick side.
"Nathan. Surprised to see you here."

"The marshal invited me. It's his house after all."

"Yeah, it's his house. But this is my wife you've been eyeballing.
Don't think I didn't see you."

Nathan's eyes narrowed. "She ain't your wife yet."

Charlotte glanced between the two men. The tension between
them was as sharp and dangerous as a knife's edge.

Isaac snorted. "I'm surprised you got time for socializing. What
with all the work that piece-of-shit ranch of yours needs."

Nathan took a step towards Isaac but as he did Marshal Meriwether appeared at Nathan's side.

"How's it going, Nathan?" His voice was soft but there was steel underneath it

"It's going, Marshal."

"Glad to hear that. Now, I'm just going to remind you quiet-like that I invited you here with the promise to my wife that you'd behave yourself."

"I ain't done nothing." Nathan shot a dark look over at Isaac. "At least not yet."

"And you won't be doing nothing or you'll have to leave," Marshal Meriwether firmly said.

"I was about to anyway. I've seen enough." Nathan looked at Charlotte, the lust still smoldering in his eyes.

"That's right. Get on out of here," Isaac sneered. "You ain't fit to be among decent folk. And if I catch you looking at my wife again, I'll shoot you down like the good-for-nothing dog you are."

"I'd like to see you try." Nathan looked over at Charlotte and the heat of his gaze was like a brand upon her soul. "As I said before, she ain't yet your wife."

Isaac rubbed his hand up and down Charlotte's hip, taking a liberty with her person that brought the color flaming to her cheeks. "She's all but my wife in name, aren't you?"

Charlotte saw the other guests staring at her and Isaac. Some of the women were frowning disapprovingly.

She wriggled away from Isaac. "Mr. Chandler is right. We're not yet married. And there's been nothing improper between us. Please do not suggest that there has."

Isaac's thick face mottled with rage. "Where the hell you get off talking to me like that, girl?"

Nathan moved toward Isaac, his jaw clenched, but Marshal Meriwether stepped between the two men. "That's enough. Go on home, Nathan."

Nathan glared at Isaac for the space of five heartbeats. Then he turned on his heel and left the house. Charlotte watched him go, then she glanced at Isaac. The look he gave Nathan's retreating back was nothing short of murderous.

He reeled toward her and raised his fist, shaking it in her face. Charlotte flinched but did not back away. She was tired of retreating before his temper.

"Don't ever take that bastard's side against me again! You may not yet be my wife but you're gonna be and you better start acting like it."

Charlotte's lips trembled with the words she wanted to hurl at him but she was aware of the other guests gawking at them. Tears stung her eyes, but she didn't want anyone, least of all Isaac, to see her cry. She quickly left the parlor and went outside.

Fat, white clouds floated across the dark blue sky. A sky, she now saw, that was the same color as Nathan Chandler's eyes. Then she heard voices coming from within the Meriwether's house toward the front door.

She turned and ran toward the livery stable. It was dark and cool inside and she found the smell of hay and horses strangely comforting. And, best of all, she was alone. She leaned against a post and drew in a shaky breath.

It was a mistake. A terrible mistake. She never should have agreed to come to Montana. And she never should have agreed to marry Isaac Smith. She hated him. Hated him with every fiber of her being.

"He ought not talk to you like that."

Charlotte whirled around. Nathan stood across from her. "What are you doing here?"

"My horse is here."

He moved across the distance that separated them and stopped just in front of her.

Charlotte was not tall and she was slight, despite her rather full bosom and rounded hips. As a result most men seemed large to her. But whereas Isaac was big because he was mostly fat, Nathan was big because he was tall and powerfully built.

"You ain't going to marry him."

Charlotte's mouth opened. "What? Of course I'm going to marry him." Her throat tightened and she looked down. "I have to," she added, the words falling like stones from her mouth.

"Why?" Nathan demanded. "Why do you have to? He don't deserve you."

Her head shot up, and it wasn't just anger that made Charlotte clench her fists. It was panic. "I don't see what concern that is of yours."

"You don't want to marry him."

"You presume a lot, Mr. Chandler. How dare you claim to know what I want or don't want."

"I reckon I dare because you know it's the truth. You don't love him. As a matter of fact you hate him. I can see it in your eyes."

"That's none of your business."

"That's where you're wrong, Miss Charlotte Babington. It's very much my business."

She turned away from him. She didn't want to hear anymore. Until this day she had not even known Nathan Henry Chandler existed. He didn't know anything about her, just as she didn't know anything about him. Except he fancied himself a rancher but in fact was kin to thieves and murderers.

She picked up the hem of dress and ran out of the livery.

"You ain't going to marry him," Nathan shouted after her.

Charlotte only shook her head at his words. She went back inside the Meriwethers' house. Back to where the man she was going to marry, the man she now knew she despised with all her heart, waited for her.

---

CHARLOTTE LOOKED AT herself in Mrs. Meriwether's mirror. The wedding dress she wore was modest enough with its high neck and long sleeves. But it also fit her in such a way that it emphasized her generous bosom, slim waist, and curved hips.

She did not think herself vain about her looks. At least she hoped she was not. But she knew she possessed enough of whatever particulars it was about a woman's body that drew men's attention. Whether wanted or unwanted. For Charlotte, since the day she had blossomed into womanhood, that attention had been unwanted.

She shuddered as she recalled the days of enduring her uncle's lecherous groping whenever her aunt was away from the house. And the dread that gripped her at night when he paced past her bedroom door. Mercifully he had never gotten up the nerve to actually enter her room but Charlotte had feared it was only a matter of time before he finally did.

That's what Isaac rescued her from when he came to New York. Her parents had died in a fire when she was eight and she was sent to live with her aunt, who had treated her like a slave instead of a niece. Isaac had been a friend of her parents and, upon learning of their deaths, had gone in search of her.

When he finally found her she had just turned eighteen. He straightaway asked her to marry him. And she, wanting to escape from her aunt's house, had said yes, despite the fact he was old enough to be her father.

But she soon discovered what kind of man she had so hastily agreed to marry.

The day before Charlotte had been walking past the saloon on her way to the general store. Isaac was inside drinking with some of the men of the town. Hearing his voice, she stopped but made certain she kept out of sight.

Horrified, she listened as he boasted of her virginity and then, with the men's drunken encouragement, bragged that come their wedding night he was going to brand that virgin pussy of hers. He would fuck her so hard and so long he would make her scream and he didn't much give a shit if she screamed from pleasure or from pain.

The men had laughed and slapped Isaac on the back, congratulating him on being such a lucky son of a bitch.

Charlotte's wide gray eyes stared at her reflection in the mirror. She did not want to marry Isaac. But what other choice did she have? She had no money, no prospects, and no family. She was alone. A stranger in a strange land.

Then she thought of him.

Nathan Henry Chandler.

Since the day she had met him at the Meriwethers' party, she had not spoken with him again. But she had seen him often enough for he seemed to appear whenever she happened to get out from under the eagle eyes of Mrs. Meriwether or Isaac.

One day she saw him riding through town on a big black horse that looked as fierce as he did. He wasn't wearing the fancy clothes he'd sported the day she met him. Instead he wore his regular cowboy clothes, and he had looked wild and free and utterly handsome.

Another day she saw him striding into the saloon, his gun belt low on his lean hips, his scuffed boots clattering on the wooden steps.

And then there was the day she saw him at the general store picking up supplies for his ranch. With him had been a short, bowlegged man named Hiram Boggs. According to Isaac, Nathan's piece-of-shit ranch had only two hands. Nathan and Hiram, and Hiram was worth about as much as the ranch, being that he was old, arthritic, and crazy to boot.

Every time Charlotte had seen Nathan, no matter what he was doing, he would, at some point, stop and look over at her. And his dark blue gaze, regardless of how far the distance was that separated them, pierced her like an arrow and burrowed down to the very core of who and what she was.

And she would recall the words he had shouted after her when she ran from him in the livery stable.

*You ain't going to marry him.*

Charlotte turned away from the mirror and looked out the window. Just beyond that grove of trees was the river. It glittered beneath the sunlight like a ribbon of silver. The only peace she had known since arriving in Montana had been spent at the river.

As a matter of fact, just yesterday, as she had been walking along it, she had seen, up on a hill and silhouetted against the sky, the dark figure of a man on a horse. Although he had been too far away for her to see him clearly, she had known it was him.

She stopped walking and stared at him and he had sat, motionless on his horse, looking at her and, for a moment that seemed to stretch into eternity, they gazed at each other until Nathan turned his horse away and galloped down the hill and out of sight. And Charlotte had felt as if all the light and warmth of the day had gone with him.

She felt that way now. Dark and cold. She stared out the window and, almost as if it had a voice, as clear and bright as it was, the river called to her.

Mrs. Meriwether was downstairs in the kitchen finishing up last minute preparations of the meal she was cooking for the party after the wedding. Charlotte left the room, descended the stairs, and quietly opened the front door.

Once outside she lifted up the long skirt of her wedding dress and went toward the river. The wind blew hard and she feared it would spoil her hair, but now that she could smell the river she no longer cared what she looked like.

She stopped at the edge of the river. The water rushed past her, bubbling over the rocks. Charlotte imagined herself a fish, swimming with the swift current, heading toward the open sea. But her reverie was interrupted by the rapid hoof beats of an approaching horse.

She whirled around. Nathan raced toward her on his big, black horse. The sun shone behind him so he appeared to her like some dark specter, comprised of both man and beast.

She instinctively turned back toward town but Nathan rode past her and reined his horse in front of her. He looked down at her, his black Stetson shading his eyes.

"What do you want?" She knew he hadn't been invited to the wedding. Mrs. Meriwether had made certain of that.

"You know what I want."

His chin and jaw were stubbled with what looked like a week's growth of beard and his eyes were red-rimmed and haunted as if he hadn't slept in days.

"No, I don't, Mr. Chandler. I have no idea what it is you want."

"I want you not to marry him."

"And what does it matter to you whether I marry him or not?"

He edged his horse closer, forcing Charlotte to take a step back. "He don't deserve you."

"And who are you to be the judge of that?"

"He's a pig."

"He's going to be my husband. And there's nothing you can do about it. Now go. Please."

Nathan shook his head. "He ain't gonna be your husband. He ain't gonna have no part of you."

Charlotte took another step back. Then she turned and ran. Nathan rode up behind her. Her wedding dress twisted about her ankles. She stumbled, scrambling to keep her footing. His horse galloped along-side her. Charlotte turned so that she could run the other way but Nathan's arm reached down and snaked around her. She cried out as he pulled up onto his horse and settled her in front of him.

"Let go of me!"

"Be still," he growled.

He held her tight against his broad chest with one arm and guided his horse with his free hand. She felt his hard thighs tighten as he dug his spurs into the horse's sides. It reared, then dashed across the ground, running so fast that the world flew past Charlotte.

After awhile she stopped struggling, and she let Nathan spirit her away, like the fish she had yearned to be as it was swept by the river to the sea.

<hr />

NATHAN URGED HIS horse up a hill. As they had rode, clouds had swelled in the west but as they reached the top of the hill the sun suddenly broke from behind the clouds.

Charlotte looked down into a valley and in the center of it was a ranch. Even she, who knew as much about ranching as she knew about anything in Montana, saw that, although it was small, it was well tended and not at all the way that Isaac had disdainfully described it.

Nathan rode his horse down the hill. As they approached the ranch, Hiram Boggs came out of the barn. He stared at them, then threw down the bucket he was carrying.

"You just had to go and do it, didn't you? You just had to go and do it."

"Don't start in with me, Hiram," Nathan warned.

"And why the hell shouldn't I?" He pointed at Charlotte. "That ain't exactly a sack of taters you got there." He shook his grizzly head. "But I should have figured you was planning on doing it. The way you've been moping around here."

Nathan got off his horse. He looked up at Charlotte. "He don't deserve her."

Hiram looked at her. "And what you got to say about that? Is that what you think? That your husband don't deserve you?"

"He ain't her husband," Nathan said stubbornly.

Charlotte glanced down at him but he was looking at the ground and she couldn't see his face from beneath his hat.

She looked back at Hiram. "I don't . . . I mean, I'm not—"

"Well, speak up," Hiram barked. "Cat got your tongue?"

Nathan's head snapped up. "Don't talk to her like that!"

He put his hands around Charlotte's waist. She resisted only for a moment, then let him help her off his horse.

Hiram frowned. "Ain't nothing coming from this but bad."

"You let me worry about that." Nathan took Charlotte by the arm and led her over to the house. Before they entered, she glanced back at Hiram. When he saw Charlotte looking at him ,he slowly shook his head. Then he turned and went back toward the barn.

"Where's he going?" Charlotte asked.

Nathan shrugged and opened the door. "Don't know and don't much care."

"You don't mean that."

Nathan snorted. "He ought to be thankful I ain't run him off before now. Ain't worth the air he breathes." He looked over at her "But since you seem so all-fired concerned, he's got his own little domicile down by the creek. He'll go down there and stew I suspect."

Charlotte entered Nathan's house and looked around. It lacked what one would call feminine accoutrements but it was neat and relatively clean. Nathan started at her and Charlotte was surprised to see apprehension in his eyes.

"It's very nice," she finally said.

He visibly relaxed at her words. "Are you hungry? Or thirsty?"

She shook her head. He leaned against the wall and dug his hands into the pockets of his pants.

"Wanna sit down?" he asked.

"I want you to take me back."

He pushed away from the wall, his eyes wide. "What? You still want to marry him?"

"Hiram is right. Nothing good will come of this. You have to take me back."

Nathan turned away from her. Then, startling her, he slammed his fist into the wall. She ran over to him and took his hand. He snatched it away. She looked up into his eyes. They were blazing. But not with lust or even anger. What she saw was fear.

"I'm no better than they are," he said, his voice thick and raw. "I see something I want and I take it. Don't think of the consequences. Don't think about whether it's right or wrong. I just take it. Just like them."

"Like who? Nathan, what are you talking about?"

Nathan barked a harsh laugh. "Don't try and tell me that Mrs. Meriwether failed to acquaint you with my notorious family tree 'cause I won't believe you."

"You're talking about your father and brothers?"

He nodded. "The Chandler gang." He laughed again, bitterly and harshly. "They set their eye on something, whether it's money or cattle or a woman, and they take it. Don't matter if they have to kill somebody to do it. They just take it."

"You haven't killed anyone, Nathan."

"The day's still young, darling."

"I don't want anyone hurt," she said. *Least of all you*, she thought. "But it's only a matter of time before Isaac finds out it was you that took me."

"You really want to go back to him?"

Charlotte bit her lip. She thought about Isaac, his coarse manner, his vile language, the vulgar way he had talked about her to the men in the saloon.

"No," she whispered. "I don't. But I can't stay here."

Nathan put his hands on her arms. "Why? Why can't you stay?"

"Because I have to marry Isaac."

"But you just said—"

"I said I didn't want to marry him. But I have to."

"No, you don't, Charlotte. You don't have to do anything you don't want to."

"You don't understand. If it weren't for Isaac I'd still be in New York, living like a slave in my aunt's house. And my uncle." She shuddered. "He . . . he wanted . . . he tried to . . ."

A sob choked her throat. Nathan pulled her into his arms. She let herself sink into his embrace.

"That ain't any reason to marry him," he said, stroking he hair. "Any decent man would have taken you away from that. He wouldn't have made you marry him."

"He didn't make me marry him. He asked me to marry him and I said yes."

"Because you felt grateful. Not because you loved him."

She pulled away and looked up at Nathan. Lord knows she had felt indebted to Isaac for offering her an escape from a life that for the past ten years had been unbearable. Had that truly been enough of a reason to marry him?

Nathan gently touched her face. "Charlotte, darling."

His eyes were so full of desire they looked almost feral in the gloom of the darkening room. She glanced toward the windows and saw the sky was now full of thick, black clouds. Nathan followed her gaze.

"Going to storm." He looked back at her, his eyes flaring with lust. "Probably last all night."

She stared at him. Is that what he wanted? Just to bed her? Is that all men would ever want from her? She put her hands on his chest and tried to push him away but he was so big it was like pushing against a mountain.

"Is that what you want?" he asked. "You want me to let you go?"

He quickly released her and stepped back. "I ain't going to take nothing from you that you don't give me willingly. And if you want me to take you back to town, I will."

Charlotte had no doubt he would do exactly as he said. He would give her that choice, and she could go back to the wedding where all the townspeople waited for her to become Mrs. Isaac Smith, the wife of the wealthiest man in these parts.

She flung her arms out to him. "Nathan."

He moved swiftly back toward her and placed his large, callused hands gently about her face. He stroked her cheek with the pads of his fingers. She gazed up at him, her heart beating hard and fast in her chest.

"Nathan, I . . . I've never. Despite what Isaac said at the party I've never . . . been with a man."

"I know, darling, I know." He traced her lips with his thumb. "Do you want me, Charlotte darling? Because I want you. I want you so much that sometimes I fear I'm going to die from wanting you so." His throat worked. "And I ain't talking about just in a purely lustful manner. Though Lord knows I do want you that way, too."

He smiled at her and it was such an infectious grin she couldn't help smiling back. "But I also want you to be mine," he went on. "I want you as my wife."

She looked away from him. Fat raindrops splashed against the window and the wind had picked up. It slammed against the trees, bending the branches and scattering the leaves.

"I don't want to be anyone's wife."

She hadn't even known she was going to say those words until she did. She looked back at Nathan and saw the hurt in his eyes. She cupped his face, her fingers brushing across the dark stubble on his jaw.

"But I do want you, Nathan Henry Chandler. In a purely lust-ful manner."

He gazed gently down at her. "I don't want to disrespect you."

"You won't."

He lowered his head until his lips brushed against her hair. His warm breath tickled her ear and his voice took on a calming lilt.

"I'm going to take my time with you, darling. And when I'm done you're going to be so soft and wet you're going to feel noth-ing but sweetness when I claim you."

Charlotte felt a powerful wave of desire wash over her and she shuddered in response. Nathan slowly moved his hands over her body as he pressed her against the wall. He slid his lips up and down her throat, his stubble scratching her skin. Her legs trembled as another swell of desire surged through her.

"Tell me you want me. Charlotte. Tell me you want only me."

"I do, Nathan," Charlotte whispered. "I want only you."

She undid the buttons and clasps on her wedding dress and let it slide to the floor, leaving only her corset and chemise. Nathan stared hungrily at her. She nodded, giving him permission to touch her. He unhooked the corset, and she found herself moved by the fact his fingers were trembling. Once her corset was gone, he eased down the shoulders of her chemise, baring her breasts.

"Lord have mercy," he breathed as he gazed at her.

Charlotte blushed. Then she gasped as he moved his hands over her bare breasts, molding them between his palms, his callused fin-gers tugging at her nipples. They throbbed and tightened under his skillful touch. He lowered his head and covered her mouth with his, even as his hands continued to squeeze her breasts. She moaned when he parted her lips with his tongue and shoved it deep inside her mouth. Clutching her breasts, he rasped his thumbs over her pouting nipples, his erection bumping against her belly.

Nathan picked her up and, still kissing her, he carried her into the bedroom. He set her on her feet next to the bed. He cupped her bare bottom with both hands and, as he pulled her close, she felt his thickening erection.

"Can you feel me, darling?" he murmured. "Can you feel how much I want you?"

"Yes, Nathan. I do. And I want you just as much."

She unbuttoned his shirt and pushed it off his broad shoulders. His skin was warm and smooth, and she eagerly explored his muscled arms and torso. She fumbled with the buttons of his pants. Nathan chuckled and helped her undo him. She tugged at the pants and pushed them down his lean hips. His sinewy cock jumped free. Charlotte closed her hand around it, moving her palm and fingers up and down it.

Nathan groaned and pulled her against him. He seized her mouth in another punishing kiss before he pulled away, shucked off his pants, and kicked off his boots. Then he was back at her, ravaging her lips and neck and shoulders with his mouth and his tongue and his teeth. He quickly stripped her of her chemise and drawers and laid her gently onto the bed.

He kissed her naked body slowly and attentively, his tongue sweeping across her skin. He cupped her breasts, circling the stiff nipples with the tips of his fingers. Lowering his head over her breasts he brushed his lips over each nipple before drawing it deep into his mouth.

Charlotte threw back her head and shoved her fingers into his thick dark hair. She held him tight against her breast, begging him not to stop. He did stop, but only to move to her other nipple in order to bestow upon it the same delirious attention he had given the other one. He continued to ravish her breasts while his hands moved down her body. He stroked her belly, her hips and the tender skin of her inner thighs. Then he slowly circled her sex with his fingers. Charlotte wantonly threw open her legs.

Nathan raised his head from her wet breasts and smiled down at her.

"You want me to touch you there?" His dark blue eyes burned. "You want me to touch that virgin honeycomb of yours?"

"Yes . . . oh, yes. I do. I do."

"Then tell me, Charlotte, darling. Tell me what you want me to do."

"I want you to touch me, Nathan. Please, touch me."

He slid his fingers over her soft, wet folds. Then he slowly moved them in and out while his thumb caressed her sensitive root. Charlotte writhed and moaned against the bed. She rocked her hips against his hand, longing for more.

Nathan grinned as her movements became more and more frenzied. "You might be a virgin, but you're the most passionate virgin I've ever heard of."

"And how many . . . Oh, God! How many virgins have you had?"

His dark brow arched "Well, to be honest, you'd be the first, but from what I've heard virgins are supposed to be shy and bashful."

"And is that what you want me to be? Shy and bashful?"

In answer, Nathan thrust his fingers deep into her, stroking her inner walls. Charlotte moaned, her body shuddering, and as the storm raged outside, he brought her to the brink of bliss three times, stopping just before she climaxed. The last time he did she cried out.

"Why are you doing this?"

He looked down at her. "I'm just making sure that when I break that cherry of yours it's going to be nothing but sweetness for you."

"Oh, Nathan, I'm ready. Please . . . I want you inside me now."

He rolled on top of her and pressed the tip of his erection against the opening to her moist and eager sex. He looked deep into her eyes. "Now, darling?"

She threw her arms around his broad back. "Yes, now, Nathan. Please!"

He eased inside her, melding their bodies together. Charlotte twisted her head on the pillow. He was so hard and thick and long, and she felt so full and so wanted. He moved inside her, slowly thrusting back and forth.

"Lord, you're so tight." He stopped moving, his heart slamming against her chest.

"What's wrong?" she asked, fearing she had done something wrong.

"Charlotte, darling, forgive me, but I can't . . . I mean . . . Oh, honey, I just want to fuck you."

She thrilled at the sound of that illicit word on his lips. "Then do so, Nathan. Just don't stop. Please don't stop."

"I don't want to hurt you."

"You won't."

He buried himself back inside her, his thrusts coming hard and fast, and as he did Charlotte felt a tearing inside her. But the pleasure she now felt was so entire the pain lasted for only a moment. Nathan moved his tongue into her mouth, thrusting it between her lips in rhythm with the hard strokes of his cock.

She twisted wildly in his arms and, since she was already primed as a result of the impassioned attention of his hands and mouth, when her orgasm finally gripped her, Charlotte screamed, but it was a scream of pure pleasure.

She clasped his broad back, her fingernails raking his sweaty skin, her legs locked tight around his thrusting hips as he rode her as hard and fast as she had seem him riding his horse. Then she felt his body stiffen, and she listened blissfully to his long, drawn out moan of release as he spilled himself deep into her sex, his cock throbbing with each powerful spurt.

"Sweet Jesus," he moaned against her ear, his breath hot and hard. "Sweet Jesus Almighty."

———∞∞∞———

CHARLOTTE AWOKE AND saw that not only had last night's storm broken but it was now morning. She yawned, stretched, and reached over for Nathan.

His side of the bed was empty.

She sat up, the blanket falling and uncovering her naked breasts. The air made her nipples harden and she recalled Nathan's tongue and lips and teeth on them. She shivered, as much from the coolness of the air as from the memory of his ravishment of her breasts.

Then she heard what must have woken her up.

Shouts. Curses.

She looked around for her clothes. All she had to wear was her wedding dress. She saw Nathan's shirt on the floor. She quickly put it on. He was so tall it hung down to her knees. She left the bedroom and went into the front room. The door was open, which accounted for why it was so cool in the house.

She peered through a window. A group of men sat on horses in front of the house. She shuddered when she saw one of them was Isaac. Marshal Meriwether was also with then. Nathan stood just outside the door. He wore only his boots, pants, and a gun belt around his waist.

Isaac leaned forward, his big face mottled with rage. "You fornicating son of a whore. You bring my wife out right now before you get your head blown off."

"Last I saw she wasn't yet your wife."

"That's because you stole her before she could become my wife, you goddamned son of a bitch! Now bring her on out here!"

"C'mon, Nathan. Do as Isaac says. Bring the young lady out and turn her over to her rightful husband."

"Rightful," Nathan sneered. "Isaac Smith ain't been rightful since the day he was born."

"And what do you know about right?" Isaac bellowed. "You're just like that no-good pa and those no-account brothers of yours.

Bad blood all around." He looked over at Marshal Meriwether. "Well? Aren't you going to arrest him?"

"Before I can do that," he replied, "I have to determine if in fact a crime has been committed."

"What you mean you have to determine?"

The marshal gave Nathan a long, meaningful look. "How do we know Miss Babington didn't willingly go off with him?"

"Why the hell would she go off with a no-good son of a bitch like him?"

Charlotte stepped outside. All the men's eyes widened except the marshal's. He just looked at her as if wondering what had taken her so long. She moved next to Nathan, conscious not only of the warmth of his body but of his scent, which was a combination of her smell, and it filled her with courage she had not known she possessed.

"Look!" Isaac shouted, pointing at Charlotte's disheveled hair and half-naked body. "The bastard raped her! I want that son of bitch hanged."

"He didn't rape me."

Isaac stared openmouthed at her. "What?"

"I gave myself to him. Just as I went with him. Willingly." She looked directly into Isaac's face. "He branded my . . . my womanly parts. I'm his now."

Isaac stared at her and, from the look in his eyes, she knew he was aware that she had heard him that day in the saloon. His face bruised a dangerous shade of purple.

"You bitch! You whore!"

He drew his pistol and aimed it at her. Charlotte jerked as if the bullet had already ripped through her body. Instead, Isaac was the one who lurched back, clutching his hand to his chest, his gun on the ground.

"You goddamned son of a bitch," Isaac howled. "You shot me!"

Charlotte looked over at Nathan. His gun was in his hand. He had drawn it so fast she hadn't even seen the movement. Isaac continued to howl as he clutched his bleeding hand to his chest.

Marshal Meriwether looked over at Nathan. "Guess we've had enough gunplay for the day."

"Yeah, Marshal, I guess we've had."

He tugged his hat at Charlotte. "Ma'am." He looked around at the rest of the men. "All right. We're done here. Somebody wrap something around Issac's hand. The doc can have a look at him when we get back to town."

"Go on, you bitch!" Isaac shouted. "I would have made you respectable instead of the whore you've become, but if that's what you want, so be it. Be his whore and goddamn you both!"

The men turned their horses around and galloped away. It wasn't until they were gone that Charlotte let herself once again breathe.

"You could have told them I kidnapped you," Nathan said. "That I raped you. They would have believed you. I'm a Chandler after all."

"And I'm a whore." She shrugged. "Perhaps we're deserving of each other."

Nathan gently took her chin. "We make ourselves what we want to be, Charlotte, darling. And I meant what I said yesterday. If you don't want to stay with me, I'll take you back to town or wherever it is you want to go."

Charlotte looked around at Nathan's ranch. As far as ranches went, she supposed it was rather small. But it was a beginning.

She looked back at him. "There's no need for that. I'm where I want to be."

"Are you sure? I won't be able to give you the things Isaac could. At least not for some time. And it's a hard life working a ranch."

"I'm not afraid of hard work. At least here I'd be working on something that's mine." She looked up at him from her under lashes. "I'm sorry. What I meant to say is I'd be working on something that's—"

Nathan picked her up and whirled her around. "That's yours!"

Charlotte laughed and begged him to put her down. The tail of his shirt was flapping about her bare bottom. He ignored her and swung her around even harder.

"Everything I have is yours, Charlotte darling."

"Don't you figure that before you go giving the ranch away you'd best get to working on it?"

Hiram stood at the foot of the steps, a rifle slung in his arms. Nathan put Charlotte down. She hurriedly smoothed his shirt down over her legs.

"And where the hell was you?" Nathan asked.

"Where I always am. Watching your foolhardy back." He jerked his head toward the barn and raised the rifle. "Had a dead aim on Isaac the whole time."

"A dead aim? Hiram, you're as blind as a bat."

"Don't need no eagle eye to see that melon head of Isaac's." He looked over at Charlotte. "You all right, Miss?"

"Yes. Thank you."

He looked back at Nathan. "You have any idea what you're getting yourself into?"

Nathan laughed, a strong, joyous laugh. "Nope. No idea whatsoever."

He put his arm around Charlotte's shoulder and drew her close. She slid her arm around his bare waist and nestled against his strong, warm side.

"How about you, Charlotte, darling?" he asked her. "Have any idea what you're getting yourself into?"

She smiled up at him. "Absolutely none."

Hiram grunted and shook his head. "Damn fools. The both of you. Well, I got work to do, and I ain't gonna ask what you two are gonna do 'cause I got a pretty good idea what that is. I don't wanna know no more than that."

He turned and headed back toward the barn. Once he was gone, Nathan looked down at Charlotte. "You still set on not being my wife?"

"Well, before last night I would have said yes. But"—and she slowly drew the tip of her finger down his broad, muscled chest— "I've had cause to reconsider my position."

"Oh, you have, have you?"

She nodded and tilted her head. "And, well, perhaps I could use a little more persuading."

"More persuading?" He grinned wickedly. "Well, Charlotte, darling, I'm more than happy to accommodate you regarding that."

He picked her up and carried her back into the house.

# Celestial

STEPHEN DEDMAN

T HE WALLS OF the parlor house were thin enough that Tao could hear the argument down the hall almost as clearly as if the Earps were standing in the room with her. Wyatt was keeping his voice low, mostly, but Mattie tended to become shrill when her supply of laudanum was running low, and sometimes he had to shout above her. "Goddamnit, woman, nobody's going to pay more than four bits for a bath just so they can—"

"You ain't the one who has to fuck 'em!"

Tao glanced up at the mirror on the wall, which showed the man thrusting into her from behind. If he was listening to the altercation, he didn't let it disturb his rhythm. Tao's serene smile was largely genuine. Diego was neither big enough to be uncomfortable or small enough to be irritating, and if he sometimes took long enough that the madam had suggested charging him by the minute, that was fine by her. Most important, he treated her like a person, at least before he started and after he finished, and the only other man who did that was Johnny. She did not love her job, but it was more pleasant than working in the family's laundry.

Diego closed his eyes, threw his head back, and gripped Tao's hips more tightly. She felt him gush inside her, a torrent, a veritable flood that almost made her come in harmony with it; it felt, strangely, like being washed clean.

"Water's two, three dollars a barrel," said Wyatt, "and we need's most of it for the whiskey, not for washing things as is about to get dirty again real soon anyway." He was walking along the corridor, probably hoping to get away from the nagging, but Mattie followed him.

Diego's breathing gradually returned to normal, and he opened his eyes. He looked into the mirror at Tao's face, and climbed off the bed. "Did I hurt you?" he asked, looking at the fading scarlet handprints on her ivory-pale skin.

"No," she said, knowing he wanted to be assured that he hadn't; other men, usually smaller men, sometimes wanted to be told that they had. Diego pulled his dusty Levi's up and fastened his braces—like most of the brothel's clients, he didn't waste valuable time undressing for sex—and looked at Tao's face. "I'll be back when I got more money," he said, with a hint of a stammer in his voice. "You're the prettiest girl in town."

Tao bowed her head slightly to hide her smile. Diego was younger and better looking than most of her regulars, though not as handsome as her beloved Johnny. He was part Mexican, part Apache, with thick black hair and strange dark eyes. He smelled of sweat and dust and horses even after the obligatory fifty-cent bath, but never of beer or whiskey. After he said good-bye, almost shyly, and walked out, Tao washed as much of herself as she could in the basin of scented water she kept beside the bed. The pleasantly slippery sliding feeling brought her back to the edge of orgasm—and beyond. She put her left hand over her mouth to muzzle her cries as she continued to rub with the right, her slender fingers reaching farther and farther inside herself until she hit that perfect spot at just the right angle and just the right amount of pressure.

Then she pulled her shift down from where it had bunched about her waist, and waited a moment before dressing. She heard Wyatt walk past her room, with Mattie following him—and then stopping outside the door. "And another thing," Mattie shrieked. "Why we got to charge as much for her as we do for whites? Other places only ask two bits for their chinks and niggers, and the other gals is getting jealous."

"'Cause folks pay it," said Wyatt, as Tao heard Doc Holliday laugh, then immediately burst out coughing. "Chink men only fuck chink women, and you know it. They think white women are ghosts, or something. And it's not just the chinks. You know how many men ask for her every payday. Her cunny may not be slanted, like some of them think, but it's got almost no hair on it and it's tight as a nun's. Leastways," he said, verbally backpedaling, "that's what Father Gallagher tells me. 'Sides," he continued, "she's not a chink. She's a Celestial."

"And what the hell's the difference?"

"A Celestial costs the same as an American," Holliday wheezed.

Wyatt chuckled, and the two men walked down the stairs to the gaming tables. Tao finished dressing, and followed them downstairs.

"Maybe you should let the women take a bath first, then let the men wash in the same water," Holliday suggested to the Earps, between pouring himself a whiskey and gulping it down.

"What if there's more water after the women had their bath than there was before?" asked Wyatt.

Holliday grinned, and lit a cigar. "Better yet. There's men back east who'd pay more for extras like that." Mattie scowled, and the two men burst out laughing, until Holliday began coughing so hard he had to use the spittoon near the bar.

Tao stared at the swinging doors as Diego rode away, then sat at the table with some of the other women: tall dusky Cassie, the favorite of the buffalo soldiers; henna-haired sharp-tongued Ella; and Mexican Maria, who claimed to have lived in New Orleans and became French Marie when it paid better. They dealt her into their poker game, and waited for business. It was a long time until payday.

———— ∞ ————

JOHNNY RINGO WAS six foot three inches tall, with deep-set eyes and a high forehead; he had an actor's poise, and the vocabulary to go with it. He greeted the Mexican women in fluent Spanish, then turned to Tao, "'The most celestial, and my soul's idol, the most

beautified Ophelia,'" he quoted. His right hand disappeared into a
pocket in his long linen coat, and Holliday grabbed the shotgun he
kept under the table, half-expecting Johnny to draw a pistol, but
the cowboy opened his fist and dropped a small stack of half-dollars
into Tao's palm. "'To bed, to bed; there's knocking at the gate: come,
come, come, come, give me your hand.'"

"Bath first," she said.

The cowboy raised an eyebrow at that, then smiled. "Only if you
wash me," he said softly. "It's not an accustomed action with me."

A few of the women tittered; Tao hesitated, then nodded. "Come
with me."

---

JOHNNY EMPTIED THE bucket of water into the hip bath, then
reached for Tao and grabbed her by the waist. "You first," he said.

"What?"

"The bath. I'd like to see you wash, first. Naked."

Tao's eyes widened, but she obeyed, undressing quickly enough
to suggest that she was eager. Johnny watched as she sat down in
the warm water, her legs slightly parted. Tiny as she was, with skin
as pale as porcelain, she looked almost like a doll, a child's toy—
except that he'd never seen any doll with a plump cunny on display
like this one. As he watched, grinning, her inner lips began to
emerge, darkening from pastel pink to crimson, almost red-violet.
"Is that why they call you Peach Blossom?" he asked.

"It's my name," she said, with a hint of a giggle. "Tao Hua
means 'Peach Flower.'" She cupped her hands together, and poured
water onto her small breasts. Her cinnamon-dark nipples swelled
slightly. "Now your turn."

"Not yet."

She shrugged, then reached for the soap and began rubbing it
over her body languorously. He removed his linen duster, then his
red bandanna, his braces, and his shirt, before taking a step toward

the tub and reaching into the water, slipping a hand slowly along one wet smooth thigh, touching her lightly between the legs, then sliding back up the other leg almost to the knee. Tao gasped as the hand descended again, this time stroking her puffy lips and teasing her clit, getting her lubricated, then one long strong finger slid inside her, and then a second. She felt herself becoming tighter, and the warm tingling feeling rose up her body, higher and higher, as though she were dissolving into the water, until she wasn't sure whether the pleasure was growing or she was shrinking. Tighter, until he couldn't have withdrawn even had he wanted to, as though they were locked together. Tighter, though she could no longer remember the word or any other word in any language as the sensation enveloped her and nothing else mattered, not words, not names, not thought.

She recovered gradually, and when she was sufficiently sure that she could judge distances and control her own body, she reached for the waistband of Johnny's Levi's and began unbuttoning them, freeing his cock, which she stroked lovingly. She considered kissing it, but he was sweaty, even grimy, and he stank. "You bath now?"

"Later," he said, placing one hand behind her shoulders and sliding the other gently under her ass, the tip of one finger tentatively touching her anus. He lifted her out of the bathtub with no apparent effort as his Levi's fell down about his ankles, then he swung her around so that tip of his cock rubbed against her clit. She let him tease her like this for a moment, enjoying the feeling, then wriggled and enfolded him, taking as much of his length into her as she could in one thrust and wrapping her legs around his hairy butt for extra traction. They smiled at each other, nose-tip to nose-tip, as they settled into a rhythm that was comfortable, then exciting, then urgent. The shared sensation of warmth became heat, heat became fire, and the fire became volcanic, an eruption, a lava flow, an explosion that could level mountains, until he was roaring and she was babbling and wailing in her native Mandarin.

When they opened their eyes again, they looked at each other almost shyly, both feeling oddly embarrassed . . . then he slid his cock and his finger out of her, and lowered her to the floor. He turned away from her, and washed his cock and his hands in the bathwater before pulling his pants back up and buttoning the fly. "'A consummation devoutly to be wish'd,'" he murmured, almost sadly. "I'll see you again soon."

Tao watched him walk out, then sat down in the bath with a faint sigh.

---

DIEGO SAT ON top of the hill and stared up at the moon, trying to make his mind as clear as the cloudless sky. He had been raised on the reservation, and still remembered a little of what he'd been taught by their old shaman, who claimed to have been taught by Geronimo himself. Diego had never seen any sign that the old man had any magic to speak of: he was plausible enough when it came to interpreting dreams, and despite his age he still cut an impressive figure when he danced, playing a large twisted flute, but none of the love charms Diego had bought from him had ever worked. Diego stared across at Tombstone's buildings, and tried to remember how the old man had pranced about when attempting to summon the spirits. Feeling more than a little silly, he began stamping his feet and chanting, waiting for a sign.

He kept this up until he was exhausted, but saw and heard nothing that struck him as any sort of sign. He waited, and eventually fell asleep, dreaming (as he so often did) of Tao Hua, her sweetness and her scent, the sound of her voice, the little catch in her breath as he entered her, the beauty of her eyes and the muscles beneath her pale silky skin, her warmth and grace and surprising strength, the way she drew him in that made him feel as though he could never escape or want to. . . .

He woke at sunrise and walked down the hill, feeling as gloomy as the gray clouds that were slowly approaching from the west.

TAO WOKE EARLY the next day, to a sound that was both familiar and strange. It took her nearly a minute to recognize it as rain on the roof. She opened the window of her small room, and stared out onto the street. Other people from the brothels and saloons and dance halls did the same, and she heard whoops and cheers and laughter. One gambler ran out onto Toughnut Street and threw his Stetson in the air, then set it on the ground upside down to fill with water. Other men followed his lead, and one also shed his frock coat, then his string tie, collar, waistcoat, and shirt. By the time Tao had run downstairs and onto the road, two men and one woman were already naked and others were well on their way there. She stared amazed, and amused, as Ella threw her corset up onto the porch and leapt up into the air, her huge breasts bouncing merrily. She threw her head back, too, and opened her mouth wide to let the clean water shower down into it.

Tao looked around as many other townsfolk and visitors hurried outside to enjoy the rain while it lasted. Cornishmen from the mines, Chinese from the laundry, soldiers, cowboys, shopkeepers, dance hall girls. . . . Tao stared in disbelief as Ella, now naked but for her boots, trotted over to one of her regulars and pulled his face down to her breasts while she fumbled with his trousers. A can-can dancer from the Bird Cage Theatre did a handstand in the street, her skirts falling down to her chin while she waved her shapely legs in the air; she was naked under her skirt, and men goggled or applauded. Two women, their clothes wringing wet, grabbed and kissed each other. Fly emerged from his gallery with his camera, obviously hoping to make these fantastic sights immortal.

A little hesitantly, Tao peeled off her sodden nightgown and reveled in the feel of the rain on her bare skin. She pirouetted, flinging water gaily about, then looked around and saw Johnny wandering up Allen Street. He, too, was dancing in the soaking rain, catching drops in his mouth. She blushed when he saw her, and he grinned and began stripping off his own clothing as they ran toward each other. He was bare to the waist by the time he reached her, and with her help, completely naked a few seconds later. She could smell whiskey on his breath, but the rest of him smelled wonderful, clean body and dirty mind, and she steered him towards a pile of hay bales in the OK Corral.

Tao knelt before her favorite lover, kissed the tip of his cock, licking a drop of pre-come from the eye, then slowly took it into her mouth, inch by inch, swirling it around between her lips and licking it enthusiastically, while stroking the rest of the shaft with one hand and fondling his balls with the other. Johnny grinned as he saw his cock disappearing into her beautiful face, and her dark slanted eyes smiled back at him. He moaned, his knees buckled, and he crashed back onto the hay bales as Tao continued to pleasure him with her mouth.

Tao closed her eyes as she savored the moment, enjoyed the taste and the feel of him inside her mouth, there where the nerve endings were clustered together so thickly that everything was magnified; she could feel the big vein throbbing, the sensitive ridge behind the head, the rubbery texture of the glans as it emerged from his foreskin. She sucked eagerly, feeling as though it was the first time she'd ever really felt a cock, as though it were something new and astonishing and magical. Johnny tasted clean, even pure, but even more—it was as though the rain was reviving everything that had been dried up, no mere water but a medicine and a lubricant and a blessing and an intoxicant.

When Tao looked up again, she saw that another woman had joined them and was kissing Johnny while he fondled her. Tao was even more flabbergasted when she recognized the woman: Big Nose Kate, a successful madam and Doc Holliday's sometime common-law wife. Kate glanced at her, and reached for Johnny's crimson cock, but Tao was quicker and more agile. She grabbed Kate's wrist, then scrambled on top of Johnny and quickly impaled herself on his length. Even though she was ready and oh so wet, inside as well as out, it seemed to her she could feel every vein and artery as it filled her and continued to swell, seemed to her that the sheer power of it was rising up through her belly and into her chest, until she couldn't tell its pulse from her own. She sat there for a moment, outwardly immobile but internally vibrating, shuddering, then began moving languorously but precisely as a dancer. Then, unable to tease him or herself any longer, she began to ride him as energetically as though she were breaking in a horse that had never been ridden.

Kate glowered, then defiantly swung a leg over Johnny's head and sat on his face. The cowboy didn't seem to object; on the contrary, Tao felt his cock pulse inside her, and Kate began writhing in harmony with it, murmuring endearingly in Hungarian and giggling as Johnny's huge moustache tickled her. The cowboy's huge hands reached upward, finding Kate's breasts and tweaking the prominent nipples. Her giggles turned to gasps, and Tao, who'd never seen another woman have an orgasm, watched in fascination as the madam arched her back, opened her mouth wide as though she was trying to suck in the rainstorm, and turned nipple-crimson from her breasts to her face.

A moment later, Kate opened her eyes again, and the two women stared at each other as the man beneath them eagerly pleasured both. Kate, her eyes still more than slightly glazed, leaned over and licked raindrops from Tao's face, then from her tiny breasts. Tao smiled encouragingly, though she was barely aware of anything other than Johnny's cock inside her, the rhythm now filling her head as well as her heart, as they moved through excitement to enthrallment to explosive erotic ecstasy as he erupted inside her, leaving her oblivious to anything but the strength of her own orgasm, the rest of the world dissolving into a wet welcome darkness.

When Tao opened her eyes, she was lying on the straw, staring up at the sky. Kate had leaned forward and was licking Johnny's cock clean, while he continued to feast on her. Her legs shaking, Tao left them to it and returned to walking around the town, dazed by her own feelings and still bewildered by the sights around her. Her legs shaking, Tao left them to it and returned to walking around the town, dazed by her own feelings and still bewildered by the sights around her. She saw Wyatt Earp outside one of the town's ice-cream parlors, eagerly licking ice cream off Sheriff Behan's fiancée Josie Marcus. The two women who Tao had seen kissing were locked in a tight embrace, their thighs around each other's ears as if to block out the rest of the world. Maria/Marie was sprawled in the mud with Father Gallagher, fucking Italian-style. Ella was greedily sucking two cocks, while other men sat in a circle around her, most of them obviously exhausted. Tao looked up from the chaos, and saw Diego leaning up against the corner post of the porch of the Grand Hotel. He was fully clothed and shaking his head in disbelief, and Tao saw another emotion on his normally stolid face . . . something strangely like guilt.

She approached him cautiously, and asked softly, "Did you do this?"

"I . . . I didn't mean . . . didn't know . . ."

"What?"

He took a deep breath. "I was just copying something I'd seen a medicine man do, once. I thought it was a love charm, a lot of people asked him for those, but it must have been a rain dance or . . . I don't know."

"Why were you trying to make a love . . ." To her amazement, he blushed—no mean feat, with his burnt-brown complexion. "Who for?"

He didn't answer.

"Me?"

He nodded, then stared at his boots, unable to meet her gaze.

"This was for *me?*"

"Yes . . . well, I . . ."

To his amazement, she giggled, and reached for the bulging front of his rain-soaked Levis. "It's wonderful," she said. "The best thing anyone's ever done for me. Thank you."

He looked up, and saw that she was smiling. "Take your clothes off," she said. "Enjoy this. Dance. We can fuck later, we can fuck anytime, but this, this is . . ." She tried to remember one of the Shakespeare quotes that Johnny was so fond of using, and suddenly smiled. "'Love comforteth, like sunshine after rain.'"

# Cowboy Cocksucker

CLAYTON HOLIDAY

Every time I hit Oklahoma, the place is exactly six months more nowhere, like the course of a degenerative illness. Something ugly is cooking in this mongrel state of meth addicts, paint sniffers, and goat fuckers, this degraded Baptist backwater on the southern plains.

After years I return reluctantly for unfinished business. The weather is warm enough that when I step outside at high noon my white polo shirt sticks to my body like a used condom.

To escape the heat, I enter a cool convenience store, and a gregarious man old enough to be my father instantly talks to me in familiar tones. My eyes flicker the question: who is this guy? He reveals his name, and I vaguely recall him from twenty years ago. Life has not been kind; he's beat, bleary, and bloated.

We've both been dealt a bad hand or two, but he's been knocked hard to the canvas.

Although I'm married and sport a wedding ring, the man sizes me up correctly as a sexual outlaw and comes on with embarrassing flirtation. He suggests we get together.

There are times when I'm not satisfied being a straight husband and I need a man—a masculine man. I want cock. I must have cock. I scheme how to score cock. I want to be fucked and filled by cock. This excites me, and completes me. No emotions are necessary. No dialogue. Just pure animal lust between two masculine males.

Yet the man offering himself to me can do queenly hauteur like no one else. I remain outwardly unmoved: the straight WASP glacier has closed over me.

"I'd like to," I explain, "but I'm on my way to the Married Men with STDs meeting."

⁓∞⁓

LATER I DRIVE by the decaying shithouse of the daily newspaper, and pull over to reminisce about the well-hung, married cowboy I used to blow after hours in the darkroom. The nature of our sleazy introduction is not relevant.

Slim is a memorable character: medium height and physically streamlined, like a classic rodeo bull rider. He has the biggest cock I've ever sampled.

In the intimacy of the darkroom, Slim drops his tight, boot-cut Wrangler jeans to his Tony Lama snakeskins, and seductively pulls down his skimpy black jockstrap. Even in darkness, his cock is breathtaking in its size and shape. He sits on the counter so I may go down on him easily.

Of course I cannot resist this cowboy. I don't know if I should kiss him—this may violate his masculine code. Instead, I unbutton his shirt, pretending not to notice his captivating physique, but I want to touch him everywhere immediately, rub my hands across his splendid smooth, hard chest, caress him, and kiss his nipples. I'm so hot. I must have him.

Instead, he touches my face, at first with gentle strokes, and then he inserts his middle finger in my mouth, feeling all around. He directs me to suck his cock and presses my face toward his crotch. I let out a discernible moan of approval and offer total compliance. My hands fondle his immaculate cock. When I see a clear bead form at the tip, pumped out by my eager hand, my mouth waters. I must taste that drop of liquid . . . I feel compelled to put his thick, hot meat in my mouth. He instructs me to slide farther down on my knees. Is this how you treat your wife? And all the others before me? I don't really care.

Right now I have no other sense of purpose and don't understand my own desires. I'm willing to be his cocotte, his slut, his whore. I want to worship his cock, to be more spellbound than his wife, as he places his strong, cowboy hands on my head, guiding me up-and-down on his cock, fucking my face with authority.

"Oh God, yes . . . that's so good . . . take it all down, cocksucker."

And I love to feel his strong hard cock moving slowly past my lips, then thrusting as he becomes so wild to have me. His hand caresses the back of my neck, pulling me closer as he fucks my face. I smell the musky aroma of his genitals, spicy and intoxicating. I capture the sticky stuff on the tip of my tongue. It is warm and tastes sweet and I want more. I part my lips and let the bulb knob slide inside my mouth.

My cowboy moans as I offer the pleasure he loves. My mouth opens wide to surround his thick cock. Gradually I take it all in my mouth. How do I compare with his wife? Does she suck cock like this? I massage his balls. The cowboy's breathing is labored. The moans are more appreciable. Deeper and deeper his cock slides into my mouth. My head moves faster.

He tells me, "Your mouth is wonderful, keep sucking my cock."

I love it when a man tells me what to do, knowing I'll do as he wishes. This is wonderful, as his cock moves in and out, over and over. I want all of him. I can't keep my mouth off of him. I love the smell and taste of his cock, the texture of his cock, his foreskin, his bulging veins, the smell of his cologne, his sweat.

I am a shameless cocksucker. I love this submission, because it feels right to pleasure a man like this—a seemingly endless blowjob. Yet I can tell he's about to explode. I'm waiting for his orgasm. My skin shivers in expectation, my heartbeat quickens—then the pièce de résistance. And the cowboy moans without inhibition. He fills my adoring mouth with spurting hot cum, and I use my tongue to lick him clean. It's a matter of pride, and, as his fatigued cock slips from my mouth, he eases me to my feet.

For a moment, I feel my face go all red and I stand looking down, speechless and abashed. I struggle with myself. I'm married—of course this should never happen. I'm not supposed to be attracted to my own gender, yet I feel a thousand times madly alive . . . at length I raise my face to his and I want to kiss the cowboy. Kiss every part of his face, his ears, and eyes, and neck, and yet I don't. Instead his cock stirs proudly, and voluptuous thrills pass through me at the thought of sucking his cock again.

"Go on," he tells me.

In seconds my hand instinctively envelops his cock, my fingers play with it, letting him know I can't resist. He calmly watches the spectacle of my mouth moving from one nipple to another. My fingers trace the curves of his body. My hands investigate the curve of his cheeks, squeezing them gently. My hand is on his thighs, roving up and down, then round his haunches, as far as I can reach, over his smooth, sweet flesh—letting him know I'm about to travel farther down his body again. As I begin my descent, he extends his legs slightly. I can't wait until his cock empties itself into me again.

We meet like this a half-dozen times, and I can't get enough of his wonderfully thick cock.

＊＊＊

When I see my rugged yet gorgeous cowboy in Wal-Mart on the weekends with his wife and two children, we play that old Brokeback con routine and pretend we don't know each other—because we're straight, and everyone knows we're straight.

But we are not straight. We play by different rules. Slim wants me, and I want him, too. I want to give myself to him. I want a physical connection with another man that many people can't accept. Our desires are forbidden and our relationship must remain just as secretive as any place in the American West. But this doesn't stop us.

I miss Slim and his eight-inch cock. I look for him everywhere, yet he is gone, moved on, still acting straight, while offering his throbbing cock for a hungry, masculine male oral bottom. There's always another Slim, another sexual outlaw, moving cautiously across the hard-core Republican landscape.

I have stopped pretending the full scope of my desires doesn't matter, and I do have many. Now I gladly admit that I love to suck both a hard cock and fuck a hot, wet cunt. I want it both ways because I go both ways.

I finally accepted this about myself years ago in this small Oklahoma town that looks like it is left over from a receding flood.

This is where I found myself, and found I do not belong among the solid, small-town citizens with their Rotary Club memberships, and the rusty abandoned cars and pickup trucks scattered here and there on front lawns.

I belong to the world where I can be myself and enjoy the pure white heat of sex, whether the object of my lust is male or female.

# Reverse Cowgirl

RACHEL KRAMER BUSSEL

I STILL CAN'T believe Pete waited all summer, until my very last day on the ranch, to fuck me. Yes, he was worth the wait, but still, thinking about all those missed opportunities for screwing each other senseless makes me wistful even now.

My friend Janice had sent me to her brother's ranch to get away from the city that was threatening to eat me alive. "Go, relax. You need a change of pace and you know it, and with your severance check, you can afford it. I won't take no for an answer," she insisted, brown eyes blazing at me as she pressed a plane ticket into my hand. I'd just gotten laid off from my job as a photographer for a big-time magazine, and wasn't quite sure where to go next or what to do. I had my camera and was roaming the streets of New York, when I wasn't hunched over some bar doing shots and going home with men who went from bad to worse on the scale of unavailability. Everyone had noticed, but only Janice had it in her to force me to do something about it.

I'd never met her brother, had heard he was the tough loner who'd left their cozy intellectual family to strike out on his own. A real, live modern-day cowboy running a ranch. Probably the type just waiting for a sexy little wife to slip into his life and plant flowers and bake pies. So not me. But from the night I arrived, there was a spark between us. I'd been worried that Janice had badgered him into letting me stay there, but I sensed beneath his brusque bravado that he wanted the company. "Claire, right?" he asked. "I've seen your photo, and my sister talks about you all the time . . . but she didn't tell me quite how well you fill out your jeans." His eyes raked over my favorite pair, the last ones that still fit after my late nights bar hopping and ordering pizza. I'd donned my favorite boots for the occasion, stiff brown leather that clicked in just the right way.

"Can I set this stuff down somewhere?" I asked, not wanting to be rude, but tired from the long flight. He reverted back to polite Midwestern gentleman then, taking his eyes back up to my face and then showing me to a small, simple guest room, complete with a TV, dresser, and desk.

"If the sun is too much for you in the mornings, just draw the blinds. It's pretty desolate out here, and I'm working from the crack of dawn on, but come find me if you need anything. Maybe you'll want to give one of my horses a workout."

I barked out a quick, sharp laugh. "Not this girl," I said, remembering my first and only attempt at horseback riding as a budding preteen. I'd been thrown almost as soon as we'd started across the lawn, much to the mockery of the other birthday party guests. The memory made me shudder.

"Hey, you never know until you try," Pete said, squeezing my shoulder and leaving more of an impression on my skin, and my senses, than he should have. He walked out and I sniffed the air for traces of his scent, a musky odor that was like flowers topped by sweat sprinkled with cinnamon. Definitely good enough to eat. I shook my head back and forth and unpacked, then settled into my favorite comfy sweats and got into bed.

I saw him once more that night, when I slipped into the kitchen for a brief snack. I grabbed my cheese and crackers and ran back upstairs, scared of his nearness, his interest, just plain him. I'd been so busy gallivanting off to event after event, covering everything and everything, hiding behind my camera even once I was no longer on duty, I'd barely had a moment to sit and rest and think like I did on the ranch. Everything moved more slowly, and the wide-open space of it all meant that my contact with other humans, mainly him and his ranch hands, shook me up more than it probably should've.

And then a subtle dance started between us. He'd wink or gesture or throw out a flirtatious remark, but the minute I pounced on it, he'd pull back, and I'd have to wonder if I'd imagined his interest. "Rough night?" he asked when I stumbled downstairs in my big white T-shirt, black leggings, and hair zigzagging every which way.

"Wouldn't you like to know?" I asked, raising an eyebrow as I poured my coffee.

He didn't answer, and his indifference only drove me wilder. I found myself thinking about Pete every other second. I'd take my camera and stroll the grounds, sight horses through the lens, and capture them in all their raw beauty until they noticed me and wanted to become friends. I'd walk off and sometimes catch Pete looking my way. I wondered what he'd done by way of female companionship around here. There was a local pub he'd taken me to once or twice, but the male to female ratio was at least five to one.

He didn't come right out and say it, but it was implied that if I didn't at least get on a horse once while I was there, I wasn't getting into his bed—or his pants. I'd never been rebuffed by a guy quite like this before, and instead of feeling hurt, I saw it as a challenge. Unlike guys back home, I knew Pete wasn't disappointed that I wasn't ten pounds lighter or wearing the latest designer threads or more accomplished in my field. He didn't care about any of the superficial bullshit, and in a way, what he wanted from me was harder. He wanted the opposite of a pretty face; he wanted me stripped down, raw, open, and honest. He wanted to see me push myself past my limits. He wanted me to fully enter his world in a way I hadn't been prepared to when I stepped onto the ranch.

It took me a few weeks to agree. I'm a klutz when it comes to anything sports related, and have always preferred to hide behind my camera, capturing the beauty of a ball swishing into the net or a runner's final lunge across the finish line than attempt either one myself. But I decided that if the moment was right, I'd go for it.

When it finally happened, Pete wasn't even foremost on my mind, though my pussy sure never forgot him. I'm slightly ashamed to admit that the reason I finally agreed to a lap around the premises on the back of Rusty wasn't so much to impress Pete as to assuage the ache between my legs. "God, I need to get laid," I'd said to myself just that morning, two months in, as I woke up and immediately pressed my fingers to my panties, finding them wet and sticky. I'd had a dream involving me, Pete, and a leather belt that he'd chosen to wield in ways that made me shudder just thinking about them. It was getting to the point in real life where any slight interaction with him set me off so much I'm sure I blushed madly. No amount of masturbation was working and I knew it was fight or flight time, and as stubborn as I am, I've never been a quitter. I got up, shucked off all my clothes, and looked at myself in the mirror. My skin was tan, the harsh city pale gone to a toasted bronze spackled with pink and freckles on my nose and shoulders. My breasts seemed to stand higher, my back prouder. My arms had bulked out, even with my minimal efforts around the ranch. The light ripple of muscle was an unexpected benefit of long days spent stacking the occasional bale of hay and chopping wood and simply being on the ranch, a state that required so much more of me than hopping on subway trains every day.

I didn't dare ask myself if Pete would like what he saw. That was city-girl thinking, and while I was still one, something had changed. "Fake it till you make it" is a phrase I'd learned a long time ago and as I checked out my ass in the mirror, I thought I faked cowgirl pretty damn well. I crouched down in the doorway of the barn and looked up at Rusty through my camera, which had almost become another part of my body. I thought of it the way most people think of glasses—a way to improve my sight, see things in ways I couldn't otherwise. I adjusted the shutter speed, zoomed in, and waited. He was looking away from me, but I knew he knew I was watching; kind of like Pete and I all summer, sizing each other up from afar and then stammering through conversations up close. "Good show," he'd say when he caught me watching one of endless hours of *Law & Order,* his words so short and sharp I couldn't tell if he was being sarcastic.

Rusty snorted at me, as if egging me on. I smiled and he seemed to smile back, enough to coax me to put down my camera. I felt a stirring between my legs and realized the whole atmosphere around us was supercharged with masculine energy, the result of me being the only woman to grace this part of the property in who knows how long. "You'll take care of me, won't you, Rusty?" I asked, slipping my hand briefly between my legs to press against my swollen flesh. I offered him a sugar cube, as I'd heard was customary.

Then I heard a familiar voice from nearby. "He doesn't have a sweet tooth, Claire." Pete was standing far enough away that I had to have imagined his breath floating along my neck, but I shuddered nonetheless. "You're finally gonna ride him? On your last day? I wonder if that's a gift to yourself or to me, sweet city girl." He looked me up and down appraisingly and I longed to sink to my knees right there and take him between my lips. He's stolen my thunder; I'd been so proud of getting ready to ride not for him, but for myself, though if I were truly honest, separating my lust for Pete with my lust for some semblance of country bravado was an impossible task for someone as horny as I was. Lonely, too; the solitude was starting to get to me, the silence still striking. I missed car horns honking, people yelling, subway trains rumbling. I missed my city in all its grimy glory, but I'd needed this visit, that was for sure.

"It's not for either of us," I said as I leaned forward to stroke the patient horse. He looked up at me so knowingly, I almost forgot he didn't have the same kind of brain we did. *I'm ready for you,* he beamed to me with those endless eyes.

I got on, letting Pete steady me and give me a few instructions. "Relax," he said, noting the way I gripped the reins too tightly. "He'll show you." Then he kissed me, just on the cheek, but that was enough. I blushed and dug my heels into Rusty, who brayed before pushing forward. I wobbled a little at first, then settled down against him, the ache of my sex somewhat eased by the pounding of my heart. There was no time to be horny as we flew across the seemingly endless expanse, the wind whipping through my hair, this wild animal not controlled by me but working in tandem.

"Yeah," I whispered to nobody but myself, feeling a tear fall as I looked up at the majesty around me. Had I really waited so long to enjoy it?

I don't know how long we rode. It felt like hours but was probably less than half of one. I returned winded, breathless, amazed. I had done it and it was nothing like my early mishap. Maybe it was like getting that perfect shot, the one you wait and wait for, shifting and searching and posing, until it appears, out of nowhere, unbeknownst to you. Perfection, but only for a fleeting moment. You have to grab it before it disappears forever.

Pete was waiting for me in the barn. I wasn't sure if he'd been watching the whole time, and didn't really care. I'd stopped worrying about what he thought of me as Rusty took me places fucking could only dream of. He gave me back the girl I'd lost along with my pink slip, and Pete was there to usher her into her new life.

He lifted me into his arms, and I let him. My nonrefundable plane ticket was waiting for me early the next morning, but for tonight, I was his. He carried me into the house, put me down on his bed, then rolled me over onto my stomach. "Damn, that ass has been haunting my dreams since you got here, Claire," he said, and then slapped it, hard. I shuddered as he pressed his fingers against the sodden crotch of my jeans.

"You should've listened to me sooner, city girl. A horse between your legs is almost as good as a cock. Almost," he said, and I moaned as I heard his zipper come undone. He pushed me down when I rose to try to get a taste of it, and I sobbed. He offered me two fingers instead and I lunged for them while he got me out of my jeans, then stroked my wetness. "I won't say I told you so again, Claire, but I do hope you'll consider a return visit. Not all of us cowboys are the devil . . . unless you want us to be."

He had me utterly at his mercy, the result of waiting so long for his hands and lips to overtake me. "Close your eyes," he said, and I did, sinking into blissful oblivion as he took off my shirt, undid my bra, and pinched my nipples so hard I screamed. "That's what I like to hear," he whispered in my ear, and this time the shudder was all real.

He lifted me up like I didn't weigh a thing, then turned me around so I was facing away from him, before placing my pussy over his cock and guiding me down. *Reverse cowgirl,* I thought, just moments before I leaned forward, grabbing for his ankles as I slid up and down against him, his dick slamming up against that place inside me that had gone unfilled for too long. The tears streamed down my face, tears of pleasure, passion, release, relief, as he raised me up and down. I bent forward even farther, as far as I could, city yielding to country, girl yielding to boy, my bent body an invitation to plunder, pillage, pound. He didn't need an invitation, of course, knowing just how to make me come like he'd done it countless times before. "Let go. Relax, remember?" he said softly as he sat up, reaching forward to rub my clit in slow, strong circles until I came, unleashing everything I'd kept inside all these months. Sure, I'd given myself orgasms aplenty, but not like this, not ones that seemed to ricochet through my body again and again, lapping around me until I could barely breathe.

When I was done I leaned back, my length covering his, sliding downward and then back up. "Can I taste you now?" I asked, suddenly needing that contact, that connection, to fortify me before I left him forever.

He put his hand on my neck, pressing gently, making me moan again. "You're such a whore, Claire." That was all I needed to come again, releasing a trickle of my juices onto his cock. He quickly shoved me off of him, then onto my back and climbed on top, presenting his cock to my open lips. I reached out my tongue and tasted myself on him, then, as he plunged into my mouth, his all male flavor overtook my taste buds. I hummed against his cock as it penetrated my mouth, keeping my eyes open as long as I could until I had to reach for the wall behind me when I felt him nearing orgasm. "Damn it, Claire, you're too good," he said after just a few minutes, taking his cock in hand and whipping it against my wet lips before erupting against them, his hot cream covering my lips, chin, cheeks. He pushed some of it into my mouth and I swallowed it, still shaking from the power play he'd shown me he was capable of.

He held me then, neither of us needing to talk, until the sun came up. I drifted in and out of sleep, picturing myself alternately on the ranch, then back home, neither one seeming to fit just right. Was I a cowgirl now, or the reverse? Was this just a fling, or a new way of life? I left him sleeping as the hour arrived, having called the one car service within miles. I picked up his shirt off the floor, full of his sweat, his smell, his home. I slipped my arms into it, then found panties and the same jeans and boots I'd arrived with, taking him and his flavors and the feel of his body in me, on me, with me, as I went.

I've been home for three months and the weather's starting to get colder. The click of my boots on the ground still reminds me of him. He's coming to visit over the holidays, and I wonder which of us will be in reverse then. Whatever position or city or setting we wind up in, this time, I'll be ready.

# The Stake

LEE CRITTENDEN

IT WAS A September Tuesday that Mindy Chang blew into Dodge on the afternoon stage. The coach was about a half hour late because a fight had broke out among the passengers, one of the ladies there thinking to defend her man against Mindy's painted, roving eye. Ben Carrington and Hal Meadows, riding shotgun on that day, had had to stop the stage and separate the two factions, meaning them that supported Mindy and her right to look, and them that supported decency and modest behavior in the gentler sex on the other hand. The factions might've set up different if everybody had themselves all the facts about Mindy, but of course they didn't know, so the brawl went on as it did.

Once they was into Dodge and the tired horses pulled up in front of the express office, Ben Carrington climbed up on top of the rig and threw down Mindy's heavy valise outright—without so much as a by your leave, and without much concern for possible breakables that might be inside either, like expensive French perfume bottles.

"Good riddance!" he yelled at Mindy.

"Fuck you!" screamed Mindy in response, very strident.

She adjusted her hat to a haughty slant. A marvel of millinery craft, it looked like an ostrich in molt just then, covered in dust and disarrayed from the cat fight that had gone on inside the stage. Mindy grabbed up her valise and stomped off down the street toward the hotels, her taffeta skirts bouncing off the ruts and show-ing her fancy high-button shoes, and her elaborate bustle dancing from side to side with the swing of her walk. Most of the men on the street swung around to watch her prance by, their mouths hanging wide open, and the parson, meeting her at the corner, out-right blushed. Mindy winked at the man seductively and pouted her painted mouth, but actually her heart wasn't in it on that day. Mindy was some worried.

She was flat busted. Mindy needed a stake in the absolute worst way. If she didn't come up with a fortune in the next night or so, she figured to be in jail come Friday, when hell in general was like to catch up with her.

Dodge in them days was a wide-open town. It had grown up catering to the buffalo trade, and by the time the buffalo were wiped out and the Santa Fe railroad come to town, there was a general store, three dance halls, and six saloons. After the railroad come the cattle trade, and then Dodge got to be called the cowboy capital, famous for gamblers and bars and gunfights before breakfast ever day. Them that was slow on the trigger ended up on Boot Hill, and several famous lawmen were imported to keep the place in order and the cattle trade moving smooth. There was an ordinance against rid-ing a horse into any of the saloons, but never one against guns.

All in all, Mindy figured this was a good town to make her stake, and then maybe get lost back East for a while, or maybe in San Fran-cisco, where a girl was sometimes appreciated. Broke or not, she fol-lowed her usual inclinations. She picked out the best hotel in Dodge and hired a deluxe room on the second floor.

Then she pestered the manager a while, wanting the sheets changed and the floor swept, and fresh towels and hot water sent up from the kitchen, because Mindy meant to go to work that very night. She cleaned off the trail dust that had come in the windows of the stage and changed her dress to one that was even shinier taffeta. It had a tight, low-cut bodice, sewed with a pile of ruffles to disguise her lack of cleavage, the usual frothy bustle, and fashionable leg-of-mutton sleeves to hide her too-wide shoulders. She pinned up one side of her skirt to show lacy petticoats and a shine of silk stockings underneath. Then with a curling iron, she put up her glossy hair in curly ringlets that strayed down over her ears and across her high cheekbones, framing her face in sweet, girlish inno- cence. For jewelry she added a sparkly cameo on a velvet choker, and earrings that looked like rubies, but really were only glass.

All that was meant to be a distraction, because young Mindy was a world-class gambler, and had got herself thrown out of more towns in them days than most folks had ever been to. It was getting dark by then, oil lamps showing in the windows across the street, and so Mindy went down the stairs to check out the nightlife in the saloons in general, and the sharpness of the gambling concessions there in particular.

The Long Branch looked like the best bet, filled to overflowing already at dusk, and with the honky-tonk sounds of drunks laugh- ing and piano playing drifting over the swinging doors and out into the street. There was more gambling tables at the Comique, but Mindy didn't like the balcony-box arrangement of the hall, which she thought likely to complicate a quick getaway. After her tour, none of the other places looked any better than the Long Branch. Fid- dler's music from the shows was filling the streets by then, and from somewhere shots racketed, though it sounded like cowboys raising hell, and not likely a fight. Before she tried the saloon, Mindy took a chance and slid down an alleyway behind the building and found a passed-out drunk with a few dollars in his pocket. It was a sign of good luck, she thought, and maybe enough to get her into a game.

But first she had to get into the damn saloon.

She marched up to the swinging doors and pushed right inside big as life, but then she bumped into a tough that was hired by one of the owners, Bill Harris, to keep out undesirables, that man being Wes Benson.

"Ain't no ladies allowed in here, ma'am," said Wes, towering over her.

"I ain't no lady," said Mindy, and her eyes roved past Benson and out over the room. She winked and smiled at the nearest handsome man.

That gent was Bud Towner, and he was half-drunk already at eight o'clock, his heart being near broke that night from losing his girlfriend over at the Alamo to another man. Now Bud was a railroad maintenance hand, even bigger than he was handsome, kinda morally loose and definitely a man to be reckoned with around Dodge. He was fair even-tempered, but he was in a fight every week and spent most Saturday nights in the jail. He never had kilt a man, but he'd come close lots of times, and folks figured it was just a matter of time before he did, by accident if nothing else.

Well, Wes Benson went to take hold of Mindy and kind of escort her back out the door, but Mindy had already slid past him and linked her arm through the crook of Bud Towner's elbow.

"Handsome," she said, batting her innocent eyes up at Bud, "aren't you going to buy me a drink?"

"See here, Bud," said Wes, "we cain't have no ladies in here."

"Didn't you hear she wasn't no lady?" asked Bud. And then he smiled down at Mindy. "Come here, honey," he said, "and sit on my lap a while."

They found a spot at a table and Mindy worked her skirts in between Bud's legs so she could perch on his thigh, and smiled up and tossed back the double shot of whiskey that Bud bought for her.

"Honey," Bud said, frowning now and trying to focus on Mindy's face, "are you a Chinawoman?"

"Part." Mindy said sweetly, "Did you just notice?" She put her arm around Bud then and leaned over to flick her tongue around inside his ear.

Wes Benson frowned at this behavior, but he didn't say no more to Bud, nor to Mindy, either, as there was a fight broke out just then at one of the faro tables, and he had to go and throw two of the drunks out the back door to join the one that was already lying in the alleyway.

Mindy let Bud pull her up close then and massage her back to see if she was wearing the proper foundation garments, which she wasn't. Mindy didn't never much like a corset. It cut down her wind for them quick getaways, as was already mentioned.

The hugging was real pleasant, and the nearness of big, handsome Bud, so Mindy fluffed her skirt up a little more, and under cover of the taffeta, she slid her hand down Bud's crotch and unbuttoned his fly. Bud's dick fell out, already half standing up from the warm weight of Mindy near sitting on it, and Mindy commenced to feel it over. The way it felt excited her, the way the foreskin tightened and slid back, and the way the head got big and hard and pre-come oozed out right away, so Mindy begun to rub on it in real earnest. Bud gasped at that, but didn't have no real complaints about what Mindy was doing. He cussed some under his breath, and then he began kissing Mindy on the mouth and feeling for her tits. He couldn't find none, and at that he started to have second thoughts as to what he had on his lap. He cussed some more at the idea, but then he decided it didn't matter no way.

They went on that way, Bud getting more and more agitated and Mindy rubbing harder and faster—she had a real talent in that little hand. Finally Bud come, gasping and groaning. Mindy kept working at him until he was complete played out, and then she took a lace-edged hanky out of her little bag, tidied up her fingers, and heaved out a great big sigh.

The gents at the bar had totally missed what went on, as they were listening to a grisly account of the latest demise around Dodge. Mindy sat there and waited a minute for Bud to come out of his daze, meanwhile checking out the room, the ornate chandeliers, and the dark wood bar with the mirror behind it reflecting nothing much but a haze of smoke. But most of all she was studying the gaming tables. She was real serious about making a stake, and taken as she was by Bud's charms right then, Mindy figured she could always pick up with him later on. Bud seemed plumb wasted, showing no signs of returning life, so Mindy buttoned up his fly and

patted his dick good-bye. Then she slid off Bud's lap and headed
away into the smoky murk.

The first place she stopped was at the craps table, that being the
best place to start for them with minimal funds. Fred Logan was
running the craps game that night, and he looked around when
Mindy bellied up to the table, but he figured if Wes Benson had let
her in, it wasn't his call to throw her out. So when Mindy put a ten
dollar piece down on the five, Fred threw craps and then paid up
when the five won the toss. Mindy just let the money lay, won again,
and then moved her pile to the seven and won again. After a while
she had a tidy pile of cash, winning some and losing some, and then
she reached up and took off both the earrings that looked like they
was set with rubies.

"These are worth a thousand," she said.

Now, Fred Logan never could tell fakes. Mindy had cleaned
them earrings with vinegar so the jewels shined like they was the
real thing, the cut facets catching the light and sparkling and
throwing it back, and the gold looked like it was fine and solid, and
not plated on at all.

Fred squinted at the things in the lamplight, and looked around
for one of the owners to help him out, but wasn't neither of them
on the premises just then.

"They were my mama's," said Mindy, standing there real innocent with tears forming in her eyes. "All I've got left from her in this
world. She was a fine lady over in San Francisco. . . ."

Which was a pure lie, as Mindy's mother had been a waitress in
a mining camp over in Oregon, and destitute all her life. Mindy's
dad now, she wasn't real sure about, only that he had been a half-
breed Chinaman.

Well, Fred was no better hand at appraising gurdy girls than he
was at jewelry, so he decided to let Mindy bet the earrings for a thousand. Mindy won again, and then a couple more times.

She was getting a big enough roll to join a poker game, so she
winked and said, "Thanks, honey." Then she deserted Mr. Fred

Logan, and with him the crowd that had gathered around the craps table to follow her bets.

Over at the poker table they was some real hard cases playing five card stud that night, and the atmosphere was downright different from the craps table. Actually, it was kinda tense. Hollis Cole held one of the hands. He was a famous gunman out of Abeline that folks suspected of being likely to hold up the stage or the railroad when he come up short—though nobody was going to come right out and say that. Hollis Cole was a gaunt man, tough as rawhide, bleached all over to the color of bone, with a death's head grin when he was like to start a gunplay. His eyes was black as coal, burning like embers in his cold face just then, because of the way the game was headed.

On his right was Lew Grace, as near to Hollis's opposite as you was like to find. He was a big, fat jolly man with a red face, always with his sleeves rolled up and sweating like a field hand, even in the deepest dead of winter when most folks was huddled close around the pot-bellied stove and were feeding it wood and coal 'til it was like to bust. Lew's jolly face was deceptive, as he was about as quick as Hollis Cole to leave dead men strewn about the room. Folks were suspicious where he got his cash, too. Lew was quiet just then, watching the cards and the other men at the table with a smirk now and again.

Across from Cole was the worst of the lot—though it didn't show much 'til you looked real close—a man name of Doctor James. At first glance he seemed like a city dude, with a pale, consumptive complexion and long-fingered hands pretty as any woman's. They were slender and fine like they'd never known a day's work in all his life, but those hands had intelligence in the fingertips that could read the cards almost by touch, and they could flash a gun out faster than most men could even think of doing it. Over the years he'd accounted for more dead folks on Boot Hill than either of the other men. The good doctor was wearing a black suit and a virgin shirt that night with a starched collar, and a broad, striped necktie with a diamond pin. His black hair was combed back slick and smooth as you please, with not a hair out of place, and his mustache was trim and neatly waxed. There wasn't no sweat on him either. He was cool as a cucumber, regardless of the way Lew Grace was sweating.

The fourth man at the table was a Wally Craft, a local rancher and complete done up, pale and clammy like he'd just lost his life savings—which he had. He choked as he lost that last hand to Hollis Cole, and he pushed up out of his chair, shaking and unsteady, to stare down into the gunman's hollow eyes.

"Damn you!" he said in a terrible voice. "You'll get your due in hell!"

Cole didn't answer him, only his gun hand twitched where it lay on the table. Friends of Wally Craft laid hold of him then and pulled him away from the table, got him out of harm's way. Mindy broke into the cold, smoky silence that hung in the air behind his departure.

"Gentlemen," she said, cocking her chin up in the air, "may I join your game?"

Hollis Cole's eyes flicked around at her, and Lew Grace started and giggled and shook his fat all over at the very idea. The doctor grinned at first, too, as he had noticed Mindy sitting in Bud Towner's lap over at the bar, and the glazed look on Bud's face which had come of it. But then the man stopped and looked Mindy over more close and serious, seeing maybe the solid set of her jaw under the black curls, and the supple, strong quality of her hands.

"Sweetheart," he said, narrowing his eyes, "let's see the color of your coin."

Mindy opened the strings of her little purse and spilled some of it out for him to inspect. The doctor looked at it, and at Mindy again with some speculation, and then at the crowd that was forming around at her back.

"All right with me," he said finally, with a sardonic little smile. He leaned back and stroked his smooth mustache, looked around the table. "Okay with you boys?" he asked, raising his eyebrows maybe a tiny fraction higher in his pale face.

The two of them nodded, following the doctor's lead, though Lew Grace scowled something fierce. One of the gents standing by pulled out a chair then for Mindy, and she sat into the game.

The smoke haze got thicker, drifted over the table like unnatural fog. There'd been something of a sigh of relief and a let up of strain when there was no gunplay between Hollis Cole and Wally Craft, and then a stir of interest and a few snickers at Mindy's brashness, thinking she could sit into a game with serious gamblers like Doctor James, Lew Grace, and Hollis Cole. But after the first couple of hands the snickers died down, and the watching got to be serious business again. There was a different kind of tension after that—mostly between Mindy and Doctor James, watching one another over the cards.

It was Lew Grace who took to losing now, and Mindy to winning strong. The cards went dead against Lew, and he went from laughing and joking to frowning mighty quick. An hour later he threw down a final losing hand and shoved back his chair.

"That lets me out, boys," he said. "I ain't got no more luck tonight."

Then he heaved up and swore something foul about playing cards with damn women and Chinks to boot, and plowed out through the crowd toward the bar. Mindy didn't blink, didn't glance up from watching the deal, or from making sure it was honest. The ring of men opened to let Lew's bulk pass through, and then closed back again into a solid, silent mass.

The doctor was dealing, and his hands were a white glimmer in the lamplight, moving so fast it was hard to see what he did. He was keeping two cards in the air at a time, and had all of them dealt in a flash. They raked in the cards, and it looked like Hollis Cole aimed to throw down his hand, but he didn't. He took three and the doctor took three. The bidding was heavy, high-rolling game as it was, and even if the cards weren't good, Mindy took in about five hundred with her three nines.

It went on that way, and Hollis Cole got grimmer and colder, as his pile got to be smallest of the three. The doctor dealt again, the cards streaking out, and this time Cole kept one card to draw to. He got nothing and threw down the hand.

"The girl's cheating," he said. "She's got cards up them damn fancy sleeves."

"Hush, Cole," said the doctor. "And let the woman play."

Hollis Cole flushed some at that, and then went white. His eyes burned hot in his skull face, looking murder back at the doctor, and over at Mindy, too. He leaned back in his chair and lit a cigarette, but it didn't fool nobody. He was wound tight as a fiddle string.

Mindy had kept two cards, and so had the doctor. They both drew, and then Mindy started off conservative, betting a measly five. The doctor raised her by ten dollars. Mindy thought about it some, and then she covered the ten and raised five more. Pretty soon they was raising back and forth a hundred at a time, and then a thousand, causing little gasps and heated whispers from them that was watching, and a certain shifting of feet. Quiet hung over the table heavy as the smoke, and the rustle of bills and the clink of gold sounded loud.

Then the doctor run out of funds.

"My dear girl," he said to Mindy, "I'd like nothing better to keep this up, but I'm afraid I'll have to drop out now."

The two of them appraised one another through the haze of smoke, Mindy with her black eyes and solid jaw, and the doctor, with his pale, hard face and mocking, elegant smile. It looked like they had come to the call, but then Cole moved, leaned to throw his wallet on the table.

"Five thousand," he said, "for the doctor."

That was against the rules. The doctor considered it, and raised his arched eyebrows at Mindy Chang. "My dear?"

"All right with me," she said, with the faintest of pouts. She fluffed her silky curls. "I can damn well cover it."

So the doctor bet Cole's five thousand against Mindy's wad.

Mindy called, and the crowd leaned in as the doctor spread out his hand. On the draw the man had filled out a pair of queens with

three sweet treys. He laid down that full house, and the crowd
gasped and murmured, and Hollis Cole's eyes burned hot with tri-
umph to see Mindy beat.

"Beautiful," Mindy smiled, but then she laid down her cards.
Damn if it wasn't a flush of hearts. The pot was hers.

"Bitch. You cheated!" Cole hissed, and he went for his gun. It was
easy to see that Hollis Cole wasn't used to playing poker with no
gurdy girl.

The crowd scrambled back, men falling over one another, and
Mindy dropped, agile and quick as a flash. The doctor shot Hollis
Cole dead through the center.

For a second there was only quiet and the acrid smell of powder
drifting up to the ceiling. Then the doctor got up, calm and cool
as you please, and went around to help Mindy up from where she
had slid under the table.

"My dear girl," he said, "are you all right?"

It seemed he was going to take his losses like a man. Pale as he
was, it seemed no paler than usual, and his smile was as easy and
smooth as ever. He helped Mindy to track down the coins that had
fell on the floor and stash them in her little bag. Then he gracefully
accepted a drink, as Mindy offered to buy a round for everybody
there. Somebody went for the sheriff, but they just left Hollis Cole
where he lay, and the bar in general got down to riotous
celebrations.

Now Mindy was some pleased to have made her stake this quick.
Even at a rough count she had near fifty thousand in that little bag,
and things looked good for her to get out of Dodge and on to some-
wheres else before that aforementioned trouble caught up with
her. As a result she drunk more whiskey than she'd meant to, and
then she made a mistake. She took the doctor up on an offer to see
her back to the hotel.

Doctor James was a good-looking man, smooth and sweet talking, and he'd turned more than one woman's head in his time. He
held Mindy discretely by the arm and helped her across the dark

street and up the hotel steps. They collected Mindy's key at the desk
and climbed on up the stairs. There in the hallway the doctor made
his play.

He pushed Mindy up against the wall and started to kissing on
her and running his hands up through her hair. Mindy was a mite
surprised, but it wasn't long before she was a willing participant in
the kissing, and then the doctor eased out his gun and walloped
Mindy on the side of the head with it.

Down she went, and then the doctor collected his money, blew
out the lamps in the hallway, and went on down the stairs. He nodded and smiled at the hotel clerk like he'd just seen the lady to her
door, proper as you please, and then he was gone out the door.

Now about that time, Bud Towner was back over at the Alamo
getting serious drunk. He decided he was missing something. A
taffeta queen, he thought it was, that he'd had on his lap a while
ago. Plus that, he was missing his daddy's gold watch, something
of a heirloom, that he'd had in the pocket of his vest just before the
girl had come along. Bud figured, and pretty rightly, that the queen
he'd had on his lap had something to do with the sudden way it
had disappeared, so he headed on back to the Long Branch.

He checked around the saloon and found out Mindy had won at
poker a while back and bought drinks all around and then gone back
to her hotel room. A few more questions produced some specula-
tions as to what hotel that was, but nothing definite, so Bud had to
stagger out and check at a couple of places before he found the one
where Mindy was actually staying. He climbed uncertainly up the
stairs from the lobby and headed down the hallway, and he did think
it was mighty dark. He figured the lamps had just burnt out of oil,
and he figured the proprietor, Sloan McGill, was too cheap to fill
them up again, so he just kept going, feeling his way along, looking for the right room.

Bud Towner come around the corner, and drunk as he was, and
dark as it was in the hallway, he didn't see Mindy laying there, just
starting to stir, so he tripped and fell right down on top of her. That

knocked Mindy's head against the floor right smartly and KOed her again.

Well, Bud picked hisself up and lit a match to see what it was he had fell over, and found it was the girl he'd been looking for. He noticed the key sticking in the door, and figured it was Mindy's room, so he just turned the knob and shoved the door open. Then he stooped down and heaved up Mindy like she didn't weigh no more than a sack of nails, stepped inside, and dropped her on the bed.

He felt around for the lamp then and lit it with another match, fitted the chimney back down over the flame. In the dim lamplight he looked around the room for his watch and felt through Mindy's clothes. He couldn't find her bag though, because, of course, the doctor had took it. Well, Bud was damn sure where his watch had gone, and he was some perturbed not to find it. Being an outgoing sort of gent, Bud wasn't one to bottle up his passions, so he decided Mindy owed him a little something for his trouble.

Bud got to working through all the skirts and petticoats and lacy drawers that Mindy was wearing, and that confirmed what he had thought before. It turned out Mindy was a man.

Now Bud Towner was an adaptable fellow, and not one to let a little thing like that get in his way, so he just went right ahead. While he was still tussling with the petticoats, Mindy woke up and noticed what he was doing.

"Honey, what's your name?" he asked, remembering who Bud was and the feel of his cock, and how he'd been so hot for the man just a few hours back.

"Towner, ma'am," Bud said, real polite and still pretty drunk. "Bud Towner."

"Well, Bud," said Mindy, "there's better ways to go about this. Get up a minute and I'll take my clothes off."

Bud did and he did, and he got Bud's off to the bargain. Now underneath the frills and ruffles of the dress Mindy was a little thing, and slim, like Chinese boys mostly was, but he had some manly charms, after all.

Mindy was hung like a horse, and the muscles of his body were smooth and hard as polished teak. His skin had that kind of warm glow that good dishes have in the light, and his round nipples and thick dong had a rich, earth-brown cast. His long hair run like silk over Bud's chest and shoulders as the boy lay down on him and kissed him hard on the mouth.

Bud wasn't so bad himself, being the big, hairy, muscular sort of gent that he was, and Mindy was right away in love and eager to please. Mindy ran his tongue in and out of Bud's mouth and bit his ear and then moved his attentions lower down, as his own dong got hard and started to lift with what he was doing.

He sucked and pulled on Bud's nipples as Bud felt him over and squeezed his butt, grinding their bellies and their cocks together, moaning with the feel of him. Then Mindy slid on down, ran his tongue around the edge of Bud's foreskin and squeezed his cock hard, nipping at his balls.

Bud jerked and swore at that, being as the nips was a little hard, but Mindy just grinned. He started to probe the sensitive spot up behind the balls, sliding his fingers up into Bud's asshole and back down to tease at his balls, as his other hand massaged his own cock, making it harder and longer as Bud watched in amazement.

"Lord, kid," he groaned. "Let me have a feel of that thing."

Mindy grinned again, and got up and let him touch it, rub it up and down and even take it into his mouth. The boy started to thrust some, in and out, warming up, but right away he was trembling and winding his hands into Bud's hair and gasping and shoving harder and deeper, so he was like to choke Bud with the size of his dong.

After a while Bud backed off to catch his breath, and then he said, "Sit on my lap again, kid, like you did earlier tonight."

So Mindy turned around and sat down, gasping some as he slowly impaled himself on Bud's erect rod. Bud put his hairy arms around the boy and held him down tight as he started to thrust, raising the boy's weight without any effort and then rocking back and again fucking hard and deep up into him.

Bud's cock wasn't no little thing, and Mindy couldn't complain about the way it felt ramming up and down inside of him. He arched his back and started to jerk himself off then, but Bud pushed his hands away and took over, pinching his tits and beating his rod with one hand, still holding him close with the other. Bud was getting hotter and hotter then, down to serious business. He pulled out a second, rolled the boy over onto the bed, and shoved into him again, harder and faster still.

The bed springs was squeaking in a pure frenzy, and the bed was banging and thumping into the wall with every stroke, and they was both moaning and groaning fit to be tied. They had waked their neighbors, a brush salesman and a prostitute in the next room, who was banging on the wall and yelling at them to keep quiet. Instead they raised up to a peak, both yelling and shooting off with a ruckus like to have waked the whole hotel.

Run down finally, they laid still and listened to the salesman and the prostitute start up next door. It was at least another half hour before the hotel was quiet enough for sleeping again.

"Bud Towner, you ever want to see the East?" asked Mindy, laying against Bud's shoulder in the lamplight. "Or maybe San Francisco?"

"San Francisco," said Bud, looking up at the shadowy, white-washed ceiling. He was getting to be almost sober by then. "Yeah, I'd like to see that town."

"Well," said Mindy, reaching over and closing his fist possessively in the thick mat of hair that grew on Bud's broad chest, "in these days and times a girl needs a man around."

"Where's my daddy's gold heirloom watch?" asked Bud.

"I don't have it," said Mindy, taking his hand away. "Doctor James took it, and he stole my poker winnings, too. Help me to get 'em back, Bud, and we'll go to San Francisco together."

"Take on Doctor James?" asked Bud.

"Why not?" asked Mindy, sitting up and throwing back his hair, pretty arrogant for such a kid. "There's two of us, isn't there?"

That did change things a mite to Bud's addled wits, though it might not've if he'd been complete sober. The doctor wasn't a man to be meddled with, after all. But Mindy was awfully attractive, sitting there all muscular and slick with sweat and slime, teasing at Bud's eyes, so Bud couldn't do nothing but go for it. He was some in love, too.

Well, seeing he was to have what he wanted, Mindy got up and washed and inspected the bruises on his face. Wasn't nothing to be done about those, so he dressed in an old pair of pants and a shirt from the bottom of the valise, and braided up his hair into the Chinaman's usual queue. With his manly charms covered up by the clothes, he looked to be just a pretty, dark-headed boy, and prime deceptive.

"Kid, you got a plan?" asked Bud.

"No," said Mindy, shoving taffeta into the valise. "I'll figure it out as we go along."

He pulled out one more thing, a whopping big Buntline special, and loaded up all the cylinders with ammunition, then hid the thing inside his shirt.

"Let's go," he said.

Bud checked to find if his own gun was loose in its holster, seeing as they was like to have gunplay.

What they ended up doing was all plain brass and plumb straightforward. Bud, being a regular resident of Dodge, knew where it was the doctor had his rooms. It was getting on toward light by then, and they had to hurry if they were to get the money and get out before folks started to waking up. Mindy didn't waste no time with scouting out the situation nor working up different plans. He just sent Bud up to the door, where that gent commenced to pound and yell for the doctor to open up. Doctor James was inside, but if he was asleep, he wasn't like to be deep into it.

He come to the door and opened it and stuck out the barrel of his six gun.

"Get away from my door, Bud," he said in his smooth, easy way.

"You got my daddy's gold watch!" said Bud, leaning hard against the door and slurring his words like he was dead drunk.

"Now, Bud . . ." the doctor started off.

"Gimme my daddy's watch," Bud hollered, "or I'll call the law on you."

Now the doctor wasn't no fool, and it didn't take him a second to figure what had happened.

"All right, Bud," he said. "Hold on a minute." He moved away from the door to look for the watch, and at that, Mindy slid in from the side and through the opening like a flash. He had that Buntline special in his hand big as life, and the towering figure of Bud Towner stepped in, too, and shut the door behind them.

The doctor was caught with his britches down, in lots more ways than one—even if he had put on a silk dressing gown. He had laid down his gun on the dresser, and now he had the little silk bag in his hands instead. His eyes flickered as the thought went through them to reach for his gun.

"Don't," said Mindy, in a clear, steady voice, and the special didn't quiver none in his hand. The doctor didn't.

While Mindy had the drop on the man, Bud slid in close and got the gun, and the little bag to boot. The doctor's eyes flickered again as they roved over Mindy, this time noticing the clear bulge in the front of his pants.

"Well, kid," he said. "You sure fooled me. If I'd known that . . ." He stopped, looked Bud over critically and then turned his elegant smile back on Mindy. "My dear, are you going to kill me?" he asked.

The man had some nerve, and Mindy couldn't help but like him, much as he was in love with Bud just then.

"Nope," he said, smiling back at the doctor. "Tie him up, Bud, and we'll leave him here on the bed."

By daylight they'd hired two horses and headed out. Around ten o'clock the doctor worked loose and come down for his breakfast, cool and collected as ever. He never said too much about what had happened.

The next spring Bud Towner showed up back in Dodge, and then the doctor went off to San Francisco. Some folks said it was to meet a woman, but Bud always knew it was something else.

# The Barning

LUCYPHER

THROUGH THE OPEN window,
the silence of the cool, clear evening was pierced by the eerie sound
of a coyote. Lily's head lay on Clint's arm. His other arm was draped
across her waist, his hand cupping her breast. Sex was on the menu,
but ever since the get-together with the gals of the reading group,
Lily had been unable to concentrate.

"Clint, have you ever barned anyone?"

"What kinda question's that? Nice girls shouldn't even know
'bout stuff like that."

"Y'ain't gettin' off that easy . . . have you?"

"Some of the fellas talk like they have. Might just be talk," he
said, sidestepping her question.

"Do you know what they do? In a barnin', I mean."

"Why the sudden interest in barnin'? You gonna get one o'
them strap-ons and join the boys?"

"I'm being serious, don't make fun of me. When the gals get the
reading group together, we talk about all manner o' things. Sometimes we get carried away. Yesterday, we were talkin' 'bout things
that turned us on and Mary Anne, you know how quiet she usually
is, well she said 'a barnin'.' I was gobsmacked, but then she blurted
out all about it. How a wild bunch of boys'll catch a girl unawares,
blindfold an' gag her, and all of 'em would take turns havin' her. The

way Mary Anne talked . . . she sounded like she thought she had missed out on one o' life's ultimate pleasures."

"Lily, a barnin' ain't nothin' more 'an gang rape. The gal doesn't look back with fond memories . . . not usually anyhow."

"Yes, but . . ."

"Lily, it's violence, plain and simple. You don't git careful, considerate rapists."

"Damn it, I know that. I'm not stupid. What I'm sayin' is, it doesn't hafta be. Supposin' they were all friends."

"The gal and the boys? I don't know, probably happens sometimes . . . wait, you mean they all get together and decide they want to do it, includin' the gal?"

"Yeah, if the boys didn't get too carried away, an' the gal wanted to do it, an' someone responsible was there lookin' out for her, it would be okay, wouldn't it?"

"Well, yeah, I s'pose it could be . . . if she really wanted to."

"An' it doesn't have to be real violence. I saw on the TV last week where some people have sex play where they act out the roles of rapists an' torturers an' the like. The ladies enjoy the play actin' as much as the men."

"Is there a point to all this?" Clint asked, suspiciously.

"Well, it just sounded like . . ."

"Like what?"

Lily was silent for a bit and then said forcefully, "Fun damn it, fun. I just don't see anything wrong with it, not if the gal really wants to do it."

She was still talking, when Clint nibbled her ear lobes and kissed her neck.

Shivers ran up her spine, "Oh, Clint, are you tryin' to distract me?"

He squeezed her breast and took a swollen nipple in his fingers, squeezing and pulling on it, eliciting a groan. Lily rolled onto her back as he kissed her breasts and belly. His hot breath trailed across her mound, the tip of his tongue separating her labia, touching her clit. Lily rotated her pelvis, picking her hips up as his fingers slipped inside her.

"Oh c'mon, Clint, enough lovemaking, fuck me, fuck me like I'm the first woman you seen for years."

Lily put her legs around Clint's hips as he slid into her hot, slippery sex.

"Do it hard, Clint, I want to scream."

Clint obliged, shaking the bed so much that it banged the wall.

"Uhh . . . ohh . . . oh . . . more . . ."

"More . . . more? I ain't got no more, you gotta be still thinkin' of a barnin' . . ."

"Oh please don't get mad Clint, I don't know what I mean . . ."

"Lily, what's wrong?"

"I don't know, probably nothin', Clint, it's just me. I'll be okay in the mornin'."

Clint looked at her, but she avoided his eyes.

"Okay, I gotta get some sleep, we're gonna have a long day tomorrow. Night, Lily," he said, kissing her.

She grunted and rolled over, her back to him, a tear rolling down her cheek to be absorbed by the pillow.

―――

EARLY NEXT MORNING Lily was serving breakfast for the ranch's ten hands. She had overcooked the eggs and almost burnt the bacon. She was in a foul mood, slamming the plates down and generally taking it out on anyone who acknowledged her presence.

"Whata y'all gonna do with your lives? We gonna do this 'til we get old, 'til we cain't no more? All you do is punch cows an' go into Abilene once a week, get drunk an' screwed, blewed an' tattooed. Don't you want no more?" she asked, slopping a big helping of grits onto Clint's plate.

All she got in response were a few grunts. The men were concentrating hard on their breakfast, avoiding eye contact with her, not wanting to get into a debate.

"You gonna punch cows 'n get drunk 'til you die? Don't any of you got any dreams . . . any ambition?"

She waited, there was no response, "Damn it, someone say somethin'."

After a moment she hurled the plate she was holding into the large stone fireplace. The steel plate clanged, scattering tiny shards of porcelain.

No one said anything, just hurriedly finished their breakfast and excused themselves, not looking at her, not wanting to catch her attention.

"Y'all meet me in the corral. I want to talk a 'fore you go off," Clint said to the men.

"See ya at dinner, Lily," he said, kissing her cheek.

"But Clint . . ."

He turned to face her, "Lily, this is gonna be a busy day, we gotta cut five hundred head and get 'em to the railhead. We'll talk later."

"Clint . . ."

"Not now, Lily."

He grabbed his 30-30, put his hat on, and turned to her, lightly touching the brim.

Lily was angry, but finally looked up at him.

*God, he's good lookin'.* The thought intruded on her anger like an unwelcome guest.

She couldn't help love him, but what she really wanted right now was . . . what? Something more from life, that's for sure. She thought of the conversation last night, the talk about the barnin'.

Lily watched Clint's receding form, his weathered leather chaps, his jingling spurs, his fleece-lined denim jacket, losing sight of him when he went behind the barn.

After he had gone, Lily attacked her chores, and by nine o'clock she had finished cleaning the big kitchen and had a big pot of chili on the cooker for dinner. Dinner was no easy chore when cooking for ten hungry ranch hands. She sat down, took a sip of her coffee, and made a face. Lukewarm. Damn, she hated lukewarm coffee; some days it seemed that was all she got, lukewarm coffee, lukewarm conversations, lukewarm sex.

She glanced around the kitchen, the silence was deafening. No one had even remembered her birthday. Forty . . . she was forty years old today. She thought about the last twenty-two years and back to her high school days. She had gone to school with most of the ranch hands; the rest were a few years younger or older, but all local boys that she had know all her life. And at one time or another, she had gone to bed with most of them, before finally hooking up with Clint. They were all like family, but much more. As she thought about it, she got annoyed, annoyed at what could be, but wasn't. But then she heard the milk cow. The old gal needed her attention.

"Back to reality," she said aloud, going to get the milking pail. It wasn't in its usual place.

"If one o' them worthless excuses has used my milkin' pail for anything. . . ."

Lily left the sentence unfinished and stepped out onto the porch; the cow was nowhere to be seen. She was usually waiting for her near the door and walked to the barn with her.

*Maybe she's already in the barn . . . yeah, there she is . . . that's funny.*

As she approached the cow, it was obvious that she had already been milked.

*What in tarnation?* she wondered, turning to leave.

She took a step and almost jumped out of her skin. Her way was barred by a group of men, bandannas tied across their faces as masks. They appeared out of the shadows; she had heard nothing.

"Oh . . . what's goin' on?"

"Take her arms," one said, gruffly.

"Who's that? Is that you, Clint?" she demanded, nervously.

They circled around her. She couldn't see their features, but she thought she recognized some of them.

"Shut up if you know what's good for ya," the leader said, pulling a pillowcase out of his back pocket.

"Hey, that's one of my pilla cases, what ya gonna do with it?"

He slipped it over her head.

"Now whata you gonna do?" she asked again, "Don't hurt me . . ."

"We won't, just gonna have a little fun," a voice came back, as they pulled her over to a stall.

She staggered on the uneven ground in the barn, but someone caught her and then pushed her back. She fell onto a coarse, smelly, old horse blanket thrown over the top of some bales of hay. They tied ropes around her wrists and ankles, pulled them snug, and tied them to the sides of the stall.

"Clint? Is that you? I was kiddin', Clint, you wouldn't really . . . you know . . . would you?" she asked, from inside the pillowcase.

There was no answer, but a moment later she felt a pair of rough hands reach in the neck of her cotton dress and pull it apart, tearing it down to her waist.

"Hey, that was a good dress . . ."

She could feel his rough hands at her waist then he tore it down, through the hem. She was lying on the blanket in her bra and panties, the shredded dress underneath her.

She gasped when she felt the touch of cold steel on her skin, but then the blade slid under the shoulder straps of her bra. They parted easily. The blade then slid between her breasts, under the center strap. A quick flick of the blade and her bra sprang apart.

*Oh no, please don't,* she thought, trying to will her nipples not to stand up, but she failed.

"Hot doggy!" someone exclaimed, among murmurs of appreciation.

Then the blade slid between her skin and the sides of her panties, cutting first one side, then the other. The man reached between her splayed legs and taking hold of her panties, pulled them out from under her.

*Oh shit,* she thought.

"Y'all be nice, y'hear?" was all she could think to say.

There was no response.

After a moment she asked, "How long ya gonna keep me like this?"

Still there was no response.

"Y'all there?" she asked.

Minutes later, she jumped when something touching her labia. She could feel it separate her sex, touching her clit. It was a tongue.

"Sure you wanta do that?" she asked, squirming, "I ain't had a bath for a while. You're gonna taste the sweat, grime, and pee o' the last few days . . . oh . . . ohh . . . oohhh . . . never mind . . . forget I said anythin'."

The man was obviously enjoying himself, as he pulled her lips apart and wrapped his tongue around her clit. Her orgasm rapidly approached as her clit engorged, becoming more sensitive. She couldn't help groaning, writhing, trying to force her legs together

"Oh yeah! Lookit her, like two rattlers goin' at it, man she loves it. That's it, eat that pussy, eat her, eat her!" one of them yelled. Some of the others joined in, cheering.

Then he stopped. She could feel the air on her clit and then something soft and warm rub over her clit and cunt. She was taken by surprise when all of a sudden he forced his cock into her, pushing her against the ankle ropes.

"Oh . . . ohhh."

"Go, go, go," she could hear the others chant as the man fucked her.

His rough hands were on her hips as he pulled himself into her and came. When he was done, he pulled out and she could hear murmurs.

"I should go next, I'm younger."

"No, I should go next, I'm older, more experienced."

"No, you should go last, your dick's too big, you gonna stretch her." They finally decided to draw straws.

"Hot damn, I'm next, I'm next . . . little lady I hope you're ready for this . . . and apologies in advance to your boy friend, 'cause you won't be little any more," the man said laughing.

*Deke, that's gotta be Deke . . . he's always braggin',* she thought.

"Clint? You there? You gonna let him do that? Clint?"

But there was no response and she could hear the man undo his belt and unzip his trousers. In anticipation she held her breath. The head of his cock separated her labia and pushed into her vagina.

Then in one thrust, he forced his erection into the hot, slippery orifice vacated by the first man.

"Oh . . . oohhh, ouch, it's too big . . ."

"Hey damn it, you're stretchin' her. Ya shoulda been last," someone protested.

The man pulled almost completely out of her and then drove into her, one hand on her breast, the other on her mons, his thumb circling her clit, occasionally squeezing it. After a very short while, Lily could feel his cock pulsating as his white-hot come spurted into her.

When he was done, number three stepped up to fill the void.

"You gonna rattle 'round in there now, boy," the previous man said, laughing.

The younger man's cock slid into her.

*Wes, that has to be Wes,* she thought, clenching her pelvic muscles.

What the man didn't have in size, he made up for in enthusiasm. He ground his cock into her, pulling her against the ropes.

After the seventh one, Lily began to wonder, *I hope they didn't go and get the rest of Abilene.*

"Man, talk 'bout sloppy seconds, I wish I had sloppy seconds," the last one said as he slipped his cock into her.

After they had all had her, those that wanted to had her again. The only one she was sure she could identify was the one with the big cock; she was sure it was Deke. His cock slipped into her well-lubricated cunt, much easier than the first time. She raised her hips up, wanting as much of him in her as she could get. As he pumped her, he rolled her clit between his fingers.

"Oh . . . ohhh, don't stop, please . . ."

It took him a while to come, allowing her multiple orgasms. As his climax approached, he leaned over, clamping his teeth on a nipple, pulling it, stretching it. The other men were silent, watching, more than a little envious.

*Age does have its advantages,* Lily thought.

"You stay here five minutes 'fore coming out," the leader said, as he untied her hands.

She listened intently and could hear them leave, their boots on the hard ground, spurs jingling.

*Five minutes ain't enough,* she thought, as she reached up and pulled the pillowcase off her head.

The hot sun lanced through the many gaps in the barn's siding, making it difficult to see into the shadows. She looked around, shading her eyes; she was alone. The lingering smell of sweat and come assailed her nostrils as she lay there, thinking about what had happened. Sitting up, she reached down and untied her ankles. She was a mess; there was half-dried come everywhere. Reaching down, she pulled the dress up between her legs, holding it over her pussy, with her other hand, she held it wrapped around her shoulders. Then she got to her feet and walked unsteadily to the house.

Up in her bedroom, she looked at herself in the mirror. She wanted to clean herself up, but didn't want to remove the lingering evidence of their exertions. It would be like trying to erasing the event from her being and she didn't want to do that. She dabbed a damp wash cloth at her vulva and pulled clean panties on, stuffing them with toilet paper. Then she pulled a clean dress on and went down to the kitchen. Forty-five minutes later, she had dinner on the table.

<hr />

"HEY LILY, SOMETHIN' sure smells good," Clint said, kicking his boots against the side of the door frame before coming into the kitchen.

Normally she would chide him for that, but not today.

"Hi Clint," she said, throwing her arms around him, kissing him.

"What's that fer?"

"The birthday surprise."

"How'd ya find out about that? I tol' no one to tell ya. Mary Anne's gonna be disappointed, she's expectin' to surprise ya after dinner."

"No, in the barn, this mornin', after breakfast . . ."

"Barn? This mornin'?" Clint asked, a puzzled look on his face.

"Yeah, in the barn . . . that were y'all . . . weren't it?"

"Why, what happened?"

She looked at him, hesitated, and then said, "Oh . . . just that someone milked the cow for me."

At that moment, the ranch hands came into the kitchen. There were both murmured and shouted greetings, but no one said anything about the morning. Lily was busy for the next ten minutes, serving everyone.

"Did you get the cattle to the rail line?" she casually asked when she finally sat down with them to eat.

"Yeah, we been in the saddle all mornin'. I'm beat," Clint said, tearing off a large piece of homemade bread and dipping it in a steaming bowl of chilli.

*He couldn't be lyin' . . . could he?* Lily wondered.

"You got the chit from the rail yard?" she asked. "I'll enter it in the books."

"They gonna mail it to us."

She glanced at him but she couldn't tell if he was telling the truth or not.

Looking around the table, everything seemed normal. She had to smile, a better bunch of guys she couldn't hope to meet. Any of 'em would gladly give her the shirt off his back. Lily always enjoyed mealtimes. They would all get together in the big kitchen and talk and joke about everything that happened that day, but there was no mention of the barn this morning.

When the meal was done, the men starting to get up, Lily spoke up, "Hey wait, you're not done yet, we're havin' dessert."

She gathered their plates and started setting out bowls of strawberry shortcake.

"Dessert? What's that fer?"

"'Cause any of y'all 'll come when I need you . . . some of ya more than once."

# Contributors

**ANNA BLACK** resides in the Midwest. She has previously been published in *The MILF Anthology* and has another story in Zane's upcoming *Caramel Flava 2* anthology. She enjoys reading, writing, researching history, and collecting tarot cards.

**RACHEL KRAMER BUSSEL** (www.rachelkramerbussel.com) is senior editor at *Penthouse Variations*, writes for Gothamist.com and Mediabistro.com, hosts In The Flesh Reading Series, and wrote the popular Lusty Lady column for the *Village Voice*. Her erotica has been published in over one hundred anthologies such as *Best American Erotica 2004* and *2006,* and her books include *Naughty Spanking Stories from A to Z* volumes 1 and 2 and the recent *He's on Top: Erotic Stories of Male Dominance and Female Submission* and *She's on Top: Erotic Stories of Female Dominance and Male Submission*. Her novel *Everything But . . .* will be published by Bantam in 2008.

**LANEY CAIRO:** When Laney Cairo isn't writing erotica, she works in a science fiction bookshop, an employment option known as "subsidised reading." This is the first time she's sold a hetero-normative story, and the first time both she and her partner have had stories in an anthology together.

**M. CHRISTIAN:** For the last decade M. Christian has proven himself to be a true literary chameleon, establishing himself as a master of multiorientation erotica with stories in anthologies such as *Best American Erotica, Best Gay Erotica, Best Lesbian Erotica, Best Fetish Erotica, Best Transgender Erotica,* and two hundred other publications as well as in the collections *Dirty Words, Speaking Parts, The Bachelor Machine,* and *Filthy.* He is also the editor of over twenty anthologies, including *Amazons, Confessions, Garden of Perverse* (with Sage Vivant), *The Mammoth Book of Future Cops,* and *The Mammoth Book of Tales of the Road* (with Maxim Jakubowski). Recently, he has also shown himself to be a master of humor and suspense with novels such as *Running Dry, The Very Bloody Marys, Me2,* and *The Painted Doll.*

**LEE CRITTENDEN:** I was born in the South and have worked at a variety of different jobs over the years, from pumping gas to drafting at the Kennedy Space Center in Florida. I've always loved the West and the outdoors, and I'm currently working on a farm in Tennessee that raises beef cattle. I've been writing seriously for about fifteen years, and my stories have been published in several anthologies.

**ANDREA DALE** lives in southern California within scent of the ocean. Her stories have appeared in *Best Lesbian Erotica 2005, Dyke the Halls,* and *Sacred Exchange.* Under the name Sophie Mouette, she and coauthor Teresa Noelle Roberts have sold a novel, *Cat Scratch Fever,* to Black Lace Books, and stories to *Sex on the Sportsfield, Sex in Uniform,* and *Best Women's Erotica 2005.* In other incarnations, she is a published writer of fantasy and romance. Her Web site is at www.cyvarwydd.com.

**STEPHEN DEDMAN** is the author of the more than one hundred short stories published in an eclectic collection of magazines and anthologies. His supernatural cross-dressing lesbian erotic western romance "'Til Human Voices Wake Us" was shortlisted for the Gaylactic Spectrum Award. He has also been nominated for the Bram Stoker Award, the British Science Fiction Association Award, the Sidewise

Award, the Seiun Award, and a sainthood. He can vouch for the erotic skills of at least one other writer in this collection.

**SHANNA GERMAIN** is a poet by nature, a short-story writer by the skin of her teeth, and a novelist in training. Her award-winning work has appeared in publications such as *Absinthe Literary Review, Best American Erotica, Best Bondage Erotica,* and *Salon.* Visit her online at www.shannagermain.com.

**CLAYTON HOLIDAY** is a middle-aged misanthrope. He's an American expatriate who lives in the Far East with his wife. In the paradise they call home, he writes, reads, and slowly dips further into insanity. Originally from the Midwest, Holiday's early life sent him drifting along the Continental Divide, from the border of Canada to Mexico, with lengthy stays in Montana, Wyoming, and Oklahoma. Eventually, he took an unexpected turn toward the Middle East and western Europe. For many years Holiday worked at various newspapers owned by alcoholics or sexual degenerates. Late in life Holiday decided to get paid to read literature by highly acclaimed misfits and became a teacher. He remains a constant source of concern among family members and law enforcement.

**LIVIA LLEWELLYN** was born in Anchorage, Alaska, and currently lives in New Jersey. Her fiction has appeared in *ChiZine, Short and Sweet: Original Novellas by Erotica's Hottest Writers, Subterranean Magazine,* and is forthcoming in *The Field Guide to Surreal Botany* and *Sybil's Garage.* She attended the Clarion writers' workshop in 2006. You can find her online at http://liviallewellyn.com.

**LUCYPHER:** I am a writer, artist, and single parent. I write erotica, science fiction, and computer programs. I also draw, life drawing, mm-mm, love people. I am on the far side of fifty, but I figure that once past fifty, a body starts back down, so that makes me forty-three. I live in Edinburgh, Scotland, the best city in the world to live in (as long as sunshine and temperature don't count for too much). I have three children, one still at home, whom I love dearly, and one cat.

**AUGUST MACGREGOR** is the pseudonym of a writer and freelance graphic designer. The sensual world of erotica offers him steamy and refreshing breaks from design projects, and it gives rich life to his fantasies. His stories have appeared online in the swanky Ruthie's Club, as well as in the print anthologies *Naked Erotica, Wicked: Sexy Tales of Legendary Lovers,* and *The MILF Anthology: Twenty-one Steamy Stories.* He lives in Maryland with his wife and two daughters.

**ELSPETH POTTER**'s upcoming publications include "Poppies Are Not the Only Flower" (*Lipstick on Her Collar*); "Silver Skin" (*Periphery: Erotic Lesbian Futures*); and "Place, Park, Scene, Dark" (*Tough Girls 2*). Her work has previously appeared in *Best Lesbian Erotica, Best Women's Erotica,* and *The Mammoth Book of Best New Erotica.*

**TERESA NOELLE ROBERTS** has been in Texas on business, but was far more influenced by watching too many John Wayne/Maureen O'Hara movies. Her erotic fiction has appeared in *Best Women's Erotica 2004, 2006,* and *2007; The MILF Anthology; Garden of the Perverse: Fairy Tales for Twisted Adults;* and many other publications. She's also one-half of Sophie Mouette, whose novel *Cat Scratch Fever* was published in 2006 by Black Lace Books.

**DAVID SHAW** is a fully qualified village idiot, a hereditary wheel tapper, and a genuine gongoozler. *Gongoozler* is an ancient British word for somebody who can happily spend an entire day watching a river flow by. The difference between a gongoozler and a fisherman is that gongoozlers don't have enough ambition to drop a hook into the water. David prefers to catch strange thoughts and turn them into offbeat stories. He has jumped out of aircraft, sailed a yacht along the Great Barrier Reef, driven the longest and heaviest trains in the world, and joined the ten-foot-high club on the back seat of a Greyhound bus. David likes to write about those ladies who believe, in Shakespeare's words, that it is no dishonest desire to desire to be a woman of the world.

**CECILIA TAN** has edited many erotica anthologies for many publishers including *Sex in the System* (Thunder's Mouth Press), *Best Fantastic Erotica* (Circlet Press), *SM Visions* (Masquerade Books), and *Erotica Vampirica* (Blue Moon Books). Her own erotic fiction can be found everywhere including *Penthouse, Ms., Best American Erotica, Best Women's Erotica,* and in the e-book *Edge Plays.* All the details are at www.ceciliatan.com.

**RAKELLE VALENCIA** has coedited *Rode Hard, Put Away Wet: Lesbian Cowboy Erotica* (a LAMBDA Literary Award Finalist); *Hard Road, Easy Riding;* and *Lipstick On Her Collar,* with Sacchi Green. Upcoming is the project *Drag Kings: Tales of Lesbian Erotica,* coedited with Amie M. Evans. Her stories have been published in *Blood Sisters; Red Hot Erotica; Ultimate Lesbian Erotica 2005, 2006,* and *2007; The Good Parts: Pure Lesbian Erotica; Best Lesbian Love Stories 2005; Hot Lesbian Erotica 2005; Best Bondage Erotica 2; Best of Best Lesbian Erotica 2; Naughty Spanking Stories from A to Z; Best Lesbian Erotica 2004* and *2005; On Our Backs: The Best Erotic Fiction Vol. 2;* and *On Our Backs, October/November 2003, Vol. 18, Issue 3.* Rakelle is also a 2006 semifinalist in the Project: Queer Lit Contest with her western novel, *Mail Order Bride.*

**CONNIE WILKINS** writes in western Massachusetts, and, along with her alter ego Sacchi Green, has published short fiction in publications ranging from two of Bruce Coville's kids anthologies to *Penthouse, Best Transgender Erotica, Best S/M Erotica 2,* six volumes of *Best Lesbian Erotica,* and four volumes of *Best Women's Erotica.* She's also coeditor of the anthologies *Rode Hard, Put Away Wet: Lesbian Cowboy Erotica, Hard Road, Easy Riding: Lesbian Biker Erotica,* and several others slated for publication in the next couple of years.